a novel

Melissa MacVicar

To my children
Eileen and Joel

Lizzie

MY BROTHER SHOULD BE DEAD. Death was what he wanted, and his death might have made everything that came after that day less painful. After succeeding in so many terrible things, however, he failed to complete this one final act.

Despite these harsh words, I do not take the possibility of his death lightly. Even now, when the thought of it enters my mind, I resist it, and immediately following the shooting, I hated myself for it. My insides ached, and my head throbbed. He was my brother. My baby brother. I was supposed to love him, not wish him gone from the planet.

Standing in his room before we left for Nantucket, I considered what to take. I wanted something of him. A talisman. An object from the scene of this crime, my own personal family tragedy, that would allow me to remember him as the boy he was before. The boy who laughed at sitcoms on Nickelodeon and swam in the pool with neon green floaties. The boy who called me Wizzie. The little brother who couldn't possibly be locked up in a jail cell for murdering four people.

The room itself was not special—double bed, blue

walls, built in book shelves stripped of their contents. Boxes littered the floor, filled with the personal items that populated Thomas' life. Out his windows, the picturesque view of the pool and the fir trees beyond was still lovely.

I forced myself to try to see it as a stranger, like someone who only heard about Thomas on the news. Were there clues in the paint color? The books he read or the framed poster of Tony Hawk? No matter how hard I searched, no answers to my infinite questions were revealed. Nothing there explained what happened to us.

I spotted it then, atop a pile of books in a still open box. The horseshoe. I forgot all about it until that moment, but I knew instantly it was what I'd been looking for. We both received one on the vacation at the dude ranch with Dad although I had no idea where mine was anymore. On that trip, we rode horses and square danced and ate all our meals together. Good times. We had some good times. The rust speckled piece of metal, satisfyingly heavy in my hand, was my proof.

Turning to leave, I caught a glimpse of Thomas' cork board. Removed from the wall, it leaned against the side of a box near his old desk. Weird drawings of scary faces, death metal concert leaflets, and a few pictures of a scowling Thomas were pinned haphazardly across it. In one corner, however, an unexpected pop of color peeked out. Without thinking, I reached to expose it.

Thomas—a four-year-old Spiderman, me—a six-year-old Cinderella. We both smiled as we clutched our bags of trick-or-treat candy. With a little effort, I unpinned it from the board and gazed down at our grinning, childish faces. When exactly had Thomas stopped smiling for pictures?

When was the precise day and time that occurred? That was the day I should have known. I should have noticed. I should have realized that something was not right with my baby brother.

Chapter 1

Lainey

SLEET CLICKED AGAINST THE WINDSHIELD of the Volvo. From the passenger seat, I peered out at the gray shingles and beige trim of Nantucket High School. Students rushed inside, trying to escape the wind-driven ice pellets.

"You remember where to go?" Mom asked.

I nodded, but I still didn't get out of the car. I kept waiting and staring at the façade, hoping I'd feel something. Excited would have been nice. I would have settled for optimistic. After all, I had been looking forward to that day and that very moment for four months. This was my start over day. I got a second chance at a normal life where no one knew me. Instead of giddy enthusiasm, however, all I felt was the same numbing sadness. It descended on me like a spell on September twentieth and held me in its clutches still.

When the feelings I wanted didn't come, I decided to just make my move. I inhaled a huge breath and pulled the door handle.

"I'll text you for a ride," I said to my mother.

"Good luck!" she called after me as I hurled myself out into the precipitation.

I jogged to the entrance, backpack slung over my shoulder. Once inside, I shook off the moisture that collected on my fleece jacket and recalled my mother's directions. *Go straight through the Hall of the Whale and take a left at the stairs. Guidance is the first door on the right.*

I had no idea what a Hall of the Whale would look like, but once inside, I was too distracted by the other kids to care. They thronged the hall like a species unto themselves—saggy pants with boxers showing, mini-skirts with knee high boots, low-cut tops that revealed brightly colored bra straps. I knew public school was like this. Despite my sheltered, private school life, I still grew up in Los Angeles. I went to clubs. I had a twenty-year old boyfriend. But on that day, their displays disconcerted me.

For my part, I tried to choose clothes that would help me blend in. Jeans. Uggs. North Face jacket. I wanted as little attention drawn to me as possible. But as I made my way through the Hall of the Whale, aptly named for the giant whale skeleton hanging from the ceiling, I realized just about everyone was looking at me. A new girl in the hall the first week of February was probably not something that happened very often in Nantucket, and it didn't help that I had the face and body of a model. My mother, a former actress, gave them to me. My tall, willowy body combined with high cheekbones, full lips, and vibrant green eyes made me stand out—made boys especially notice me. Perhaps I should have gone with an uglier hair cut like my mother recommended. To keep my identity a secret, I cut six inches off my blond hair and dyed it brown. Along with my new hair, I had unintentionally lost about ten pounds since the shooting—gone from a four to a two and not in a good way; bony compared to my healthy body from before.

Navigating the gauntlet of students, I managed to find the guidance office. I asked the secretary if I could see Mrs. Duncombe just as my mother told me. This Mrs. Duncombe and the principal were supposed to be the only people in Nantucket who knew my identity. Someone had to know because of my transcripts.

A few seconds later, a woman emerged into the waiting area from an office off to the side. "Good morning, Lainey. I'm Mrs. Duncombe." She shook my hand. "Come in and I'll go over your schedule with you."

She had short, dark hair streaked with gray and wore a cardigan sweater along with corduroy pants and black clogs. Once inside the office, she shut the door and took a seat beside me.

"How was your trip here?" she asked.

"Fine," I answered.

Nervous energy surged through me. People that knew who I was were generally not nice to me, not anymore. Before the shooting, my father's fame as an award-winning movie director ensured most everyone liked me—or at least they pretended too. Afterward, we were shunned—ignored and cast off by most of our former friends.

"I have a student coming in to take you to your first class," Mrs. Duncombe said. "She'll be in several of your classes."

I held my hands tightly in my lap making them tingle and sting. "Okay."

"She's a soccer player and an honors student," she

continued. "I know you played tennis, but unfortunately, we don't have a tennis team here."

"It's fine," I said.

Truly, I didn't care if I ever picked up a tennis racket again. Despite my interest in it before the shooting, it was the last thing on my mind since.

"And if you need to talk, I'm here. I can only imagine how hard this must be for you and your mother. She asked me to find you a good therapist."

I didn't want a new therapist. I lucked out with Belinda back home, and I doubted I'd be as lucky again. Plus, talking about what happened was something I avoided. Talking about the blood-shed and horror in the cafeteria at Beaton Prep only made it more real and more terrible. I wished everyone would stop encouraging me to do it. We left so I could forget. We were here so I could start over.

"Why don't we go meet Alex," Mrs. Duncombe said.

The moment of truth—or in this case, the moment of the first lie.

Alexandra Wilcox was a tall, athletic looking girl with wide set eyes and a largish nose. She smiled politely beside the secretary's overflowing desk when we were introduced.

"Everyone calls me Alex," she told me. "And we better get going because Rapisardi's a pain about tardies."

I slung my backpack over my shoulder and nodded to Mrs. Duncombe like a soldier headed into battle. Everything about my life had become a battle. That was what depression felt like, according to my mother, and that was why I took my pills.

"So, California? This must be a big change for you," Alex said.

We climbed the open staircase in the Hall of the Whale amidst a crush of other students trying to get to class.

"Yeah, it's okay."

Minimal details—that was the protocol. Whatever questions people asked about the past, I told them as little as possible.

"Hey Alex, you got a new friend?"

A pack of four boys surrounded us as we reached the second floor. Two of them wore navy and white letterman jackets with their numbers and names on the sleeves.

Alex gestured at me. "Yeah, this is Lainey."

"Hi Lainey," one of the jacket boys said.

He had a sly grin, and he took his time examining me. All of me. Up and down and back up again. *Real subtle*. His jacket sleeves proclaimed him to be *Wick 87 TE*. He had deep brown eyes and dark, perfect hair.

"Michael Wickersham. Are you headed to English?"

He finally met my eyes, having finished his surveillance of my body.

"Yes, we are," Alex answered, trying to maneuver past them.

Thankfully, Wick and the others stopped at a row of nearby lockers. "See you there," he called after us. Then, to his friends, "Dude, I call it."

He didn't even attempt to be quiet about it.

"Don't worry about them," Alex told me. "We don't get many new kids here."

I cringed at how universally stupid boys were. As if a boy could call dibs on you. As if I'd date a boy in a letterman jacket who tried. For a moment, my old sense of ego rose up inside me. *How dare he? Who does he think he is?* Boys at Beaton Prep would never have treated me that way.

They knew better than to mess with Lizzie Berringer. But I needed to remember who I was in Nantucket. Things would have to be different for Lainey Darwin. Lainey Darwin was a whole new girl—a girl with no past and no friends. She'd have to make it up as she went along.

Chapter 2

HANNAH AND I LOUNGED IN the family room watching Next Top Model.

"Kiara's going to get sent home," Hannah said.

"I don't know. I think Heidi really likes her."

"Yeah but that shoot was horrible."

Thomas came in from the kitchen with a plate of food. We both ignored him.

"This show sucks," he finally said after a few minutes of standing behind the sectional and watching with us.

"Then go away," I said rudely.

"Like who cares about fucking models? You should be more concerned about falling into the ocean and dying when the big one hits. Could be any day now."

Thomas's latest obsession was the San Andreas fault and how an earthquake would break California in half.

"Shut up," I told him.

"Fine. Don't come crying to me when you're stuck under a pile of mansion rubble. I might save you, though, Hannah."

"Oh, gee, thanks," she answered and rolled her eyes at him.

Thomas walked away toward the stairs. "Fine. I won't save you then either," he called over his shoulder.

Lainey

When we reached English class, the twisting vine of anxiety that lived in my chest began to grow and spread. I was only vaguely aware of the other students around me. They sat at desks and chatted with friends, but they were all blurry and misshapen. I only saw a small focus area directly in front of me.

"You should go check in with Mr. Rap," Alex said.

I blinked several times in rapid succession to try to clear the tunnel vision. When unsuccessful, I pressed my thumb and index finger into my eyelids. Alex was looking at me when I stopped, her head cocked to the side. Thankfully, however, my vision was restored. I walked on shaky legs to the teacher's desk.

Mr. Rapisardi smiled and said hello when I arrived. Black hair and grayish sideburns framed his ruddy face.

I handed him my schedule, and after checking it, he said, "Welcome to Nantucket. You have good timing. We're reading short stories so it shouldn't be too hard to catch up. We are in the middle of *The Awakening* by Kate Chopin. Have you read it?"

"No," I said, but it came out as a whisper. Sometimes, my voice failed me.

"Great. I'll grab you a copy and give you the code for Google Classroom."

He headed for a cabinet in the corner where he retrieved a battered paperback with a Victorian woman on the cover.

"You can sit right here," he said as he handed me the book and tapped the top of a nearby desk.

Once seated, I scanned the room. Twenty desks were

arranged in a circle. The kids seemed like a varied group—*Wick TE 87* and some other athletes along with Alex and some other trendy looking girls. A nondescript girl read a fantasy novel with a scary looking beast on the cover, and a few geeky looking guys were deep in conversation around a Chromebook. The seating arrangement meant that everyone would be able to examine me for the entire class, including Wick and his friends. This idea reignited my panic, and I knew I needed to think about something good. Something happy. That's what Belinda taught me.

In my mind, I went to Malibu Beach with Dylan. He shredded a wave while I watched from my towel, lying in the hot sand beside Hannah. Dylan's tan torso was ridged with muscles, his biceps and shoulders perfectly flexed. As the wave broke, he timed his jump-off perfectly and disappeared under the foaming surf. I watched him do it hundreds of times, and like always, I hoped this was his last ride. I hoped he'd join me on the beach, lying beside me on his towel, intermittently kissing me and touching me and whispering sexy things to me.

I wore my favorite bikini with the navy and purple swirls. Hannah giggled. We just smoked. I tried to remember what I used to giggle about with Hannah when we got high. I could hear her in my head—soft, rolling silliness. A small smile lifted my lips.

A loud tone sounded over the PA system. I flinched, drawn back to the here and now. A very bored sounding woman droned the morning announcements, and when she finished, Mr. Rapisardi started class. As he spoke, I drifted away again, and this time, Dylan came out of the water to see me.

Lunch was inevitable. Two blocks before, the anxiety started to build. For me, anxiety was not just butterflies in my stomach. It was not just a racing heartbeat. Anxiety was a full body illness that pervaded every inch of me. Before that day, I thought I was ready. I longed to return to some sort of teenage normalcy, but eating lunch in the cafeteria now seemed as difficult as climbing Mount Everest.

Would I go full on post traumatic? Lose my nerve and run screaming from the building? Maybe I'd start crying and hear non-existent gunshots like a war veteran. In the time I'd had to think about it and imagine how it would go down, I knew anything was possible.

"Don't talk about Wick in front of Amber," Alex advised as we approached the double doors that led into the cafeteria. "In fact, just stay away from Wick if you can."

Wick and this Amber person were the last people on my mind. Seriously, I wished high school relationship drama was my biggest concern, but it wasn't. Getting through the next ten minutes was my only goal.

"I wasn't planning on it," I mumbled.

"Okay, good. Because trust me, you don't want to get in the middle of that on your first day."

Alex pulled open the door, and the cacophony of voices inside seemed to hit me like a wall. Despite feeling as if my legs weighed two hundred pounds each, I still followed her through the doors. Right away, I noticed that it was different than Beaton—smaller and not as nice. Adrenaline flooded my system, and I had to fight the urge to turn and leave.

"So this is the lunchroom," Alex said. "The other side, by the back door, is the middle school side so don't go over there."

Ahead of me was the food service area. Lines formed at various places, but I only saw one cashier. Alex and I stood in a middle aisle with long tables extending in rows on either side. Many of the tables were already full.

"That's where we usually sit," Alex pointed at a table on the left, all the way down by the windows. "Did you bring your lunch or do you need to buy?"

I exhaled the breath I was holding. "Brought. Thanks," I said softly, glad the words were willing to come.

This meant I was *coping*. *Coping* was what Mom said we had to do. Before, I never had to cope with much of anything, but after, every minute revolved around doing just that.

"Okay, this way," Alex said.

We made the short journey to our designated table and stopped at the far end.

"Hey, guys. This is Lainey. She's new."

I get various greetings and smiles from the girls. Alex introduced each of them, but there was no way I could remember all their names except for maybe the aforementioned Amber. She definitely would have stood out anyway. Clearly, these girls were cool. They wore American Eagle jeans and Patagonia jackets and Steve Madden boots. They all had long hair and well done makeup, and they were all examining me with that knowing look girls have when they recognize you're pretty, and they try to decide if they can still like you or not. It happens very fast. First impressions really do matter.

"You can sit here," Alex said.

I quickly dropped into place and busied myself retrieving my lunch from my bag—peanut butter and jelly on soft oatmeal bread. This was one of the only things I could choke down that didn't cause me stomach spasms.

When I glanced up again, I met Amber's deep blue eyes. "Where in California did you live?" She had long, stick-straight brown hair and a bitch-on-wheels pout.

"San Francisco," I lied.

"Wow. Must be weird coming here." Her tone let me know I was boring her. My presence and the day and the whole entire world seemed a terrible bore to Amber.

"Yeah, my parents got divorced." In reality, my parents had been divorced for years. I don't ever remember them together. Mom kept the Beverly Hills house, and Dad headed off to Malibu as per some secret script that ruled those matters in Hollywood.

"So who dragged you here?" a different girl asked.

"My mother. She used to summer here, and she wanted to get away."

Another lie. My mother never set foot on this island before last week. One of Dad's lawyers who grew up in Massachusetts recommended it to us. *Beautiful place, good real estate investment.*

"I guess this is getting away," Amber replied.

Wick appeared beside the table with a tray of food and another jacket clad boy I remembered from the morning, *Perk 56 LB.*

"Hi ladies," Wick said. He sat directly across from me. "You being nice to the newbie?"

"Lainey," Alex told him. "Her name is Lainey."

"I remember," Wick answered. "Did everyone have a good weekend?"

Lunch proceeded as follows: everyone shared their weekend stories, Wick eyed me, Amber eyed Wick, and I eyed my peanut butter and jelly. If Amber could have killed Wick with just her eyes, he'd have died that day for sure. I, unfortunately, was familiar with this look—the look of both love and hate. It was all the more reason to stay away from the likes of Michael Wickersham. Wick and Amber. Amber and Wick. They were the stars of that show. They were the biggest sharks in that little pond.

"So what do you think of our little island so far?" Wick asked. He kept his voice low, trying to interact with just me.

"It's okay. The weather is kind of hard to get used to."

"Yeah. Right now, for sure. It gets better though. Summer is amazing."

He held me fast in his gaze. I glanced away and back, and he hadn't waivered. He licked his lips and lifted them in a smile that was probably intended to be sexy.

"Did you have a boyfriend in California, Lainey?" The blonde seated beside Amber asked loudly.

My face flushed with heat. "Umm, no. Not really."

Dumb dumb dumb. I should have had a better answer planned.

Amber chuckled. "What exactly does *not really* mean when it comes to a boyfriend?"

Perk almost spewed chocolate milk, his body shaking with laughter. Wick tried to hide his own smile with his hand, clearing his throat and shifting in his seat.

When Perk pulled himself together, he said, "Oh I think you know exactly what that means, Amber."

"Shut up, Tyler," the blonde snapped. She and Amber stood and stormed off, probably headed for the bathroom where they could refresh their lip gloss and vent about the boys.

For my part, I wanted to melt into my seat from embarrassment. Being the new girl was bad enough without coming between the *it* couple of the whole school. I spent the rest of lunch trying to avoid looking at anyone while Wick kept trying to give me some kind of knowing look that I refused to accept. When the bell rang, I jumped to my feet and went to throw out my trash. I found Alex again near the door despite the sea of other students leaving for class.

As we walked to physics, Alex explained Amber and Wick. "She swears she's over him but they always hook up at parties and stuff. It's very dysfunctional."

"It's fine. I'm not interested in him."

"Really?" Alex wrinkled her forehead.

I should have been interested, I guess. Wick was the kind of boy that everyone was automatically interested in because of his looks and his status and his all around cocky attitude.

"Yeah. He's not my type."

Alex dropped her tone to low and conspiratorial. "What's your type?" she asked.

"Older. College boys. I only dated high school boys when I was a freshman."

This was not a lie although no one would have been able to tell from the way I behaved so far that I was ever confident and experienced enough to handle myself with guys.

"Oh," was all Alex said in response. She seemed to be

pondering my revelation as we continued walking toward the science wing.

I just hoped she'd get the word out about me not being interested. Blending in was my goal and dating the most popular junior boy would only serve to draw attention to myself. This starting-over stuff was turning out to be more complicated than I anticipated. I was not the same person I was before, and I had no idea who to become. Maybe I should have spent more time figuring that out. School used to be so easy for me—the academics, the socializing, the tennis team. But in Nantucket, it all seemed kind of overwhelming.

Alex said, "I don't have this physics class with you. When it's over, head down to the gym for P.E. and I'll see you there. That's our last class today."

"Thanks for your help. I really appreciate it."

"No problem."

Alex seemed to have good intentions towards me, and I felt truly grateful for her help.

Once alone, I tried to ground myself again. *Two more classes. Two more classes. I can do this.* Nantucket High School was better than the alternative—better than tutors and solitary confinement. I inhaled a deep breath and stepped over the threshold.

Chapter 3

Gage

NEW GIRL WALKED IN. As soon as I spied her in the doorway with her schedule clutched in her hand, I knew I'd get stuck with her. The odd number of students in physics had worked so well in my favor, but with her arrival, I'd be saddled with an unwanted partner.

She approached Smithson. He leaned on his cane near the back table, counting supplies. Kids were always stealing his crap—pulleys and magnets and steel balls. Teenagers, in general, are kleptomaniacs.

As I watched her, I could see what all the excitement was about. Her face was smooth and blemish free. Cheekbones, lips, chin, eyebrows—all stunningly arranged. Her hair was kind of plain—brown and straight and to her chin, and she was a bit skinny for my taste. Like, someone needed to give her a cheeseburger and a cupcake, quick. From what I overheard in the locker room after P.E, though, her eyes were the kicker—pure green and sexy as hell. Wick said her eyes alone got him fired up. *Smoke show* he called her.

She stopped beside Smithson and cleared her throat.

"Hello, young lady, may I help you?" he asked when he noticed her there.

"Yes. I'm new, and I think I'm in this class." Her voice was soft and not too high. She even sounded pretty.

Smithson cocked his head to the side as he peered down at her. "Welcome. Schedule?"

She handed it over, and he examined it about two inches from his reading glasses. I suspected he had a cataract, but I might have been wrong. He glanced back up at her. "I assume you were enrolled in honors physics at your previous school?" Smithson had little tolerance for weak students.

She nodded.

"Fantastic!" He thrust the schedule back at her. His quick motion and sudden excitement made her flinch. "We'll be performing a lab today. I have one student without a partner. Gage!"

I blew out my breath loudly before answering. "Yeah?"

"This young lady…" He paused to read her name again. "Ms. Lainey Darwin will be your new lab partner. I am entrusting her to your care, and I am confident that you will be an excellent ambassador of our class and school."

"Yes sir." I gave him a lazy salute.

"Fantastic. Good luck Ms. Darwin. Mr. Pike will get you everything you need."

New Girl seemed a little panicked. She glanced between me and Smithson, opening her mouth like she might object. When nothing came out, however, Smithson hobbled his way back to his desk.

"Have you done a pendulum lab before?" I asked her, figuring it was best to just jump right in. I stayed half straddling my stool, wanting to appear unfazed and uninterested in her presence. But when she looked at me (like I mean really looked at me) that's when the trouble started. Her eyes. Wick was right; there was something about them. I could see the danger in looking at her for very long. I could already feel her clouding my judgment, giving me stupid thoughts like *God she's gorgeous* and *Wow, I hope she likes me.*

"No." Her answer was quiet and sort of emerged as a sigh. She set her backpack on the floor beside her stool while I tamped down the warm feeling of nervousness in my chest. Meeting Lainey and talking to Lainey was disconcerting—her face a mix of attractiveness edged with some acute sadness she couldn't hide. She was trying, of course, as anyone would, but it wasn't working.

"Fantastic," I answered, imitating the elderly Mr. Smithson but with far less enthusiasm. "Let's get started."

I hoped I could keep myself together and get through the lab without turning into a bumbling idiot in her presence.

Lainey

Gage Pike was a cruel joke. After what I had already endured my first day, I would have much preferred a normal, run of the mill lab partner. But when this boy stood and unfurled himself for me to behold, I could see that he was anything but run of the mill. Instead, he was six foot three, at least, with broad shoulders and a lanky frame. He wore Doc Marten boots, slim cut khakis, and a faded concert tee-shirt. A tousled head of spiky, blondish hair along with chiseled cheek bones and wide set blue eyes rounded out the picture making him really hot even though he exuded a bit too much of the skaterboy/musician/rebel attitude for my taste.

"This way," he said. And, like a good partner should, I followed him to a nearby supply closet. Inside, it smelled like freshly cut wood and mothballs. Gage began rifling around on the shelves looking for materials. The aisle was narrow and the shelving was deep, so he had to lean way in. I tried not to look at his back and arms and butt when he did it, but it wasn't easy to avoid. Eventually, he found something he was looking for, and he extended his hand backward to me without turning around.

"Hold these," he said, dropping two silver discs, two stopwatches, and some string into my hand. I struggled to take it all, but enjoyed how his fingertips felt warm when they grazed my chilly palm. After that, he bent way down to pull two wooden stands off a low shelf. When he popped back up with his hands full, our eyes met, and I froze in place. He squinted down at me and seemed to wait for me to read his mind. And I tried. I really did. Unfortunately, I had nothing.

Finally, he said. "Okay, back to the table now," and bobbed his head in that direction. That's when I realized he just wanted me to move. He wasn't trying to have a little staring moment with me after all. *Dear God! What was wrong with me!*

I mumbled, "Oh. Okay," and backed out of the closet, my cheeks burning with the red-hot intensity of embarrassment.

Once we reached our table, Gage thankfully went about setting up the lab without another word except to direct me to a side table where I picked up all the hand-outs. The experiment itself required two pendulums with different lengths of string which we had to time and observe at intervals. Gage set everything up and pointed to a spot on my lab sheet for the data when he was done.

"You watch this one. Time and write down how many swings per thirty seconds."

"Got it."

As I watched, the swinging motion of the disk mesmerized me. My head buzzed and my eyes grew tired. I rested my elbow on the lab table, chin on my hand, and kept track of the swings.

After a few minutes, Gage asked, "How's your first day going?"

I shrugged and jotted down a number. "Okay."

"Just okay?"

"Yeah. But it's not over yet."

"So it could still go either way, I guess," he said. "Fabulous or suckish. Or maybe it will stay *just okay*."

I focused on my pendulum and kept counting as a small smile lifted my lips. "Fabulous is doubtful," I replied.

Gage Pike grinned in my peripheral vision. "You never know, New Girl. Things could take a turn for the fabulous when you least expect it."

"I guess there's always hope," I bantered in return.

When we cleaned up at the end of class, Gage said, "We have to do the write up for this tonight. Did you get a school Google account?"

"Yeah. I think it's with the stuff guidance gave me."

Gage slid his phone out of his bag. "Give me your number so we can text and meet up in Google docs. Have you used it before?"

"Yeah. It shouldn't be a problem."

"What's your number?"

I recited it for him and heard my phone vibrate in my bag.

"You should have mine now. Can you carry these to the closet?" Gage dropped the disks and string back into my palm. The contact only lasted a moment and really, it was no big deal, but I still liked it. Being with Gage and doing the lab with him, this was why I came. I wanted to be a normal teenager again doing normal teenage things. No one ever appreciated normal.

"I hope at least this class wasn't suckish," Gage said as the bell sounded.

"No. This class was good." And my answer was definitely not a lie.

Chapter 4

T HOMAS AND I HELD HANDS *and waited on the edge of the pool. Rosa, our live-in housekeeper and nanny, counted to three.*

"Uno, dos, tres!"

On cue, we launched from the side into the shimmering water. Thomas always grinned when he came up. "Again! Again!" he said as he shook droplets of moisture from his head.

Rosa let us jump as many times as we wanted but not our swim teacher, Kimberly. Kimberly had a job to do, and Thomas did not like that. He'd sit on a chaise and pout if he didn't get his way, refusing to go in and practice his strokes. Rosa tried to help, telling Kimberly to promise him popsicles or chocolate or candy, and sometimes, that worked. But sometimes, he wouldn't come in to swim until she let him jump as many times as he wanted. I had to hold his hand and Kimberly had to count in Spanish just like Rosa. I saw the way she scowled at him and sighed when he was being difficult, and for that reason, I never really liked Kimberly.

Lainey

Our house in Beverly Hills was a Georgian-style mansion. The story goes that my mother fell in love with number 609

North Canon Drive as soon as she laid eyes on it because it reminded her of old Hollywood. She was newly pregnant with me and had just played a prostitute in my father's film *Attachment Disorder*. A blonde ingénue fresh off the bus from Minnesota—Audrey Warner won over the audience and Roland Berringer's forty-something-year-old heart at the same time.

My father purchased the house for his blossoming family, and we all moved in when I was an infant after a meticulous renovation. By the time Thomas arrived and was a toddling around, however, my father was already gone. Apparently, my parent's relationship was not a romance that could survive the realities of family life.

Forty-Nine Madaket Road in Nantucket was cozier and homier than the Beverly Hills house. A shingled colonial, it had only three bedrooms and two and half baths. It still cost over a million dollars, though, because of Nantucket's cache. The interior was decorated in the latest coastal chic style by a designer who readied the space for us at warp speed once the decision to come to Nantucket was made.

"The plumber came today about the heat," Mom told me at dinner.

In all the craziness of my first day, I forgot about the heat issue. Clearly, he fixed it because it was nice and warm in the house.

Mom served up a new creamy chicken dish. Cooking was her new hobby despite the fact she didn't cook back home. Rosa took care of that along with many other tasks usually reserved for parents. My mother behaved more like a big sister with a bunch of boyfriends and too many parties to attend. I was still getting used to the new version

27

of her who hung around the house and asked me too many questions.

"He got it working but it needs a few new parts," she continued. "Then I went grocery shopping."

"Oh." I dabbed Italian dressing on my salad.

"So school was okay? You made one new friend at least, right? Alex?"

"Yeah." I took a bite of lettuce; unsure I could classify anyone I met that day as a friend yet. But if this was what Mom wanted to think, I'd let her.

"Do the classes seem hard?"

"No. They're fine. I need an Instagram, though."

Mom cut a piece of chicken. "Are you sure?"

"Yeah. It will seem weird if I don't have something. I can get away with not having Facebook and Twitter, but everyone has Instagram. I already set up snapchat."

"If you think you need it, go ahead. But you can't have any pictures from before."

"I know. You don't have to keep telling me."

She stabbed a cherry tomato in her salad. "I spoke with your father today."

I didn't respond with words—just a hum as I ate another bite of salad.

"He met with Thomas and the lawyers this morning."

I stopped chewing for a second but then resumed without acknowledging her.

"Dad said he looked okay. He's taking his medication."

I curled my free hand into a fist in my lap. "Are they making the deal soon?" I asked.

Mom stared at the opposite wall as if there was something important there to see. My mother's hair was dyed brown, too, and so short, she looked like an elf. "Not yet." Her gaze dropped to her plate. "They're trying, but the prosecutor's office is being difficult."

If they didn't make a plea deal, Thomas would go to trial, and I could be forced to testify. I might have to recount before a courtroom full of people and cameras what happened that day in the cafeteria. I would have to explain that my brother was a monster. Thomas was a monster, and I was his sister.

"You said it would happen, that it was pretty much a done deal." My voice cracked on the last word.

"I never said it was a done deal, Lizzie. I said most likely. But you never know about these things until the papers are signed."

I wanted to yell at her. I wanted to berate her because everything about this situation seemed unfair, and someone had to be to blame. Didn't the prosecutors see what was so obvious? Thomas was insane. He had to be insane to do what he did. Why must it be debated and hashed out any longer? Making an example of Thomas would help no one. A trial wouldn't bring anyone back.

I set my fork down. "I'm not really hungry right now."

"You have to eat."

"Maybe later."

I stood and headed for the stairs. Once in my room, I went straight to my bed and buried my face in the pillow. I wanted to cry, but that night, no tears came. Sometimes, this happened to me. I became numb and then, without warning, the tears would return — scalding torrents of shame that swelled my face and clogged my nose. Those days were some of the worst.

Four people died that day. When I focused on that, I felt like the most selfish girl in the world. I should have been grateful to be alive. I should have been grateful my brother was alive. This gratitude for life that people were always talking about was never enough, though. For me, it could not stem the tide of loss that kept rising, the guilt and regret that washed over me, the what-ifs and what-fors and painful memories of better times. Too much was lost that day for gratitude to beat it back, and despite reassurances from people like my parents and Belinda that *things will get better*, I didn't believe they ever would.

My room in Nantucket resembled that of a perky pre-teen. It had soothing blue walls, a yellow and orange flowered duvet, and white furniture. My mother must have neglected to tell the decorator that I was, in fact, seventeen and not twelve. She did, however, get the message that it needed to be a cheerful space. My room was another of my mother's not-so-subtle attempts to snap me out of my depression.

When I finished with my pity party on the bed, I went to my desk and opened my MacBook. I logged into my new school account and found an email stating Gage Pike shared a file with me. I grabbed my phone to check for a text message from him, but there was nothing. Should I text him first? I quickly decided that messaging your lab partner was no big deal and typed him a simple sentence.

Going to work on the lab report now.

I stared at the words for a few moments before tapping send. For whatever reason, I wanted Gage to like me. Not *like me* like me but to think I was cool and want to be my friend kind of like.

When he didn't answer right away, I set down my phone and opened the document. I needed to input my pendulum times on a grid. Then, there were several questions to answer and equations to solve. I was almost done with the grid when Gage logged in. A "P" for Pike popped up at the top of the document and then the chat window opened.

Hey

My insides twisted with excitement.

Hi

You got into the network okay?

Yeah. Fine.

I usually do this crap alone

I wondered how to answer this.

Okay. You can check my work? I finally wrote.

No. It's fine. I'm sure you know what you're doing.

I'll do the questions about my data.

Okay.

We worked separately after that. When I finished, I scrolled down to the page Gage was working on. He was still typing his second to last answer. I typed in the chat window: **I think my part is done.**

He answered: **Okay**

I wanted to keep chatting. To me, Gage seemed like he had the most potential to be a genuine friend. He didn't care about how I looked or how I got there. He just wanted to make me smile.

Do you have Rapisardi for English? I asked.

Not this year. Why?

Just wondering

What are you reading?

The Awakening

We haven't read that yet in Sullivan's class.

Oh

Do you have Winston for pre calc?

No. Hepps.

Apparently, we only have physics in common ☺

I smiled at his smiley. Smileys were a sign of friendship. I tried to remember the last smiley anyone sent to me. It was probably Hannah. I closed my eyes and sucked in a breath before responding with one of my own.

Apparently ☺ I wrote back. **Let me know if my answers are okay.**

Okay.

Ttyl.

Bye.

After it was over, I stared at that exchange for far too long. I didn't so much analyze its meaning or wonder if Gage and I were friends yet; I simply considered the normalcy of it. This one small interaction with Gage was a win in the fight for average. Could I maintain a relationship such as that? One that was not fraught with all my baggage? Only time would tell.

Chapter 5

Lainey

P RE-CALCULUS WAS FIRST BLOCK. I got there before anyone else, glad to have an assigned seat to return to. All my homework was completed with meticulous precision. Math had always been a strength for me, and I found it oddly comforting now—the order and definitiveness and complete inhumanity of solving the problems. Taking out my notebook, I ran my fingertips over the pencil markings on the page just as Wick plopped down beside me.

"Hey." His toothpaste commercial grin practically twinkled. "How was your first day?" he asked.

"Good."

"You get all the homework done?" He reached into his bag for his notebook.

"Yeah. Done." I rested my hand on top of the problems as if to protect them from him.

"I can help you if you need it. Math's kinda my thing."

I debated asking him why he was in the wrong seat but decided to wait and see if he planned to stay. "I did okay with it, thanks."

Other kids were arriving, and it felt like everyone was

looking at us. They whispered and stared and wore knowing expressions. Amber walked in with her death glare on and the boy whose seat Wick had taken went and sat at the back table with barely a moment's hesitation.

Meanwhile, Wick tilted ever closer to me—his body seeming to take up an enormous amount of space.

"We should hang out sometime," he said.

His offer was vague, so I saw no immediate danger in agreeing. "Sure," I answered. I could always be busy later.

"Cool. Meet me in the student lot after school. I have a white truck."

What? That escalated quickly. From *sometime* to immediately after school today? Alex warned me to avoid him. Why couldn't I follow her one simple instruction?

I tried to formulate an escape plan. Not showing up? Lying that I had to go straight home? *You see Wick, my family is very religious, and I'm not allowed to be alone with boys. Ever.*

"Alright! Notebooks out!" Hepps called from the front of the room.

I tried to calm myself through reasoning, like a math problem. Aside from Alex's advice, hanging out with Wick should have been no big deal. In fact, I should have been happy considering how good looking and popular he was. Maybe it didn't feel exactly right, but the old me would have accepted the invitation. Maybe Wick would help me regain some of myself. Single Lizzie from Beverly Hills would have gone. Single Lizzie would have seen it as an adventure.

Maybe I could recapture myself by following that old script. Just be her. Lizzie instead of Lainey. If only that was possible.

Smithson was speaking to Gage when I arrived at Physics last block of the day.

"Mr. Pike, I do not wish to see your undergarments sticking out of your trousers. Please find a way to secure them properly."

I waited for Smithson to limp away before taking my seat. Gage stood and hoisted up his khakis. "Hey," he said.

"Hi. Can I ask you a question?"

"Sure."

"How do I get to the student lot?"

"It's over off First Way. I can show you after class. I'm parked there."

"Thanks."

"Are you meeting someone?"

"Yeah."

"Who?"

"Wick."

Gage's eyes widened. "Oh. Okay."

"Is there something wrong with that?"

Gage mussed his hair with his hand and scowled "Depends on your definition of wrong."

"What does that mean?"

"Let's just say Wick has kind of a reputation."

"Yeah, like with Amber?"

"And others."

"Well maybe he and I will be just friends."

Gage quirked up his mouth in a wry smile. "Good luck with that."

I bowed my head. "Well, he asked and I didn't want to seem rude or stuck up."

"Well, you can always back out. Just text him that you have to go home."

"I don't have his number."

Smithson's voice boomed over us. "Put everything away except a pencil! We're having a pop quiz on pendulums!"

"Shit," Gage muttered.

"At least we did the homework," I said.

"At least."

The quiz took most of the class to complete and was quite difficult. When the bell rang, Gage and I packed up. "Do you still want to go?" he asked.

"Yeah. I should."

Gage and I walked through to the Hall of the Whale and then through the corridor between the library and the cafeteria. Practically everyone we passed along the way took notice, too. Gage's height and stride and presence beside me felt oddly right—like an algebra problem that produces the correct solution the first time through, no erasing necessary.

Once we exited the school, the frigid wind hit my body like walking into a wall. I shoved my hands in my pockets and bowed my head in submission to its power.

We trudged along toward a gravel path beside a basketball court. After the path, we emerged onto a dirt road across from a dirt parking lot filled with student cars.

"That's Wicks truck." Gage pointed at an older white Ford.

"Which is your car?" I asked.

"Ancient black Cherokee right there."

"It doesn't look that old," I said, smiling. Again. My only real smiles up to that point had come from Gage.

"It is. Trust me." Gage kicked at a rock with his boot. "You could still change your mind, you know. I'll give you a ride home if you don't want to go."

A ride from Gage sounded great. Wick would be furious I blew him off, but I suddenly didn't care. Unfortunately, three letterman jackets emerged from the path and headed right for us at that precise moment, before we had a chance to get away.

"Hey Lainey," Wick said as they arrived. He wasn't looking at me, though. Instead, he was staring down Gage. "Pike being a friendly guy today?" he asked.

Gage stood his ground, meeting Wick's gaze head on. The other boys, Perk and a heavy-set guy with a jacket that said *Lub RG 68*, puffed out their chests.

"Gage showed me where the parking lot was. We're lab partners in physics." I sounded defensive, even to my own ears.

"Thanks for your help, Pike." Wick said.

His words may have been pleasant, but his voice was as cold as the wind. Without answering, Gage turned his attention back to me, a stern expression on his face.

"Text me later, okay?" He backed away toward his car, keeping our eye contact.

"Okay. I will," I answered. My chest filled with a weird, warm feeling of happiness at his apparent concern for me. Feelings. Finally, I was having some that weren't desperately depressing.

Gage gave me a final head bob before turning away and striding the rest of the way to his car.

Wick and Perk and Lub all watched him go.

"You ready?" Wick asked me.

I nodded in response, glancing at the other boys and hoping they weren't coming. A group hangout was not what I signed on for, especially not with that particular group.

Wick said, "This way."

I walked beside him to his truck, relieved that Perk and Lub stayed behind.

"Have fun!" Perk called after us.

Wick smirked over his shoulder in response.

The Cherokee backed out and drove away, and I found myself wishing I had thought more about the implications of this "hang out" before that moment—before I was committed. I probably could have squirmed my way out of it at some point before then, but instead, there I was—feeling like I was about to be sacrificed to the hook-up god of Nantucket High School in his never-ending quest to prove his virility. So much for resurrecting Lizzie.

I gazed out the window of his truck as we drove away from school. Leafless trees and scraggly bushes marred the landscape. Little kids walking home from elementary school in hats and mittens and parkas provided the only pops of color. Winter in Nantucket was like a post-apocalyptic wasteland, but maybe it was only me who saw it this way. Everything looked different to me since the shooting.

I was driven to the police station in the back of a police cruiser when it was over. Because I was the sister of the shooter, I had to go. I wasn't hand cuffed or technically arrested, but I was 'taken into custody'. A female officer named Nava drove me, and as we passed all the places that should have been so familiar to me, places that I saw every day, I realized they were all different. Tilted. Fogged over. Not the same at all.

"Lainey?" Wick touched my arm and I jumped. "You okay?"

He wore an expression of genuine concern, and I realized I must have been having one of those moments. I called them zone outs, and Belinda called them episodes of disassociation. Whatever the name, it was a pretty obvious sign of my PTSD, and Michael Wickersham had just witnessed it firsthand.

"Yeah. Fine," I said weakly.

We were parked in front of a one and half story colonial on a small lot. I had no idea what part of town it was—just that it seemed to be a neighborhood where a lot of people lived year-round.

"Let's go in. It's freezing," Wick said.

I brought my backpack on the off chance we'd do homework. We entered through a side door into a mud room.

"Here, I'll take your coat for you," Wick said.

Facing me, he touched my shoulders and ran his hands down my arms. I averted my eyes from his and reached to unzip my jacket, but he leaned down and tried to get me to look at him. "Hey," he said. "Are you nervous or something?"

I shook my head *no* even though I suddenly was. My heart raced and my face flushed.

"You seem it," he said. "Maybe I should kiss you now, you know, so you won't be anymore."

And he did. He captured my lips with his and pressed me against the door to his hall closet. He was a decent kisser, too, which I guess I should have expected. A rush of hormones flooded my system. Despite my reservations about being with Wick, I enjoyed kissing him. Kissing Wick made the flat nothingness fade away.

After a minute or so, we came up for air.

"You're so hot," Wick said, his lips grazing my cheek.

"Thanks," I breathed against his hair.

"Let's go up to my room."

"Okay, but I don't want things to move too fast."

I needed to be smart. I couldn't let how good it felt physically cloud my judgment.

"Too fast? Is that like a California thing," he asked, kissing my neck.

"No. Just a me thing," I told him.

Wick pulled away and examined my face. Boys had looked at me like that before—as if I was a difficult math problem or a complex skateboarding trick that needed to be conquered. And like those boys before, Wick decided the best way to deal with me was to forge ahead.

"This way," he said, taking my hand.

He led me through his house which was small and neat with modest furnishings. Pictures of Wick and what must have been his brothers hung proudly on the wall of the staircase.

"You have brothers?" I asked as we ascended.

"Yeah. Two. I'm the youngest."

When we reached his room, he shrugged off his jacket and threw it on his desk chair. Then, he stepped close and started kissing me again. He kissed me, and I kissed him back. Against my better judgement, I hooked up with Wick. I felt sexy and rebellious and turned-on by what I was doing. I hadn't kissed a boy in five months, and I marveled at the sensation of doing it again—strong arms around me, a solid chest pressed to mine, someone's mouth hot on my neck and lips. It didn't matter who it was, and I knew I'd probably feel guilty later. All I wanted at the time, however, was to continue—to extend the sensation of being alive.

To Wick's credit, he went slow at first, but I had to stop him when he finally tried to undo the button on my jeans. I knew I couldn't let him do that. That would definitely be going too far.

"Not today," I whispered in his ear, placing my hand on his. This was a good thing to say to boys. It did not thoroughly disappoint and offend them. These two words left room for hope, and they liked that. "I should really get going. My mom will be wondering where I am."

Wick rolled away with a sigh, reaching to adjust himself below the belt. Once free of him, I swung my legs over the edge of the bed and headed for the hallway. "Bathroom?" I asked from the door.

"Down on the right," he said, barely raising his head from the pillow.

In the car, I told Wick where I lived.

"Madaket Road or Madaket? There's a big difference."

"Madaket Road. Near Main Street," I answered.

"Oh, good. Because Madaket's a pain in the ass."

Once we were underway, Wick said, "That was fun."

"Yeah," I answered, even though fun was not exactly how I'd describe it.

Before I could think too hard on the subject, however, Wick started in with some ground rules.

"Since you're new, you should know that you can't hang out with me and hang out with Gage."

41

Seriously? We made out once and he was already telling me who I could be friends with?

"What does that mean?" I asked.

"I'm just letting you know how it is," he said. "You can't hang out with me and hang out with him."

I didn't respond to him that time because there didn't seem to be any point. He'd made his stance clear. We were quiet for the rest of the ride. Luckily, my mother's car was gone when we got to my house so I didn't have to explain to her how I ended up in a strange boy's truck on my second day.

"Give me your number," Wick said once the truck was in park. I recited it, and my phone vibrated in my pocket.

"Call me or text later." Wick leaned over and kissed me one last time, smooth and seductive.

"Bye," I said, escaping as soon as I could.

And walking to my door, I wondered how I ended up in that situation—the apparent property of Michael Wickersham. I guess there were worse things I could be. I knew all about worse things.

Chapter 6

Lainey

ONCE I MADE IT TO my room, I immediately texted Gage.

Home.

Okay

According to Wick, I can't hang out with you and hang out with him?

Yeah. I can see that being a problem for him.

Why?

Um, do I really need to spell it out for you?

Yeah. That would be helpful.

Because he's Wick.

That's not helpful.

But I understand if you want to go out with him.

I don't know what I want right now.

And that was the truth. Part of me did want to go out with Wick, and part of me wanted to pretend the afternoon with him never happened.

Changing the subject...that quiz today sucked.

Ugh. It did.

I laid on my bed texting with Gage until my mother called me for dinner.

Gtg eat. ttyl.

Are you sure about that? Might be against the rules to ttyl ☺

No. I'm sure ☺

I wrote the last line with more confidence than I felt. And as I headed down the stairs for dinner, the guilt I knew was coming began to wiggle its deceitful way into my heart and mind. Going with Wick was dumb. Making out with him was wrong. He was practically a stranger. I should have been stronger, and I should have found a way out, but instead I just let it happen like I had no say. Like a doormat. I had never been anyone's doormat before, so I wasn't quite sure why I let it happen in Nantucket. I only hoped that the fallout would be minor—that I'd be able to recover from my temporary insanity that afternoon.

Gage

The walk into school Wednesday was like a walk across Antarctica. I wore a winter hat and fleece jacket, but I hadn't been able to find any gloves. I blamed Laura for this because stepmothers were easily blamed for everything that went wrong. She probably stashed them someplace safe but illogical, and she was still asleep when I left the house, so I couldn't ask her.

I was about halfway down the path beside the basketball court when Wick fell into step beside me.

"Nice try yesterday," he said. "Sorry it's not going to work out for you."

I knew he was talking about Lainey, but I refused to give him the satisfaction of an answer. Perk appeared on my other side, making me a letterman jacket sandwich.

Wick continued, "See, Pike, you need to realize you play on the JV squad. And that girl? She's way out of your league. Like division one college material."

Perk chuckled at the joke. I glanced at him and then back to Wick. "Wow, Michael," I said because I knew he preferred Wick. "Did you just create a sports metaphor to aid in my understanding of your message? I'm so impressed. I bet Mr. Rap would be too."

Lucky for me, we had reached the teacher parking area by that time. If that handful of teachers and other students hadn't been around, Wick and Perk might have tried to kick my ass.

Instead, Wick scoffed and said, "Just remember this little conversation. Time to back off." He clapped me on the back. "Nice chatting with you, Gage."

He and Perk stopped and waited for me to get several paces ahead before continuing. My face felt hot despite the cold air. I wanted to turn and rail against Wick for his attempt at bullying and belittling me, but I knew that wouldn't turn out well. Plus, with every step I took, I questioned my choice to be friends with Lainey. Maybe, avoiding Lainey was my best option. By next week, she'd probably think I was a weird, boring nerd like all the girls in Amber's clique. Plus, all the sexy eyes and cute texts in the world weren't worth getting into it with Wickersham.

But could I shake her off? Lainey already seemed to think we were friends. This was a strange twist I hadn't seen coming, but that's how it was playing out. All I could do, really, was wait and see. I knew Wick wasn't going to put up with any crap, but Lainey didn't seem like she would either. Despite her quiet sadness, she also carried with her something else. Inner strength? That sounded too cliché but I had no other way to describe it. Whatever it was, I found myself hoping she'd use it to ditch Wick. Whoever said winter in Nantucket was boring didn't know New Girl would be showing up, that was for sure.

Lainey

When I awoke Wednesday morning to my alarm, my limbs felt like cement blocks. I huddled under my perky girl covers staring at the red digits of my clock. Moving here and starting a new life was supposed to help alleviate my depression but after yesterday with Michael Wickersham, I felt worse than ever. What was I thinking?

Sometimes, when I laid in bed, I thought about when Thomas and I were little and he'd come to my room at night. He was around six the first time it happened. I felt a hand on my arm and heard him whisper, "Wizzie. I had a bad dream."

I moved over and let him crawl into bed beside me.

"Mom?" I murmured.

"Not here," he said.

That meant she was still out or staying at a boyfriend's place.

"It's fine. It was just a dream," I told him. This was what my mother and sometimes Rosa said to me when I needed them in the night.

"It was scary. Can I stay here?"

"Okay."

In the morning, Rosa found us tangled together in the sheets.

"What is this? What happened?" she asked.

Rosa was a short, round woman with long, dark hair that she wore up in a bun most of the time. Over her years with us, her hair became increasingly streaked with gray. I loved Rosa because she always seemed to have time for me no matter how busy she was with chores. If I asked her for anything, Rosa would smile and try to help.

"Thomas had a bad dream," I explained, blinking in the light as she opened the blinds.

"You come to me if you need help, little man. I in my room. Okay?" She brushed his blond hair off his face.

"Okay," Thomas said.

But he never went to Rosa. After that, he always came to me, even when Mom was home. He would get into my bed without a word and curl up beside me. His warm body and silent presence was oddly comforting to me, too. I preferred to think of that Thomas and not the one who brought a gun to school.

"Lizzie!" Mom banged on my door. "You're going to be late."

"Coming," I called back.

With great effort, I extricated myself from the sheets. I managed to throw on clothes and put my hair up in a messy ponytail. While brushing my teeth, I examined my puffy eyes and pale cheeks, but there was nothing to be done about them.

On the way to school, Mom asked, "Are you okay?"

"Fine. Just tired."

I couldn't explain this feeling to her. On top of the guilt and sadness about my crazy brother, I felt like a failure at my second chance. I painted myself into a corner already— either be Wick's girlfriend until he gets sick of me or blow

47

him off and suffer the consequences of exile from the popular group. I wished I'd kept my stupid lips to myself.

"Were you up late?"

"A little."

My phone vibrates in my pocket.

Alex: **Did you hook up with Wick yesterday?**

Crap! Wick was already bragging to everyone about getting with me. He probably exaggerated the details, too. The great Michael Wickersham must always get further than second base.

I hovered my fingers over the screen, trying to figure out what I could write back that would make this better. I'd broken the one rule Alex gave me. *Don't get in the middle of Wick and Amber.*

I still hadn't written anything when another text appeared.

Wick: **Meet me in the café.**

My heart thumped in my chest. Wick most likely wanted to show off to his friends that we'd hooked up. I shoved my phone in my pocket without answering either of them as we arrived in front of the school.

"Text me if you need a ride," Mom called after me as I got out.

"I will."

I kept my head down, and went directly to physics. The rotating schedule made it first block on Wednesdays, and I was glad I would get to see Gage. When I walked in, he already sat on his stool wearing Beats headphones. He looked good, too, clad in jeans and a blue plaid flannel shirt.

"Hey," he said. He pulled the headphones down around his neck and twisted slightly toward me on his seat.

"Hi," I answered.

I took out my phone and saw another message from Wick.

Where r u?

Gage lowered his voice slightly. "Have you seen him?"

I shook my head.

"You all right?" Gage leaned closer, trying to look at my face.

"Yeah. Fine. Do we have a lab today?"

Gage studied me, squinting slightly. "No. Lecture. And they suck, just so you know." He quirked up his mouth in one of his cute smiles.

"Okay," I answered, glad to see his grin.

"And fine is a bullshit answer. I would prefer if you were just honest. Clearly, things are not *fine* with you."

"What?"

"Don't play dumb. You know what I'm talking about."

And I found myself smiling. Gage felt like a salve on my wound. His friendship and humor were better than Prozac.

"O-kay," I said again, this time more emphatically.

"Settle down! Time to begin!" Smithson called from the front of the room.

He projected the first slide of a PowerPoint on the Smartboard. Gage removed his Beats from his neck and got ready to take notes.

Smithson stood stiffly at a lectern placed on the front table, and clicked through the slides as if we were in the speed round of a game show. I had zero chance of keeping up with the notes at that rate. Gage seemed to be writing very short bullets of information.

"It's all online," he whispered when he saw me floundering.

49

"Thank God." I stopped writing and tried to just listen.

"Collision occurs when two or more objects make impact with each other. Momentum is transferred from one object to the other. A collision can be elastic or inelastic."

In physics, we learned about inanimate objects in static environments. These kinds of events were so much easier to understand, easier to predict and write formulas about. Scientists like Smithson preferred it that way. The real world was not so simple. In the real world, chance and randomness and people made everything messier. I was stuck on a collision course with Michael Wickersham. Would our next contact be elastic or inelastic? Who'd gain the bulk of the momentum as a result? There was no way to do an equation to figure that one out. My brother's collision was most definitely inelastic. He became a solid, unchangeable force, and once set in motion, he was unstoppable.

The noise of the first shot rang in my head. Firecrackers. Who's setting off firecrackers at lunch? The first screams. Like nothing I'd ever heard before. Screams of terror. There was no mistaking them for shrieks of delight or bursts of silliness. The screams were as distinct as the sound of the gun.

I didn't see him right away from my spot on the other side of the room. He was obscured by fleeing students, and even when he emerged from the crowd with what I thought was a toy gun clutched in his hand, I still couldn't process what was happening. This was a dream. I was sure I was going to wake up any second to find it was all just a terrible nightmare.

Someone touched my arm, making me flinch. I snapped back to reality and found Gage staring at me. I shook my head to clear it, and tried to bring myself fully back to the present. I realized I was hyperventilating short puffs of air.

Thankfully, Gage went back to taking notes and didn't ask any questions.

A few minutes later, however, during a lull in Smithson's droning, Gage leaned over to me.

"Do you smoke?" he asked.

His breath was warm on my neck, and I knew by the way he said it that he didn't mean cigarettes.

"On occasion." I kept my voice low, too, so no one around us would hear. I didn't move my eyes from my binder, but my chest tingled with heat from Gage's proximity. I liked how close he was, and the soft, deep tone of his voice.

"I might be having an occasion at my house after school," he said. "You in?"

I finally allowed myself to meet his gaze. "Yeah. Are you sure though?"

After our texts the night before, Gage had to know that hanging out with me would irritate Wick.

"Yeah. Meet me in the student lot."

Day three and I had a second invitation to ponder all day long. And this one would most certainly complicate the other.

Chapter 7

"COME ON, T-MAN. JUST GET out."

"No. I hate school."

I crouched between the car door of the Range Rover and Thomas in the back seat so we were eye level. "But you don't hate me," I said. "I'll walk you in and stay as long as you want."

He squinted at me. The sun beat down my back. I hoped he'd agree soon.

Finally, he said, "They won't let you do that. You have to go to class."

His cowlicked mop of blonde hair hung limply around his face. He needed a shower. Hygiene was yet another battle Rosa and Mom and I fought with him.

"I'll make them," I told him.

Thomas eyed me again, and I prayed that at eleven years old, he still believed I was capable of anything.

"Promise?" he asked.

"I promise," I said. At thirteen, I was confident it was a promise I could keep.

"Okay." He nodded and reached for his bag on the seat beside him. Rosa smiled and waved us off as we walked in together, hand in hand. Me and my petulant little T-Man.

Lainey

"Where were you this morning?" Wick asked when I sat down beside him in pre-calc.

I unpacked my bag, trying to appear unfazed by his question. "I went straight to physics."

"We always meet in the café in the morning," he told me.

I wasn't quite sure who he meant by *we* but apparently my presence was required if I wanted to continue to be Wick's makeout buddy. Instead of questioning him, however, I simply said, "Oh."

I had to decide before 2:20 if I'd be getting high with Gage or following Wick's rules. It wasn't so much that I wanted to get high, but more that I wanted to hang out with Gage. Leaving school with Gage, however, would definitely close the door on my brief stint as Wicks' girlfriend. He made that one rule very clear to me the day before. Surely, there were other rules too, ones which had not come up yet.

I should have wanted to be with Wick. There were most likely many girls at Nantucket High School who wanted to be his girlfriend du jour including Amber. On the other hand, Gage actually seemed to want to be my friend. It appeared to be as simple as that with him, but I could have been wrong. I was wrong about a lot of things I thought I knew.

"Did you do the English reading?" Wick asked.

"Yeah, why?" I finally allowed myself to meet his eyes.

"Because I need to know what happened. Did Edna finally bone that guy?"

Now I remembered one of the many reasons I liked older guys back home, maturity being the top of the list.

"Seriously? You have to read it. I can't tell you everything that happened."

"Just an overview." Wick grinned and reached to hold my hand. "In case Rapisardi calls on me."

I looked down at our joined hands. It was sort of like an out of body experience. Why did this feel so wrong?

"Fine. Yes. She boned him," I said and pulled my hand away.

"And?" he asked. "Did her husband find out?"

"Not yet." I dug around in my bag for a pencil and wished that Hepps would start the class.

"You're not being very helpful," Wick said.

"I didn't know I was in charge of your homework now."

"Didn't I mention that yesterday?"

He had to be kidding, right? I must have looked surprised, too, because he quickly said, "That was a joke," and laughed. "Are you always this serious?"

"Only when it comes to matters of my personal freedom," I replied.

"You sound like Edna, now." he joked.

If only he knew how true that was. And before I was obligated to continue the conversation, Hepps called for quiet.

Gage

Maybe it was my pessimistic nature, but I didn't think she'd show. I shouldn't have even asked her in the first place. Inviting her to hang out was exactly what Wick warned me about. Clearly, I had some kind of a death wish. That was the only explanation.

She had that weird little episode in physics, though. The heavy breathing and zoning out were a sign something was going on with her. I would have wanted someone to invite me to enjoy a small dose of relief if I was that messed up.

But then, I saw her at lunch with Wick. They walked in together and sat at his table. I tried not to stare but found myself unable to tear my eyes away. I wanted to see how she was with him. Happy? Flirty? Miserable? It seemed like a combination of all three or something else entirely. She did smile a few times, but from what I could tell, it was fake. I tore my gaze away when Andrew asked what was up and craned his head that way.

When he turned back, he gave me a wry, knowing smile. "See something you like?"

"Whatever," I replied.

At the student lot, a pit the size of a softball formed in my stomach. I generally tried to avoid high school drama of any sort, especially girl drama. Still, I waited because I offered, and it would have been rude to stand her up. I sat and watched for her in my rearview mirror. Finally, Lainey appeared on the path from school. I stopped breathing when I saw her because she might have been going to Wick's truck.

But that didn't happen. Instead, she scanned the parking lot, and when she spotted the Cherokee, she headed right for it.

Lainey

Gage and I didn't speak. I just got in his car, and he drove us away; a whole pack of letterman jackets watching.

I made my decision to go last block. Sitting in Spanish, I imagined both scenarios—laughing with Gage and getting high or making out with Wick and feeling dirty and disgusting. That was when I knew I'd go with Gage.

My phone vibrated in my pocket. I didn't need to take it out to know who it was.

Wick: **Are you an idiot?**

Me: **No**

Wick: **Definitely!**

Me: **Sorry. I just can't be tied down right now.**

Wick: **No. You're just a fucking slut. Delete my number.**

Me: **Gladly.**

My hands shook as I did it.

"It'll be alright. He'll get over it," Gage said.

"I hope so," I answered.

But Wick wasn't the kind of guy who just got over that kind of thing. I'd only been in Nantucket for three days, but already, I knew that for sure.

After a short ride, Gage turned right into a driveway. We never left Surfside Road, the same road the school was on. I knew there was a beach parking lot just a quarter mile or so ahead of where we turned. Almost every main road on Nantucket ended in a beach parking lot, the pavement strewn with shells from hungry seagulls, a little concession shack with peeling white paint and boarded up windows nearby. Like Wick said Monday, Nantucket was supposedly beautiful in the summer, and I curiously awaited the arrival of beautiful because all I saw at the time was gray skies and dead foliage.

"You're sure no one will be home?" I asked as he parked the Cherokee at the end of a long driveway. It seemed weird to be going to his house to smoke. We should have been driving to some isolated location to do it in his car.

"Yeah. We're good," he answered.

The house was a gray shingled colonial, like every other house in Nantucket, but the landscaping and the wrap-around porch made it clear that the Pikes had money. The lot size, too, was a giveaway. There were no encroaching neighbors like at Wick's house.

I followed Gage, crunching along the white shell driveway in my Uggs. He led me to a set of stairs on the side of the house which were strategically hidden by a cedar picket fence and well planned shrubbery. We descended to a door into the basement, and I tried not to notice the sexy way Gage's pants hung from his hips as he trotted down the stairs.

Inside, he flung his car keys onto a side table and plopped himself down in a desk chair. I scanned the room, a huge area that, despite being a basement, was finished like a regular room with plastered walls and wood floors. Various areas were delineated by rugs: the sofa, coffee table, television, and gaming console area; the music area with an expensive looking keyboard and several guitars on stands; and the sleeping area with a queen-size bed. The whole thing seemed to be exclusively Gage's domain, too. No inside stairs led to the main house, but I assumed they were through the one door on the far wall.

The bed was the part that drew my attention the most. It was pristinely made as if Gage attended a military school and had daily inspections. It was covered in a puffy, blue-striped quilt and a gray down comforter. I perched on the edge and asked, "Do you have a housekeeper or does your mom come down and make your bed every day?" I smoothed my hand over the soft fabric of the duvet.

"No, I do it. I live with my dad and step-mom, but the bed making is a habit from when I lived with my mom."

He retrieved a bag of green buds from a locked desk drawer with a key he wore around his neck. While he packed the bowl, I lounged back, my body going the wrong way across the bed. I studied his music posters, most of them bands I never heard of before. Gage allowed his eyes to linger on my prone body for a few too many seconds before returning to his work. I enjoyed him looking at me that way. Unlike Wick, I wanted this attention from Gage.

When I finished taking in his posters and admiring the colorful, hippy tapestry on one wall, I slipped off my Uggs and curled up on his pillows to wait. The bed smelled faintly of dryer sheets and marijuana and his woodsy cologne. I closed my eyes and allowed myself to breathe it in. Unlike yesterday at Wick's, Gage's room calmed me. I wasn't numb, nor was I in overdrive. I felt sort of peaceful and that was before ever taking a single puff of marijuana.

"Does your dad ever come down here?" I asked.

"No." He glanced at me again before finishing up and grabbing a lighter.

When he sat on the edge of the bed, I joined him and watched while he took a long hit.

"So, no one cares that you just spark up down here?"

"Nope," he said through clenched lips, trying to keep the smoke in his lungs as long as possible.

He passed the bowl to me, and I took a long drag. The smoke singed my throat, but it was perversely pleasurable knowing the pain would quickly lead to euphoria. I handed the bowl back when I finished, and we did this passing several more times before I had enough. My head spun on my shoulders, and my vision blurred. I crawled up and rested my head on his pillow, staring at the ceiling.

I smoked too much. I was out of practice and I wanted to feel good, but a vague unease crept into my mind like a cockroach. I told myself it was only the paranoia. Marijuana did this sometimes. Getting too high made you question things you shouldn't and imagine scenarios that weren't true. I needed to keep that feeling at bay.

I closed my eyes because the room had started to spin. Against my will, my mind conjured up Thomas. What was he doing right now? Was he being beaten by a guard? Was he crying or cold or staring at a wall wishing he was dead? He wasn't down the hall in his room. He wasn't fighting with Mom in the kitchen. I couldn't bear to imagine where he really was.

I felt the bed settle, so I opened my eyes. Gage lay beside me, propped on his elbow and gazing down at me. I focused on his face, studying the lines and planes of it—the faint, blonde stubble on his chin, his wide forehead and powerful nose. He lay beside me, but our bodies didn't touch at any point. Seeing him grounded me. I returned to the present—to him and that room and the lightheaded, woozy sensation of being high.

"Are you going to kiss me?" I asked.

The words rushed out of my mouth before I could stop them. No filter. *Damn it.*

"No," he answered, firm but not unkind. He even smiled a little.

"Why not?" Suddenly, I wished he would. His lips looked so nice.

"Because I don't do random hook ups. And, you're not my type."

My heart felt like it was being squeezed in a fist. I shouldn't have been offended. Clearly, neither of us were each other's type. Gage Pike was too weird for me. Too alternative/skaterboy. Lizzie Berringer only kissed popular boys. I only kissed boys who were dying to have me and would worship me unconditionally.

Some part of me, however, was terribly disappointed by his response. Some part of me desperately wanted to know what it felt like to be kissed by Gage Pike.

"What type am I?" I managed to ask.

"The popular, cliquey type."

"Oh," I mumbled.

"Sorry."

I shrugged. "It's fine. You're not really my type either."

In reality, I had no idea what my type was anymore.

"I figured."

I attempted to focus on his face. I reached and touched his cheek, letting my fingertips run the length of his jaw. Because I was high, I didn't hold back. I'd never have been that bold if I wasn't stoned. "Why did you invite me then?"

"I don't know," he murmured. A small smile tugged at his lips again. I rested my hand on his shoulder. My face felt hot—my neck ice cold. I became hyper aware of his lips.

"Maybe, we could be friends," I said.

"Maybe."

"I really need a friend." My voice was barely audible, even to my own ears.

"I know. But I might not be the best choice."

This made me laugh. It started as a quiet chirping noise but grew into animated giggling.

"You're baked out of your mind," Gage said, shaking his head.

"Yeah. Sorry," I answered, trying to contain myself.

"It's cool," he said.

I managed to get myself under control as he dropped down to his back beside me. He was close but still not touching me anywhere. We laid like that, gazing at the white ceiling tiles, for several minutes.

Finally, I said, "Thanks for inviting me."

"You're welcome."

After a few more minutes, Gage left the bed and started fiddling with his television and game console. I languished on the bed and watched as the opening screen of Call of Duty appeared. I never played before, but I knew all about it from Thomas. Call of Duty was one of the things my family should have seen as a *sign*. *Signs* were supposedly everywhere as if all boys who play Call of Duty could predictably be expected to bring a gun to school and kill people.

Gage began a game in a war-torn cityscape. I watched as he shot men wearing head turbans, presumably Muslim terrorists. Gage's icon ducked and bobbed behind buildings for cover, blasting out rounds from a machine gun.

"What's the goal?" I didn't know if he'd hear me over all the double tapping he was doing to the bad guys. From my perspective, the killings seemed random but I knew there must be a point.

"Rescuing prisoners. They're about to be beheaded in one of these buildings."

"And if you die?" I asked.

"If I die, they die. Virtually anyway."

Virtual deaths were so much less painful than real ones.

Chapter 8

Gage

THE NEXT DAY, I STEELED myself for the repercussions, but I didn't expect them to be so swift or so brutal. I had barely put the Cherokee in park when they struck. My door was ripped open, and Wick sucker punched me in the side of the head. Then, he grabbed me by the collar of my coat with both hands and dragged me out onto the frozen ground. Two or three people began kicking me, mostly in the stomach and legs. I rolled and twisted, trying to get away but it was no use. Pain ripped through my body and disorientation took over. The whole thing only lasted about fifteen seconds but it hurt like nothing I ever experienced before. Finally, when they were satisfied with the job they'd done, Wick bent down and got in my face.

"I fucking warned you," he said, before landing one last punch in my mouth.

They disappeared as quickly as they came. Once I was alone, I rolled to my stomach, coughing and trying to get my breath back. One of the kicks had knocked the wind out of me. I rose up on my hands and knees and lifted my head to see two senior girls staring at me. When our eyes met, they scurried away. My car was still running beside me so when I could breathe again, I climbed back inside.

I considered throwing it in reverse and heading home. When I ran through the logistics of that plan, however, I discarded the idea. My step-mom was home, and the thought of having to explain to her that I just got my ass kicked by a bunch of jocks made me cringe. What I needed was some Advil for my body and an ice pack for my face. The nurse would be a bad idea because she'd report it to the office, and they'd ask me a ton of questions. Instead, I texted my friend Sybil.

You at school yet?

I cranked over my rearview mirror and examined the damage. My eye and lip were already swelling. I grabbed napkins out of the glove compartment to wipe off the blood.

Almost

Can you meet me at my car? I need help

Sure. What's up?

Just come

Sybil was a hilarious, heavy-set, drama-club girl who I'd been friends with since I arrived on island in eighth grade. She came up to me the second week of school and informed me that her friend Cassie thought I was hot and ever since then, we'd been close.

Sybil was her usual, bouncy self when she arrived until she got a look at my condition. "What the hell happened to you?" she asked.

"I got my ass kicked. Do you have any Advil?"

"Shit, Gage. Who did this?" She reached over to touch my face but I pulled away.

"Advil?" I asked again.

"Yeah. Yeah. Hold on." She started digging around in her purse, glancing up at me to check my face every few seconds. "What happened?"

"It's better if you just stay out of it. Trust me."

"Does this have to do with that new girl? Because I heard you took her home yesterday and Wick was flipping out."

I didn't acknowledge the question, and Sybil finally located her bottle of ibuprofen. She removed four tablets. "I know it seems like a lot, but it's fine. You'll thank me later. All I have is coffee to drink, though."

I swallowed all four pills with sips of coffee even though I hated the stuff. "Will you stop at the nurse and get me an icepack?"

"Yeah. Sure. But you should report this. Whoever it was should get in trouble."

"You and I both know how that would go, Syb." I raised my eyebrows at her and was immediately hit with a stabbing pain my forehead. I winced. "Ow, shit."

"We do?" she asked.

"Yeah, come on. Let's get this over with."

Everyone would know exactly what happened to me—everyone except the adults who wanted to. That's how I had to play it, though. I had to suck it up and take my punishment. On some level, I knew I deserved this. In the world of high school, Wick and I needed to fight it out for Lainey, and no matter who won, we both needed to save face. The question was: would I keep fighting?

Lainey

I tried to get to first block Spanish unnoticed but that was impossible. As I passed through the main hall, it felt like a million pairs of eyes were watching. Gage, however, didn't even glance at me when I reached physics second block. He wore his head phones and a black hoodie and positioned his body away from me.

I took my stool and retrieved my notebook, waiting for him to turn and acknowledge me. He must have been in a bad mood, and I told myself this was to be expected. Clearly, Gage wasn't always a shiny, happy person. But even knowing this, unease churned in my stomach. Gage was the closest thing I had to a friend in Nantucket. I didn't want him to pull away.

"Hey," I finally said, leaning on the table to try to see his face.

"Hey," he answered back. He turned slightly toward me, and I noticed a cut on his lip. A quick scan of the rest of his face revealed that one of his eyes was almost swollen shut.

"What happened?"

"Nothing," he mumbled.

I reached to touch his puffy eye, but he flinched away.

"Don't," he said.

Who would hurt Gage? Who was big enough and strong enough to do this to him? I quickly realized the answer and my stomach felt like it dropped to my ankles. This was all my fault.

"Wick?" I whispered.

Gage didn't respond. Other kids piled in the door, preparing for the day's lab. The bell was about to ring.

"You have to tell someone."

Gage scoffed. "Yeah right."

"Are you hurt? Anywhere else?"

"It's nothing."

"You can't let him get away with this." Indignation swelled in my chest like a balloon. Gage couldn't just sit back and be bullied. The entire situation was outrageous and wrong.

"Maybe out in California, things are different," Gage said. "But here, there's an order to things. You don't mess with the order. A sparrow doesn't nest with a bluebird. This is what happens when they try."

The bell sounded.

"Well I don't know anything about stupid birds, but I'm not planning on *nesting* with Wick no matter how many times he beats you up."

I dropped my hand and rested it on his thigh under the lab table, but he still refused to look at me. He kept his gaze focused on his binder and winced, as if my words or perhaps my touch further injured him.

Smithson gimped over and braced himself on his cane. "Gage, would you like to go to the nurse?" he asked quietly.

"Yes," I said at the exact moment Gage said, "No".

I touched the ice pack on the table in front of him. It was warm. "You should get another," I said.

"I'll write you a pass," Smithson said. "Should I call Mr. Santoro?"

Gage shook his head and rose from his stool to leave. I wished I could go with him; that it was somehow serious enough that he needed an escort. Then maybe we could just keep right on walking, past the office and past the nurse and out the door. Past the basketball court and into the Cherokee and back to the basement where we could just stay. Together. Indefinitely. Lounging and high and safe.

But that didn't happen. Instead, Gage returned and

continued to ignore me as best he could during the lab. I didn't try to engage him, either. I let him be, and I watched him storm off after class, fighting back the sickening feeling that Gage was lost to me now because of Michael Wickersham. Maybe, when the swelling subsided and his pride recouped, he'd have a change of heart.

I ate my lunch in the library, sitting out of sight on the floor in the stacks, reading Chopin for English. Wick didn't get to me until pre-calc, last block of the day. I tried to go as late as possible so he wouldn't have a chance, but he switched seats at the last minute to be beside me. Amber and Alex and everyone watched and tried to listen.

"Is it my turn again today?" he asked.

"Fuck off."

"Oh, feisty. How's Pike's face?"

He chuckled about this, like beating people up was amusing to him. I thought of several things to say, to take him down a notch or two. I was good with the comebacks back home. I knew where to hit with guys, but in this situation, I didn't say anything. This was a no win for me and for Gage. My cheeks flushed, and my head spun from the adrenaline rush. Fight or flight. I wished I could choose flight. Why wasn't Mr. Hepps starting class?

"I can get you dope, you know. Better stuff than weed too."

I fought back tears. It only took four days at Nantucket High School for them to break me. Broken and defeated.

Wick chuckled again—this time at my lack of response. "Let me know when you change your mind." He ran his disgusting hand up my arm, caressing me like a pet, and I didn't even have the energy to pull away.

Chapter 9

I STOOD BESIDE ROSA IN THE foyer listening to the raised voices upstairs. Rosa clutched a dust cloth and leaned on the polished wooden railing as if she was in pain. I had to look down at her now because she was so short. When I was younger, I thought she was a giant.

"I don't fucking care!"

"You'll flunk out. They said if you don't pass this semester, you'll have to take a leave."

"Good!"

"Thomas, you'll have to go to a special school."

"Good!"

"Your father's going to be very upset."

"I don't give a fuck!"

Rosa shook her head at me and said, "Thomas. He being so so bad."

A door slammed. We both flinched. My mother appeared at the top of the stairs, and descended toward us, her shoulders hunched.

Rosa said, "It's okay, Mrs. Audrey. He just a teenager. They be so bad sometimes."

Mom sighed, "I know. I just wish I knew what to do."

Rosa rubbed Mom's back. "He fine. He grow out of it."

Lainey

I decided to take the bus home. To most people, the bus was a normal mode of transportation, but for me, riding a school bus was a new experience. Back home, Rosa or Mom always drove us and the tennis team used vans to get to matches. But that day, I wanted to escape as fast as possible. I wouldn't be forced to wait in the back lot for my mother where Wick could find me. Taking the bus would be like disappearing, and that was exactly what I wanted to do.

I waited my turn to speak to the secretary in the office. She was a harried, middle aged woman who seemed completely fed up with teenagers asking her stupid questions all day. Her reading glasses hung off the tip of her nose—her lips pinched together in a pucker. "What do you need?" she finally asked me.

"Hi. I want to take the bus but I'm not sure which one."

"Where do you live?"

"Madaket Road."

"Bus number two. The driver's name is Harvey. Tell him your street number when you get on, and he'll let you off as close as he can."

"Thanks."

She moved on to her next tormentor, and I made my way outside.

I reached the sidewalk just as the busses were arriving. They came to a squeaky halt, and there were already elementary school kids on board. *Great*. I'd probably be getting bullied by an eight-year-old by the time the day was over.

Bus number two was the second bus in line (go figure) and Harvey was a balding man with a beard and a sly smile.

"Hi. I live at 49 Madaket Road," I informed him.

"You should get off at the Crooked Lane stop. I'll tell you when we get there if you sit up front. What's your name?"

"Li—Lainey," I answered. "Thanks." I manage to give him a small smile before heading back to find a seat.

The first open spot was beside a tiny black girl, probably in first grade, who had different colored plastic barrettes on the ends of all her braids. She looked up at me with wide eyes.

"Hi," I said to her.

"Hi," she answered, before looking back out the window.

I silently prayed that none of Wick or Amber's friends would get on and thankfully, I didn't see anyone I recognized. We left school and the bus lurched along through the narrow streets.

I found myself wondering about Gage. I hoped he was alright, and I felt terrible that he was hurt because of me. It was as if I was a walking bomb that blew up in everyone's face. Maybe now, the dust would settle with the boys, and they'd go back to living their lives like they did before I showed up on the scene. Wick with Amber; Gage with his pot.

The bus took the long way through town. Nantucket was known for its picturesque downtown. Beautifully restored, historic homes along with quaint storefronts lined cobblestone streets. I examined the glossy, painted clapboards and pretty blue door of a home on Union Street when we made a stop.

After we turned onto Main Street, Harvey had to drive at a geriatric pace because of the cobblestones. Outside the window, I watched a young mother pushing a baby stroller, and two older men in winter hats and coats sitting on a bench. The bus stopped again to let off several students, and I noticed a photographer. He snapped pictures of a storefront, his gear and a tripod nearby, but for a split second, in my mind, I imagined he was there for me. Any moment, he'd turn and aim the camera through the window of the bus.

After the shooting, the photographers were everywhere. They showed up within hours at the police station and camped outside my house for weeks afterward. When we emerged after my interrogation that first day, they screamed questions at us.

Why did he do it, Roland?

Lizzie, were you scared?

Where did he get the gun?

My parents hustled me to a car. Dad's assistant, Curtis, drove me home because Mom and Dad had to stay. They had to wait and see Thomas.

The photographers continued taking pictures as we drove out, holding their cameras close to the window while Curtis waited for traffic. I almost threw up right there in Curtis's car with the photographers snapping away. I shielded my eyes with my hand, hiding my face as much as I could until we were safely on the road.

The nausea subsided until I got home, and Rosa met me at the door sobbing.

"Thank God you're okay." She clutched me to her body

in a fierce hug. "It can't be. It can't be true," she repeated over and over again.

I didn't respond to her, though. If I hadn't seen it with my own eyes, I would have said the same thing. But it was true—a terrible, awful truth I wished I could erase.

"This is your stop, Lainey," Harvey called back to me.

I realized the bus wasn't moving. Other kids stared at me, including my little seatmate. I jumped to my feet and hustled to the door. "Thanks," I mumbled to Harvey on my way by.

Once off, I began the short walk back to my house. Despite the sun being out, the air was still chilly and the wind brisk. The wind alternated between many moods in Nantucket. These included gusty, steady, whipping, and frigid, just to name a few. For certain, it was ever present—a steadfast new companion that traveled with me everywhere.

When I reached my house, no photographers waited outside, and the shingled façade and cedar picket fence filled me with a strange comfort that day. I felt pleased to have a refuge from all my school troubles.

In the entryway, I could hear my mother speaking to someone in the kitchen.

"Cream? I have half and half or one percent milk?"

"Half and half with two sugars, thanks," a man answered.

What man was there having coffee? My first thought was a lawyer. We had so many lawyers that our lawyers had lawyers.

I quietly set my bag down and headed to the kitchen, listening along the way.

"If you go out again, you'll want to steer clear of Eddie," the man said as I reached the doorway.

"Li—ainey. Hi. How'd you get home?" Mom looked at the clock on the stove, her face reddening.

"The bus," I said flatly. I examined the man. He was tall with short, reddish-brown hair and a cropped beard. He wore work clothes, a tool belt lying at his feet. He sat on one of the bar stools, seeming to dwarf it with his massive frame, a coffee mug in front of him.

"Oh. I would have picked you up. You should have called," Mom said.

Instead of answering, I stared at Mr. Fix-it.

"This is Graham—Mr. Holt," Mom stammered. "He came to replace the parts in the furnace. So it will work. All the time."

Yes, of course, the furnace. The heat so necessary to life in this frigid place.

Graham Holt smiled kindly at me and offered up a wave with one of his giant mitts. "Hello. You can call me Graham."

My mother frantically smoothed down the hair at the nape of her neck. "This is my daughter, Lainey. How was school? Would you like a cup of coffee?"

"No. I'm fine. I'll just get some water."

Coffee upset my stomach. My mother knew this, but she still insisted on trying to entice me to eat and drink things I didn't want, especially if it was something I liked before the shooting. I used to love lattes, but after, I only drank water and occasionally tea.

"Yeah, the year-round bar scene is pretty limited. Once the season starts, though, it picks up," Graham said.

"Well, I'm not really that interested in the bar scene," Mom told him. "I was just out for one drink that night, that's all."

I realized she must have run into him when she went out on Monday night. That was the night I got upset about the plea deal.

After filling a glass with water, I headed for the front hall and stairs. I almost made it without having to speak again, but Graham Holt was too polite.

"It was nice meeting you, Lainey," he said.

"Yeah, bye," I mumbled without turning around.

My mom had many admirers in California, so one handyman in Nantucket did not really phase me. I did, however, wonder if my mother would be able to pull off the lies. She seemed to be having a harder time navigating one guy in our kitchen than I did dealing with a whole school of nosy teenagers.

When I reached my room, I curled up on my bed and found myself wishing it was Gage's bed in Gage's basement. If I was there, I'd tell him how sorry I was for what happened with Wick. Maybe we'd get high and maybe he'd lie down beside me again. Even though he didn't kiss me yesterday, I loved being close to him. That moment we shared felt more intimate than a half hour of making out with Wick.

I toyed with the idea of sending him a message. Gage made it pretty clear in class that he didn't want to have anything else to do with me, but I still wanted to say something. The fact I was even pondering this was pathetic. Since when did I chase boys? I guessed since I came to Nantucket and started pretending to be Lainey Darwin. Lainey Darwin was a hot mess.

It took ten minutes to decide on three little words, four if you count the contraction as two. Finally, I sent them.

I'm really sorry

After it said delivered, I tossed my phone on my side table because I knew the chances of him answering were slim to none. He was probably high and lying on his bed or high and playing Call of Duty. I wondered what my old friends in California were doing that very second? Still at school, maybe even at lunch. I heard Beaton was renovating the cafeteria so it would look completely different. They set up a tent on the nearby quad so kids would have a different place to eat, undisturbed by the memories or the construction.

My phone alerted with a text. I only had two friends, and I was confident Alex wasn't texting me that very moment.

Why?

I stared at the word, and its punctuation because it was so Gage. Gage didn't put up with bullshit. He didn't tolerate words like fine or nice and he certainly didn't let people apologize without knowing what for.

My hand shook as I typed my answer.

For what happened...

He answered back almost immediately.

Wait...did you kick my ass this morning?

I smiled. I knew his pride was damaged. He didn't want me to see him hurt and vulnerable, and I hated that Wick was able to humiliate and injure him. Finally, I wrote back the only answer possible. The truth.

No

And then came his.

Then stop apologizing for things you didn't do

Chapter 10

Lainey

I DIDN'T HAVE PHYSICS THAT FRIDAY which completely sucked because I wanted to see Gage. I wanted to see his face and ask how he felt, but I had no idea the rest of his schedule or where he hung out or why I never seemed to see him in the halls. I knew he'd be in the lunchroom at his regular table with his regular crowd, but I couldn't go there. So once again, I headed for the library where the librarian thankfully took pity on me and pretended not to notice that I ate my sandwich in the midst of her books.

Like a robot, I made it through the day. Based on how bad it was going, I considered telling my mother to forget this whole thing. We could call it new life failure. Why did we think it would work? Plus, if we stayed, she couldn't visit Thomas. Because of the move, she had to chose me over him—one more item on the guilt list that haunted me. Her choice was a hollow victory in the war of sibling rivalry which I had no business still fighting anyway. Feeling superior to someone as sick and lost as Thomas was hardly satisfying.

Last block was Rapisardi's circle of doom. Wick sat two seats over, leering and smirking at me every chance he got.

It disgusted me that I ever let him touch me. I counted down the minutes until the bell, literally watching the seconds hand stutter an arc around the wall clock. I grew so intent on watching it that the sound of the classroom phone on the wall made me jump.

Mr. Rap answered it. After listening for a few seconds, he hung up. "Lainey, Mrs. Duncombe wants to see you."

Shit. My mind raced through all the potential reasons for the call. My failure to connect with Alex. My hiding in the library at lunch. My new lab partner getting his face smashed. There were any number of reasons I might be called down after my first week.

Since only ten minutes remained in class, I packed my bag and brought it with me. Once in the hall, I walked as slow as possible, but the guidance office wasn't far enough away to save me no matter how lackluster my pace. When I arrived, I claimed the same seat across from Mrs. Duncombe in her office.

She crossed her legs and asked, "So how's your first week been?"

"Fine." I kept my gaze averted. I didn't want to look at her kind eyes and sympathetic expression. Mrs. Duncombe could not help me. I was a lost cause.

"I hear you've become friendly with Gage Pike?"

I shrugged. "Not really."

"And I hear someone beat him up yesterday morning?"

I shrugged again, tapping my toe against the side of her desk.

"Lainey, I know this is hard for you. Coming to a new school in the middle of the year. Going through what you have with your brother. Perhaps you could work on establishing some friendships with girls, with Alex and her friends."

"Okay." This was my go to answer for everything. Easy-going, agreeable Lainey. That's who I wanted to be.

"Is there anything you want to talk about with me? Everything would be confidential."

I finally met her gaze, trying to read her intentions. Did she really want me to talk or was this just going through the motions for her?

"No," I answered finally. "My mom's picking me up and I really just want to go home. It's been a long week."

"I understand. I have the name of a therapist for you. I've already called and given it to your mother." She reached across her desk to handed me a card. "I know it seems overwhelming, but you're going to have to work through what your brother did. Better to get it done now and move on as best you can."

I eyed her coolly. "Okay."

What did she even know about it? How could she presume to understand what it was like to be me?

"Do you know what happened to Gage?" she asked.

I shook my head and looked down at my hands. The best thing I could do for Gage was to keep quiet, so he could plot whatever revenge he wanted in secret.

My response, or lack thereof, elicited the big counselor sigh from Mrs. Duncombe before we both glanced at her clock. Four minutes until dismissal.

"Okay. You can stay until the bell," she told me.

She left to talk with the secretary while I resumed my counting down the seconds.

I took the bus again, and my mother was out when I got home. I retrieved my usual glass of water and curled up on my bed with my phone. Selfies and flashback Friday photos lit up Instagram. I, of course, had no flashbacks to share. Maybe I should have taken a selfie Monday because that's as far back as Lainey Darwin went.

I only followed five people at that point: Wick, Alex, Amber, Kaitlyn (the blonde from the first lunch), and Gage. They all followed back, too. My cover story, if anyone asked, was that my old Instagram was hacked and I had to start over—hence why I had so few followers and no one from my old life. If anyone really thought about it, however, they'd realize I most likely would have re-followed my old friends.

When I grew bored with my phone, I decided to grab my laptop and search for any new stories about Thomas. The coverage of the shooting had waned with time. Gradually, there was nothing new to report so it slipped out of the headlines on television and online. As far as I could tell, we had it slightly worse than other families of shooters because of my father's celebrity status. Being an award-winning director was not the same as being a movie actor or reality star, but it still drew some tabloid-type attention to us.

The first live report I saw from in front of Beaton Prep was a surreal experience. A blonde in a gray pant suit held a microphone and told the whole world about my brother. I became transfixed by the coverage that day, my compulsion to watch taking root and keeping me in its grip for weeks.

The night of the shooting, when my parents finally came home from the police station, I was glued to helicopter footage showing the chaotic parking lot of

Beaton immediately after the shooting. Was I there? Had I already left with Nava?

My mother whipped the remote off the coffee table and switched off the television.

"I was watching that," I protested, my voice hoarse from all the crying.

"Your father and I need to talk to you."

My father sat perfectly still and straight, his face in a permanent grimace as if he was in pain. Other kids envied me my famous father, but I always wished I had a normal one. Someone who wasn't twenty years older than my mother. Someone who wasn't abnormally thin and abnormally tan and currently gay and in relationship with his thirty something personal assistant.

"How many people died?" I asked. "The news isn't saying."

After a pause, my father answered. "We don't know."

My mother sat still and stoic as well. They were still unable to feel or accept what was happening to us. Processing something like this took time. It may have happened in seconds but the repercussions would ripple outward for days, even years.

Mom asked, "Can you tell us what happened? What you saw?"

I dropped my eyes to my lap; the vine of terror and shame beginning to wend its way around my heart. That was the first time I felt it trying to choke the life from my body. "No," I whispered. "I can't talk about it."

"Just tell me," Mom said, her voice cracking. "Are you sure it was him?"

I fixed my eyes on her, needing to be sure she was

81

looking at me before giving my answer. When I had her attention, I simply nodded my head. Using words felt too powerful. If I said it, it would be true, but if I kept silent, I could pretend a little longer. Maybe. Maybe, I could pretend it into oblivion, turning back time and making it all come out differently.

Tears spilled from my mother's eyes. "This can't be happening," she said, gasping for air. "How can this be happening?" She bent over at the waist and held her face with her hand.

I wondered the exact same thing myself. My brother. A murderer. The little boy who came to my room when he had a bad dream and curled up beside me in his superhero pajamas. The same one who loved cheesedogs and Oreo Blizzards from Dairy Queen and playing dominos with Rosa. It was incomprehensible. Fresh tears began to roll down my cheeks. My mother was crumbling before me. Losing it. I wanted my father to do something to help. He should have comforted her. He should have told us both that everything would work out, that we'd get through this together. But that didn't happen.

Instead, he asked me, "Are you sure?"

My father was intensely focused on me. I had never seen him look at me in the way he did that day. Roland Berringer's attention was precious, and I was finally receiving it. But what was he asking? Was I sure I couldn't talk about it? Then I remembered Mom's last question. Did Thomas really do it? That's what he wanted to know. They were both still in denial mode. They didn't witness it for themselves like I had. They wanted to believe it was all just a terrible mistake.

"Yes," I answered through my tears. "I'm sure."

I tried to inhale a breath, but it felt as though all the breathable air was gone from the room.

A text from Alex alerted on my phone, drawing me back to reality.

Sleep over tomorrow night at my house. You in?

Is this you or Mrs. D asking.

Me ☺ It'll be fun.

No boys?

No boys. Promise ☺

Okay. ☺

Smileys. More smileys in my life was progress, right?

Later that night at dinner, I asked my mom.

"Can I go to my friend Alex's tomorrow? She asked me to sleep over."

My mother looked up, surprise registering in her eyes. "Sure. That's great you're getting closer."

I moved fettuccine alfredo around on my plate. I knew I was most likely a mercy friend to Alex. Mrs. Duncombe probably put her up to the sleepover, but at least it was better than spending the whole weekend alone. I'd save curled up and depressed on my bed for tonight and Sunday. Plus, Alex promised no boys. No boys might have to be my new motto.

Gage

They insisted I go to Kitty's with them. We sat in the pub area, and some of the patrons checked out my shiner. Laura was more upset about my altercation than my dad. She didn't have kids of her own and didn't understand that these things happen with boys.

"Did you win at least?" Dad asked when he first saw it.

I shook my head. "No. There were three of them."

"Please tell me this wasn't about drugs?"

"Nothing to do with drugs," I replied, glad it was the truth.

He examined me, trying to determine if I was being honest or not. He must have decided I was because he asked, "A girl then?"

I was actually kind of proud that I could nod my head yes.

Dad grinned. "Well better luck next time."

And that was the end of that.

My dad and I look alike. As a teenager, it became more and more a thing, and everyone liked to comment on it. *A clone* they'd say which annoyed me. I didn't want to be just like him. I didn't want to care about money and appearances and have a phony salesman smile when I was showing someone a new house.

At dinner, I listened to Laura recount some business with one of the boards she served on. I sipped my ginger ale and wished I could leave. I hated when they made me go out with them.

Even for a casual dinner like this, Laura looked primped. She had full makeup and her dark hair sprayed into a perfect bob. When I was younger, I thought she looked like Katy Perry because of her big blue eyes and bubbly personality.

My dad had been married to Laura for five years. She was twelve years younger than him, and my mother originally told me Laura was after his money. But once I moved in with them, I realized that wasn't true. Laura and my dad really did love each other. Despite my desire to dislike her for taking my mother's place, I knew she made him happy.

After dinner arrived, Dad said, "Your mother called me today."

I tensed up momentarily and stopped squeezing ketchup onto my fries. I didn't like talking about my mother, and I especially didn't like talking about her in front of Laura.

"She's stable and home. She'd like you to call her when you get a chance."

I set down the ketchup and popped a fry in my mouth. "Okay."

My mother was a bipolar alcoholic. That's the real reason I lived with my dad, the honest to God truth that no one in Nantucket knew, not even my closest friends. She had been away at rehab (again) and hadn't been able to contact us.

I felt Laura's eyes on me, but I waited for her to speak. I didn't talk to Laura about much of anything if I could avoid it, and I especially didn't talk to her about Mom.

"Your eye looks better. Not as swollen," Laura finally said.

"Thanks," I mumbled back.

"I still think you should report what happened to the school."

"It's fine. It's better this way," I said.

"Do you have any plans for the weekend?" Dad asked.

I shook my head.

"Maybe you should call that girl." He chuckled.

I gave him the most pissed off look I could muster.

"What girl?" Laura asked.

This was exactly why I didn't like doing dinner with them.

When we got home, I laid on my couch and worked up the courage I needed to call my mother. It's not that I didn't want to speak with her. Of course, I did. She was my mother, and I loved her. The problem was all the fears I had about what condition she'd be in when she answered the phone. Dad said she was stable, so I figured she'd be fine that night, but usually, I had no idea how she'd be. I preferred not to be disappointed and upset by the way she might act, so I just avoided her altogether. My avoidance, however, made me felt guilty, and a whole vicious cycle between us spun into motion. The way I reacted to my mother's problems was normal, according to the counselors I'd been forced to talk to, but that didn't make it better in my mind. They told me I shouldn't feel bad for my feelings, but I still did. Most of the time, I just accepted it.

Finally, after much thought and even contemplating getting high before making the call, I inhaled a deep breath and hit send.

"Hi Mom," I said when she answered.

"Hi! I'm so glad you called!"

"How are you?"

"I'm good. How's school?"

"It's school. The usual."

"Tell me about your classes. Still all honors?"

"Yeah. Physics, English, U.S. history, pre calc, Spanish, and gym."

"What's your favorite?"

"Um, probably physics."

"Really? That surprises me. I would think it would be really hard."

"It is, but I still like it. I like doing the labs."

She sounded good. Normal. Not drunk or manic or depressed. I wished she could just stay like that. I wished she'd stop messing up her life.

"What about a girlfriend? You need someone to take to the junior prom, right?"

"Seriously, Mom? Do I seem like the prom type to you?"

She giggled about this. "No. I'm just teasing you. Your dad said maybe you could come visit in April. If everything goes well. Would you like that?"

"Yeah. That would be great."

I didn't want to get my hopes up about April. I'd looked forward to visits before that didn't end up happening.

"He said he's worried, though, about the marijuana. He said he still smells it on you sometimes."

I roll my eyes at this even though she can't see them through the phone line. "I'm fine, Mom."

"So you're not smoking?"

"Mom, let's talk about something else. Tell me about Grandma."

"Oh, your grandmother." I could hear the hint of mock annoyance in her voice. They lived together in Connecticut. "She's fine. She's..."

I laid back and listened. Hearing my mother in this condition was like a gift. It was a relief to know she was doing well, and I wished she could always be this way. I wished she could figure out how to make the changes stick and never go back to drinking again. If only.

Chapter 11

"I HEARD ABOUT YOU AND THAT guy," Thomas said as I pulled out of the parking lot at school.
"What guy?"
"That guy from the beach. J.P. said you're a slut."
"J.P.'s an asshole," I said.
"How old is he?"
"Are you talking about Dylan?"
"I don't know his name. Some guy you met at the beach."
"Yeah. He's twenty."
"And you're seventeen."
"Whatever, Thomas. It's none of your business."
"I'm gonna tell mom."
"No, you're not."
"Yeah. I might."
"How about you shut up about Dylan and I'll shut up about the skatepark."
"What about the skatepark?"
"About you smoking with the older kids."
He narrowed his eyes at me. "How do you know that?"
"I know. Some of those guys are my friends."
"You're such a bitch."

Lainey

The sleepover turned out to be sort of fun at first. We played Wii games in Alex's finished basement—*Dance Off* and then *Bowling* and then *Mario Kart*. It didn't matter that I sucked because they did too. Amber was the best at everything, of course. We ate pizza and drank soda and giggled about our dumb moves.

"Did you hook up with Gage?" Amber asked me during a break in the action.

She gazed at me with a sweet smile, as if getting the nitty-gritty details about me and Gage fascinated her.

"No. We just got high."

"You didn't even kiss?"

"No. Why?" I asked.

"Because he's kinda hot," she said, lifting one shoulder up in a small shrug. "And he's like the king of the nerds. All those girls at his table worship him."

Bile rose in my throat. I didn't like Amber talking about Gage.

"Has he hooked up with any of them?" I tried to keep the high pitch out of my voice, realizing in that moment that I was jealous of any girls that Gage may have dated or liked.

Alex answered, "I think he fools around with Cassie. She's the skinny one with the piercings that always changes her hair color."

Alex and Kaitlyn lay sprawled out across the floor, trying to share one throw pillow, their hair enmeshed.

Kaitlyn said, "Why just Cassie? Maybe he likes all of

them. Maybe they have huge nerd orgies." She tried to embrace Alex in a fake amorous hug.

"Ewww," Alex rolled away. "Stop!"

Kaitlyn laughed at her. "I almost kissed him in eighth grade at Sadie's graduation party. We had to go in the closet together but I told him I didn't want to because I didn't want him to be my first kiss."

"Yeah, Wick was a much better choice for that," Amber quipped and rolled her eyes.

I wondered if Wick was all of their first kisses. How incestuous.

Alex's phone alerted with a new text. She grabbed it off the coffee table. "Oh shit! It's Wick. He's outside."

"Tell him to come in," Kaitlyn said.

Alex glanced at me. "No. My mom will freak."

Amber grabbed Alex's phone and started to send a text. "No, she won't. Your mom loves Michael."

Alex promised, but I knew a promise meant nothing in a situation like this. If the other girls wanted Wick to come in, Wick would come in.

"He's at the door!" Amber grinned at the phone. "He's with Perk."

They sprung to their feet and stampeded up the basement stairs. I stayed on the couch and wondered who told Wick about the sleepover. Probably Amber. But did he know I was there too? This would be so awkward. I needed to get the heck out of there.

Before I had time to formulate my escape plan, I heard them returning. The television still had a blue screen from playing Wii, so I couldn't pretend to be watching it. Instead, I pulled up my Instagram and made believe it had something interesting to look at as they came around the corner.

Wick's eyes locked on me immediately, but even as he stared at me, he grabbed Amber and steered her toward the recliner. He sat and pulled her into his lap, nuzzling her neck like they'd always been a couple and they couldn't resist each other. Kaitlyn and Perk did the same on the other end of the sectional from me.

"Are you okay?" Alex asked, dropping down next to me.

"Yeah, but I think I'm going to go home," I answered even though that was not my actual. My plan was Gage Pike. I wanted to see him and lay on his bed and listen to music and get high. Maybe if I asked, he'd pick me up.

"I tried. I'm sorry," Alex said.

I knew this wasn't her fault; I just wished I'd anticipated it would happen. I glanced over to see Wick sticking his tongue down Amber's throat, and I knew it was time to make my move.

"It's okay. I just texted my mom, though. She's coming to get me. I have to wait outside."

Alex's house was in a nice development off the airport road. The houses were all new but made to look old like downtown.

"It's freezing out. Just wait upstairs until she pulls up," Alex said.

"What is the main road she takes to get here?"

I pretended to be sending the text.

"Old South Road. What am I going to tell my mom?"

"Tell her I wanted to go home, and my mother picked me up. It's fine."

I rose and grabbed my tote bag off the floor.

"Where are you going?" Kaitlyn asked, still entwined with Perk.

"Home. See you guys Monday."

Amber and Wick stopped kissing long enough for Amber to say goodbye.

Alex was right about it being cold. I had no gloves and no hat because I wasn't expecting to be outside. I strode along her street with my head down and stopped at the corner to text Gage.

Can you come get me?

He had to answer. As I trudged on, I silently prayed that he would. I could actually call my mother if he didn't respond or if he refused to pick me up, but I hoped that wouldn't happen. An ache had formed in my chest, and it had something to do with Gage. I couldn't explain it, even to myself, but now that the thought of seeing him was in my head, I desperately wanted to. I was rarely ever desperate for any particular boy back home, and since Thomas, I felt very little except sadness. But in Nantucket, I had developed this intense desire to be near Gage Pike.

My old friend the wind bit my cheeks and dried my lips. I continued to walk and wait for my phone to sound. Finally, it did.

Where r u?

With numb fingers, I typed my answer.

Old South Rd.

What?!

Please? It's freezing.

Meet me at the market.

Thank you!!!

I stood in front of the closed convenience store, hoping

there are no weirdos lurking around. In LA, there were always dirtbags and weirdos hanging around convenience marts but not here in the land of the frozen tundra. I guessed frozen tundra kept the lurkers away.

Thankfully, I didn't have to wait long. Gage careened into the parking lot in the Cherokee. His headlights temporarily blinded me. I shielded my eyes with my hand and hurried to the passenger side. Once inside, the heat blaring from the vents was my new best friend.

"Why are you out here alone?" Gage turned and backed out.

"I was at Alex's for a sleepover and Wick and Perk showed up."

"So you just left?"

"Yeah. I told Alex my mom was picking me up. Could we go to your house? Please?"

He ignored my request. "And if I hadn't come?"

I shrugged, just glad to be in his car. Just being in his presence made some part of me okay. Sitting in his crappy Cherokee, driving back to his house (I hoped) a twisted piece inside of me smoothed out. A fraction of the deformed mess that I was unraveled and laid flat.

"Was Wick rude to you?" he asked.

"Not really. He mostly ignored me."

I realized he was taking me to his house when we turned left on Surfside. I smiled and covered my mouth with my hand so he wouldn't see. Once we arrived, I followed him to the stairs, noticing one other car in the driveway this time.

"Parents?" I asked.

"Out."

In the basement, I dropped my bag and headed straight

to his bed. I slipped off my boots and curled up while Gage started some music.

"You wanna smoke?" he asked.

"Sure."

The first lyrics began to play and I realized the song was *Ripple* by the Grateful Dead. How did I not recognize it right away?

"You like the Dead?" I asked him.

He sat at his desk preparing the bowl. "I like good music. Genre is irrelevant."

I forgot how much I liked the Dead.

"Your eye looks better," I told him.

He didn't answer, and when he returned to sit on the edge of the bed, I joined him just like the other day. This time, however, I only took two hits. After the second one, I curled back up on his pillows and closed my eyes, waiting for the effects of the marijuana to take hold. It wasn't long before the bed settled. I opened my eyes and found Gage lying beside me.

"Thanks for picking me up," I said.

"You're welcome."

"What were you doing?"

"Gaming with my friend Andrew."

"Oh. Sorry I interrupted."

"No worries. He was killing me anyway."

I felt woozy and silly from the pot. It made me bold enough to touch his hand. He watched me do it and didn't resist when I took it further and actually held his hand. His skin was warm and soft and touching him felt so right.

Gage said, "You probably should have chosen Wick. Life here would be easier for you if you did."

I scowled at him. Why did he have to try to ruin this moment between us? He was the one who warned me about getting close to Wick, and now he suddenly thought I should go back to him?

"Too late," I told him.

"Maybe not."

"Can we talk about something else?"

"Like what?"

I examined his face. "You. Who have you dated?"

His cheeks turned pink. "We are definitely not talking about my love life."

"Why not?" I asked playfully.

"Because. And you and I are going to be friends. That's it."

"Why?" I asked.

"Bluebirds and sparrows. That's why."

I felt a renewed sense of disappointment at his words. I had a terrible crush on this boy already. Gage was strong and kind and a little rough around the edges. Plus, he seemed to get me. I didn't even get me anymore, but Gage somehow did. He could see right inside me to all my pain, and he wasn't even scared by it. Not one little bit.

He must have noticed my sadness at his words, too, because he inched closer on the bed and wrapped me into his arms. My cheek came to rest against his chest, the thin cotton of his t-shirt unable to muffle the beating of his heart or the smell of cologne and soap and marijuana. And he held me like that. For a long time, we just laid there, his arms wrapped around me, our breathing synchronized.

"Can I stay here tonight?" I finally asked him.

Gage exhaled. "That's probably not a good idea."

"Please?" I tightened my grip on his back ever so slightly before pulling back to search his face.

"Okay," he said. "But I'll sleep on the couch,"

He rolled away, breaking the contact I was enjoying so much. Once he was up, he walked to a closet and began pulling out blankets.

"You don't have to," I said. The marijuana made me bold. I didn't care if he knew I wanted him. I wanted him to know, and I wanted him to hold me like he just did all night.

He lifted a comforter off the top shelf. "I can't stay with you, Lainey. I don't trust myself. I'd probably do something dumb."

"Why would it be dumb? Everyone already thinks we are."

He stopped and looked at me. "Who thinks that?"

"Everyone."

Seriously, did he not know what high school was like?

"Well, everyone can sometimes be wrong."

He grabbed a bed pillow before heading for the couch.

Not what I hoped for, but at least I was there. I was in Gage Pike's basement on Nantucket Island after a week full of drama. Even through all of it, I was still happy I came to Nantucket. It might not have been the fresh start I was hoping for, but at least it was something.

Chapter 12

Lainey

THOMAS WALKED IN, THE GUN clutched in his right hand. This was one of those dreams that I knew was just a dream, but I still couldn't drag myself free of it. It was Dad's gun from the display case at his house, the one from his movie *Deadwood Falls*. A silver, cowboy gun. Thomas raised his arm and shot out the wall of windows in the cafeteria. I screamed, but no sound emerged. No one heard me. Everyone else in the cafeteria acted like he wasn't there. Like he was a figment of my imagination. *Wake up, Lizzie. Just wake up.*

I jolted awake. *Thank God,* I thought. Beads of cold sweat soaked my neck. I lifted my head to scan the room. It was not my room in Nantucket nor was it Beverly Hills. It was a basement—I was in Gage Pike's basement.

I rested my head back down on the pillow and waited for my heartrate to return to normal. Then, remembering Gage was on the couch, I rolled to my side to look at him. He lay sprawled on his stomach, still asleep; his face pressed into the cushion. If he'd awoken first, he might have examined me this way, and I decided that would have been terrible. I might have snored or snorted or drooled, and he might have decided I was, in reality, a very unattractive girl.

The Thomas dream ended earlier than usual. Sometimes it continued. Sometimes I saw Hannah again. I saw her, and I held her hand, and I told her she was going to be all right just like I did that day. But that was a lie. The last thing I said to her was a lie.

I banished Hannah from my mind. I couldn't go there. Instead, I focused on the present. I rubbed the soft edge of Gage's blanket between my thumb and index finger. How was I going to get home without my mother knowing where I was? When I plotted staying with Gage the night before, I planned to text and see what her plans for the day were. I'd have Gage bring me home when she was out, but that might be more complicated to pull off than I anticipated. For the moment, I decided to just enjoy sleeping Gage. He looked so peaceful and unaffected in his sleep. His forehead was smooth and his lips full. His hair stuck up at an angle, and I wanted to go over and run my fingers through it. If only I could. Instead, I pushed back the covers and headed for the bathroom.

Gage

The sound of someone in my bathroom woke me. It took a few seconds to realize who it was. Lainey. The hottest girl in school slept over, and all I did was hug her. Truly, I was a poor excuse for a teenage boy. According to any rule book on being a guy, she was fair game. She was a little high, she wasn't drunk, and she was quite literally begging me for it.

Thinking about it that morning, I wished I'd kissed her. My sexual frustration got the best of me because I knew that touching her and being with her would probably be a better high than any drug imaginable. Too bad Wick was right when he said she was out of my league. She was. And I needed to remember that. Letting myself get involved with her like that would only lead to problems.

Lainey quietly eased the bathroom door open and peeked out at me. Her eyes widened when she realized I was awake. Then she smiled—a devastatingly cute smile.

"Hi," she said, stepping out, still wearing the leggings and t-shirt she slept in. She smoothed down her hair with her hand. "I think my Mom's going out around nine thirty. Could you give me a ride home then?"

I sat up, making sure I kept the quilt covering me since I only wore boxers. "Yeah. Sure. How'd you sleep?"

"Fine. You?" She stopped several feet away and hugged herself with her arms. Her eyes focused on my chest. She might have been checking me out because I didn't have a shirt on.

"Yeah. Good. I gotta go to the bathroom though. Do you mind turning around?"

"Oh," she said. "Yeah. Sure." She spun and faced my bed.

I jumped up and grabbed sweatpants off the floor before heading for the bathroom. I had no idea why Lainey was so interested in me. At first I thought it was just the pot. She wanted to get high, and I was the man for that job. After all, ninety nine out of a hundred girls would have chosen Wick. That was just a fact. But I won't deny that her attention inflated me with an embarrassing amount of joy and new found confidence in myself. Like maybe I wasn't such a loser with girls after all, even though very few at Nantucket High School had ever noticed me.

As I looked in the mirror and brushed my teeth, I marveled at the fact that this had to be one of the most awkward morning-afters ever despite the fact no sexual activity took place. Neither of us needed to be embarrassed about anything, but we'd probably have been less embarrassed if we'd actually hooked up.

This was the time I needed to remember the logic of my decision not to make out with her. Making out with Lainey would lead to falling for Lainey which would lead to having my heart crushed by Lainey. She was just not the kind of girl who stayed with a guy like me. It just didn't happen. Someone needed to explain this logic to my lower half, though. It was quite obviously not cooperating with my logical plans that morning.

What I really needed to know about Lainey was why. Why was she a cross between tragic emo girl and most popular prom queen? Something must have happened to her. When I tried to imagine what it might have been, every scenario was pretty bad. Abusive boyfriend? Perverted step-dad? Rape? Whatever caused Lainey to be the way she was, I knew getting close to her was a dangerous thing. In the face of all my efforts to put the brakes on us, however, she kept pulling me back in. Like a magnet to metal, when I came within a few feet of her, I couldn't step away. And I realized I should probably just stop trying.

Chapter 13

Lainey

I ARRIVED AT SCHOOL ON MONDAY morning with blue hair. You could say I was trying to make a statement about who I planned to be there. Jeans and a black hoodie rounded out my new rebel look. The color was no accident either. Blue. Oh, the irony.

Before I walked in, I thought I wanted everyone at school to see my new hair, but when I entered the building, I kept my hood up. Confidence eluded me. That was, until Santoro saw me.

"No hoods," he growled in my direction as I passed.

I slipped it partway down, revealing my bluebird hair to the world. Mr. Santoro was unfazed. The whims of teenage fashion could not deter a grizzled veteran like him. Other people were looking, though. I strode through the Hall of the Whale and down to my locker in the basement, ignoring all the rubber-neckers along the way. I hoped they thought me the ugliest, weirdest, most unstable person in the whole entire world.

Wick sat beside Amber in English first block and eyed me with a sly smile. He leaned in and whispered something in her ear. I was now that crazy, unpredictable girl who couldn't be trusted. I might fly off the handle at any time and pierce myself. *Good*. Stick with Amber and all your mutual dysfunction.

By the time I reached physics, Gage already heard about my new look.

"Well if it isn't my little bluebird of happiness," he said, grinning beside me.

I perched on my stool wondering if he really just claimed me as *his* with the personal pronoun *my*?

"You like it?" I asked. I hoped he did. Gage's approval seemed monumentally important.

"No. I liked it before. Brown or whatever it was yesterday when I drove you home."

"Maybe if I get my lip and brow pierced, it'll look better."

Gage stopped smiling. "No," he said. "No piercings. Your face is too pretty for piercings."

A blush flooded my cheeks with heat. I peeked over at him to see if he was serious and noticed his eyes smoldering with intensity. He didn't look away either. He met me head on. "Definitely no piercing," he repeated.

"Just my nose. Do they have a piercing place here?"

Gage broke the look and bent over to get his binder from his bag.

"Come over after school," he said, ignoring my question. "We'll dye it back. How about blonde? You look like you should be a blonde."

I gulped. How did he know this? Had he really looked at me enough to see?

"No. Not blonde. Red maybe?"

Gage furrowed his brow. "Why not blonde?"

I gave him a wan smile. "Blonde is for bluebirds."

"If the shoe fits."

"I need a favor."

He began doodling on a blank page in his binder. "Oh no. What?"

"Can I sit with you at lunch? Please?"

He stilled his pencil. "My table, they're a tough group."

"I can handle it. I survived Wick, right?"

I admired his biceps when he rested his arms on the table. They were the perfect blend of bulging yet not too big. I had known very few boys whose biceps were this close to perfect.

"Okay. But they might be rude to you. Cassie and the other girls, I can't protect you from them."

Yes! A small victory. I could return to the lunchroom today.

Smithson blinked the lights, his signal to sit down and shut up so his lecture du jour could begin. Gage and I endured the seemingly endless PowerPoint, and I caught him sneaking looks at me a few times, his eyes flitting away when I tried to meet them. Afterward, I walked silently beside him to the cafeteria. I kept my head down and hood partially up. The vine started its familiar twist in my chest as we approached the doors.

The smell of burnt food seeped into the hall from the kitchen, and my body reacted without my permission. Gunpowder. The stench of burnt anything reminded me of that day. I inhaled a deep breath through my mouth and tried to calm myself. If I could focus, I would have tried a visualization but the hall was too chaotic. My knees wobbled, but I managed to stay upright.

My vision switched to tunnel-like for the short walk to

his table. It seemed the eyes of the whole room were on me. What would New Girl do? The politics of the lunchroom were complex and inflexible, like a maze with only one solution, only one way out. Luckily, I could see well enough when Gage gestured to a seat, and I quickly dropped into it. He claimed the one across from me, as Cassie stared at me with her black lined eyes.

"Cassie, this is Lainey." He made me being there sound as boring as possible.

Cassie didn't respond. She simply scowled and glanced back down at her food, some soy or veggie patty with cheese melted on it.

"Hi," I said, not wanting to sound too friendly or too rude. Being friendly could be a sign of weakness.

My vision returned to normal, as others took their places at the table. A boy with light brown skin and short, curly hair sat next to me. Gage said, "This is Andrew. Andrew, Lainey."

"Hey." Andrew bobbed his head at me. Then to Gage he asked, "Did you see that Vinny guy in the game last night?"

"Yeah. What a tool."

I listened and considered taking out my sandwich.

A girl set a tray of food down beside me and stared at my head. "You didn't leave the dye in long enough. It should be darker."

She had several skirts on, one layered over another, and boots with a ton of buckles. Her face was round and her boobs were so big they seemed to form a shelf. She flounced herself into her seat.

"If you're going to go blue, it should be electric blue," she continued. Her own hair was a vibrant orange.

"Sybil, Lainey. Lainey, Sybil," Gage said. "And it doesn't matter because she's dying it back today."

"Why?" Sybil asked, scrunching up her face.

"I haven't decided that yet," I said to Gage.

"You should keep it. I could help you next time." Sybil thrust a hand with black painted finger nails at me. "Nice to meet you."

"You too," I said.

She untwisted the cap to her water bottle. "Brave choice, by the way, with Wick."

Everyone froze. I heard Gage choke on his food. Sybil glanced around at them. "What? It's true, right?"

I smiled at her. "Thanks."

If Thomas could see me here with my blue hair and new alternative style friends, he would find it hilarious. Back home, I was the golden girl—a fact which he grew to hate the older he got. Puberty, I think. That was when things started to go wrong. Gradually, we drifted apart. He didn't look to me to be his protector anymore. He viewed me with contempt and I responded in the worst possible way—I didn't care.

"If you really want to, I could help you dye it back after school."

"That'd be great," I gushed.

To be honest, I wasn't loving my new look. Plus, I wanted to be Sybil's friend. I wanted her to like me and talk to me and take me under her substantial yet confident wing.

"Cool," she said. "Meet me at the back door at dismissal."

I sat on the toilet in Sybil's tiny bathroom while she swirled together the ingredients of a box of brown hair dye.

We stopped and bought it at a pharmacy on the way to her house.

"This is going to be really pretty. A little lighter than before, I think. Gage is going to love it."

I met her eyes in the mirror. "We aren't going out. We're just friends."

Sybil scoffed. "Yeah, because he's being a gutless wonder." She adjusted the towel draped around my shoulders. "You like him, though, right?"

"Yeah. I do."

I said this without thinking because being honest just felt right with Sybil. I could see no reason to lie to her, and speaking the truth about my feelings for Gage helped solidify the idea in my own head. I liked Gage. I wanted him in a romantic way, not just as friends.

"I knew it!" Sybil said. "He'll come around then. Just give him some time to get used to the idea."

She began painting the solution on my blue head. "You're going to be all Natalie Portman gorgeous when this is done."

"Hardly," I said. "Hey, do you know the deal with Gage's parents? Why is he so neglected?"

"From what I can gather, he started getting into trouble in seventh grade in Connecticut, so his mom made his dad take him. But his dad is too busy with his trophy wife and being a bigwig real estate loser so Gage just does whatever he wants."

I pondered this. It was good information to have, and it made me wonder about his relationship with his mother now. He hadn't mentioned her at all. Then again, I hadn't mentioned my family either.

"I don't think Cassie likes me," I said.

"Well, Cassie's in love with Gage, so yeah, of course she doesn't like you." Sybil worked intently on my hair, sectioning it and painting it meticulously. "Gage seriously offered to help you with this? Like he knows how to dye hair?" She laughed at the idea.

"Right?" I giggled in return.

"That alone tells me he's half in love with you already."

"You think?" I stared at her, watching her face as she worked.

"Yeah. I know. You're perfect for him. Tortured but beautiful."

"But he doesn't think so. He said I'm all wrong for him. I slept over his house Saturday night, and he stayed on the couch."

Sybil stopped painting and lifted her eyebrows at me in the mirror. "Poor Gage. He loves to be a martyr."

"Is that it?" I asked.

She gets back to work with the brush on my roots. "Let me think. I'll come up with something. Are you sure you're all done with Wick?"

"Totally sure."

"Alright. I'll work on a plan. But maybe he'll come around on his own. You are sort of dreamy."

My cheeks turned pink in the mirror, but Sybil didn't seem to notice. Her comment did make me wonder about her orientation on the sexuality spectrum, not that I really cared one way or the other. I wasn't a homophobe, and Sybil was a very cool person. She was one of those people who seemed incapable of not being themselves, of lying and

107

putting on airs. I really didn't care one way or another who she liked sexually. Clearly, she knew I was straight.

"Do you have a boyfriend?" I asked.

"Me?" She laughed. "I'm not really the boyfriend type. Guys don't exactly flock to date large, weird girls on Nantucket."

"Stop," I said. "You're pretty, and you're cool. You're the best girl I've met here."

She pretend swatted at me in the mirror. "I bet you say that to all the girls."

"I'm serious."

"Why? Because I'm doing your hair and helping you with Pike?"

"Yeah, and because you were nice to me at lunch. I was really nervous to sit at your table."

"The question is why? Why didn't you just go with Wick and Amber and Alex like you should have?"

I sighed. "I don't know. I just couldn't do it. Wick thought of me as a piece of meat. An item to claim at auction. I literally heard him call me my first day. I just couldn't do that anymore."

"Anymore?"

"I know being popular seems like it's really great, but it can be totally awful too."

Sybil nodded. "Oh, trust me, I wouldn't want to live by those rules. I'd flunk out of that class on day one."

"Yeah. It's no piece of cake being anyone in high school. I used to think I had it all, and then I saw how fast it could be taken away."

"Sound like some serious drama."

"The worst," I mumbled, knowing I should shut my big mouth. I had said enough.

"Do you have plans for the summer? Do you have to go visit your dad?"

"No. Not that I know of anyway."

"If you're here, you have to find a good summer job. I work at Young's on the strip renting bikes. A lot of kids work down there. It's fun."

I didn't want to tell Sybil I had never had a job before.

"I'm not sure I would know anything about renting bikes. What does Gage do?" I asked.

"He works for a landscaper, weeding and mowing. Bikes are easy. The managers train you. But I could see you as a hostess at a restaurant wearing a miniskirt and smiling pretty at the tourists." Sybil pouted out her lips like a model which made me laugh again.

"That sounds horrible. You do realize I'm not a bubblehead, right?"

"Honors physics? Yes. I'm aware."

"Will you tell me about everyone at the table?"

"Yeah. Sure. So there's Cassie, as you know. She and Gage went out for almost all of eighth grade and part of ninth before he dumped her, but she's still not over him."

"That's a long time not to be over someone."

"I know. She's kind of obsessive. Then there's Andrew, the black kid who usually sits next to Gage? Actually, he's half black. His mom's white. He's the closest thing to a best friend that Gage has although I can't really figure them out. They game and get stoned together. They're tight in their own stand-offish way."

She put the finishing touches on my hair and stepped

back to examine my head. "I think it's done. Let's check the box for timing."

"Thank you, Sybil." I met her eyes in the mirror. "For everything."

"You're welcome. For everything."

Chapter 14

Lainey

G AGE EXAMINED MY NEW HAIR the next day in physics. "Much better," he said, tilting his head to one side like it would help him see the real me better.

"Thanks." I smoothed it down near my temple. "Wanna hang out after school?"

He clicked his pen twice. "Sorry. Can't. I have to go somewhere."

"Oh."

"You can come if you want. I'm not sure you'll like it, though."

What was it? Errands? Doctor's appointment? It really didn't matter. Doing anything with Gage was good with me.

"I'm sure it'll be fine."

"There's that word again."

I exhaled and hung my head in shame. "Sorry."

"Meet me at my car."

Later, as we drove away from school, Gage said, "Remember, I warned you."

Gage wore his navy-blue fleece that made him look sort of preppy. He could totally have been a preppy boy if he wanted. He was handsome enough and blond enough that it could work for him. But the skater look was hot too, especially the tightish pants and Doc Marten boots.

Since I didn't really know the island very well yet, I could not predict where we were headed. We drove past the Stop and Shop to the first rotary and on to the second rotary where Gage steered us toward town. Then he took a right beside a huge, older building. We didn't go to that building, though. We drove around the back of it and parked outside another newer structure covered in gray shingles. The quarterboard over the door said "Our Island Home." Beyond the parking lot, the deep blue water of the harbor rippled with white caps.

"What is this place?"

"A nursing home. My Grandpa Pike lives here."

I glanced between him and the entrance. I'd never been to a nursing home before.

"I'll take you home first if you want," Gage offered.

But curiosity combined with my desire to do anything that involved spending time with Gage made me want to stay. "No. I'll come along."

We exited the car and were buffeted by a cold, salty wind off the water. Gage held the door for me on the way in. We entered a small lobby with linoleum floors and a reception desk. One of the nurses there recognized Gage.

"Well it must be Tuesday if I'm seeing you," she said. She was a pretty black lady with long, straight hair and a gap between her front teeth.

"Hi Anise," Gage greeted her.

"Your grandpa's in the community room, You and your friend can go right in." Anise gestured to a hallway and gave me a once over with her eyes at the same time.

"Thanks." We proceed down the main corridor before taking a right into a large room decorated in beige with accents of red. Elderly residents, some in wheelchairs, were scattered about the room at tables and on sofas. Some watched television while others just stared blankly at the walls. A plain clothed lady with an ID badge on a lanyard around her neck sat with two ladies at a table, helping them play checkers. There was a large fish tank on one wall and a side board with coffee, tea, and snacks on another.

Gage approached a gaunt man in a wheelchair and touched his shoulder. "Hi, Papa." The man's jaw was slack, his mouth sagging open, but he looked up at Gage and tried to smile. "How's it going?" Gage clasped his hand and shook it.

The man grunted and cast his gaze my way. "This is my friend, Lainey," Gage told him.

Mr. Pike examined me with large, blue eyes that reminded me of Gage's. Because of the way his skin hung, his eyes seemed huge. He nodded at me and lifted his twisted hand to shake mine. I shook it, even though he couldn't uncurl it for a proper handshake. "Nice to meet you Mr. Pike."

He gestured for us to sit at a table nearby as he walked his wheelchair closer to it. From across the room, a man and a woman began moving their chairs toward us. They were slow but purposeful in their efforts.

Mr. Pike grunted a few words I didn't understand.

"No. Lainey and I are just friends, Papa. Just friends. She just moved to Nantucket."

Mr. Pike bobbed his head at me, and I think he was trying to say welcome.

Gage said, "She's from San Francisco."

Mr. Pike said, "Ohhhhh," and gestured at himself with his gnarled hand.

"You've been there, Grandpa?" Gage asked.

"Mmmmm."

"Probably after Korea," Gage told me.

Mr. Pike nodded again.

"Grandpa served in Korea."

The worker who was playing checkers arrived at our table at the same time as the other two residents. "Nice to see you, Gage," she said.

"Thanks. This is Lainey. Lainey, this is Carol."

"Hello."

"How's it hanging, Hank!" the other man in the wheelchair shouted. He was so loud, it startled me.

"Fine, Mr. Kemp. How are you?" Gage shouted back.

Mr. Kemp was large and had a chubby, red face. I shot Gage a confused look.

"Grandpa's name is Hank, so he thinks my name is too," he told me.

"I'll get you some refreshments," Carol said.

She disappeared, leaving us alone with the three expectant faces. I felt sort of terrified of them but also fascinated.

"Hello dear," the elderly lady said to me. "You look like my granddaughter, Tammy."

She had a bright yellow afghan over her legs, and gray, thinning hair swept up in a bun. Her cheeks were still sort of full, but her eyes were cloudy and gray.

"Oh," I said, not sure how else to respond.

"Hank is such a nice young man. I'd love if he met my Tammy."

In response, Gage said, "I'm really not very nice, Mrs. Sharpe. Ask Lainey. She'll tell you."

Mrs. Sharpe twittered with laughter. "Oh oh oh, I don't think so. I know you. I know you're a gentleman. When I was a girl, I used to go to dances at the Legion. I knew boys who weren't nice. They tried all manner of things with a girl." Mrs. Sharpe raised her eyebrows at me. "Hank is not a boy like that."

A small giggle escaped me. Perhaps it was her talking about dances at the Legion or calling Gage Hank, but this whole situation struck me as kind of adorable and kind of hilarious all at the same time. This spontaneous laughter acted like a drug on my body. Endorphins. I think I read somewhere that happiness releases endorphins that give you a slight high.

"She's very pretty, Hank!" Mr. Kemp shouted at Gage.

Gage sighed and hung his head. Carol reappeared with several foil-topped juice containers and oatmeal raisin cookies from the sideboard.

"Here we go. Now, this is for your Grandpa, Gage." Carol handed him a straw and juice. "And would you mind helping Mr. Kemp, Lainey?" She gave me a juice and straw without waiting for my answer.

I prepared to do as asked while Gage somehow managed to have a discussion with his grandfather. How this happened confused me because Mr. Pike could only grunt and gesture to get his points across. Somehow, though, Gage understood and answered him.

"Dad's doing fine. Don't worry about him." Gage held up the juice and aimed the straw near Mr. Pike's mouth.

Mr. Pike managed to corral the straw between his teeth and drank.

I had to try with Mr. Kemp even though I had no idea what I was doing. I never fed a child in my life never mind a full-grown man in a wheelchair.

"How're you sleeping?" Gage asked Mr. Pike.

I adjusted the straw and stood up to get closer to Mr. Kemp. "Would you like a drink?"

He edged closer in his chair, using his feet. He reached to help me guide the cup and straw to his mouth. As he drank, he smiled up at me, and I felt oddly proud that I managed to do this simple task.

Afterward, as we walked to the Cherokee, a strange sense of satisfaction filled my chest. I still don't know what to call it. The only thing I could think at the time was I felt proud—proud that I was finally useful. That was a new feeling for me. I couldn't remember another time in my life that I ever felt that way other than tennis and even that was different.

Once we reached the Cherokee, Gage said, "If you even think about calling me Hank, I swear to God…"

But I had no teasing comeback. I could only smile over at him because Gage being called Hank by those sweet people made me happy. The whole experience was pure joy.

"I want to come back," I told Gage. "Next time you come, please bring me again."

He wrinkled his forehead at me. "You are one strange girl, you know that?"

"Yes," I replied. "Thank you for finally noticing."

Chapter 15

WE MADE IT TO THE church steps just as the ruckus began.

"Lizzie! Lizzie! Are you sorry about what happened?"

"Why are you here, Audrey?"

"Do you feel like you are somehow to blame?"

"Why this funeral and not the others?"

We reached the vestibule, and the funeral workers shut the doors behind us. One of them peered out through the window like he was waiting for the reporters to try to breach the doors.

"Can we sit in the back please?" Mom said breathlessly to one of the ushers.

"This way."

We were escorted to the second to last pew in the packed church. Despite proper etiquette, I caught glimpses of other mourners turning around to look at us. A rumble of whispers raced through the gathered crowd. I removed my hat and sunglasses, smoothing down my hair before reading the program. There was a beautiful picture of Hannah on the front. Tears burned my eyes.

The service was a full mass with communion. I had attended a full mass once before when Hannah was confirmed.

This time, I tried my best to actually pray when it was expected. I wanted to be able to pray. I wanted to know how, and I wanted to feel like it meant something, but no one had ever taught me the proper way to do it. I cried quietly throughout Hannah's service, and I prayed for everyone I could think of who needed it, even Thomas. Even myself. At the end, the polished wooden casket was wheeled down the center aisle with Hannah's mother, father, and sister walking beside it. The sight of them all was too much for me. I broke down into sobs, unable to catch my breath. Mom wrapped her arms around me, to try to comfort me.

Lainey

By Wednesday morning, a new routine was starting to emerge. When I awoke, my room did not feel so foreign. After only three times hitting snooze, I extracted myself from the warmth of the covers. The ride to school, peppered with my mother's thinly veiled questions about my mood and feelings, was downright boring. Even the rambling structure of Nantucket High School seemed far less intimidating. My rocky first week was over, and Nantucket might yet allow me a fresh start—at least as fresh I could muster or deserved.

Inside, I hurried through the Hall of the Whale. I needed to go to my locker in the basement. Upperclassmen lockers were usually on the first or second floor, but there were none left for me there.

The hall was particularly packed because of a function that morning in the cafeteria. I weaved my way through the clumps of students. At the top of the stairs stood a crowd of Lettermans, including Wick. I kept my head down and dashed for the stairwell, but for some reason, Wick followed.

"Hey Lainey. How's it going?"

Oh no. I glanced back at him but didn't answer. Why was he talking to me again? I preferred the cold shoulder.

"You don't have to look so concerned. I just wanted to said hi." His voice was quiet—not goading or taunting like he was after he beat up Gage.

"Hi," I said as I trotted down the stairs.

We reached the bottom, and I glanced back to see if Perk or the others were along for this rodeo. They were not, but I couldn't decide if this was a good or bad thing for me.

"You look pretty today. I like your hair. The blue was kinda fun too, but I'm glad you went back to brown."

Despite speeding up, Wick kept pace with me. When we arrived at my locker, two freshman boys scurried away.

"I was thinking that maybe we got off on the wrong foot." Wick leaned his shoulder against the locker beside mine, his muscular arms folded over his chest. "And I really wish we could just start over. Maybe we could hang out after school today. I could give you a tour of the island or we could watch a movie or something."

I spun my lock. "I don't think Amber would like that."

"Oh, don't worry about her," he said casually, as if there was anything casual about him and Amber. "We had a big fight and it's totally over now."

What was happening? Why couldn't he just leave me alone? I snapped my locker open and grabbed my history binder.

"Can I carry something for you?" He smiled like a used car salesman giving his best pitch.

I slammed my locker, hoping the noise would back him off. Unfortunately, it did not. In fact, he leaned in even closer as if waiting with rapt anticipation for my answer.

"I'm fine," I told him with a scowl.

"Well at least let me walk you to class."

I didn't answer. I just began walking back to the stairs, hoping Wick would take it as a no. Instead, he trailed me again and managed to stay beside me on the stairs despite other students trying to come down.

"You got plans this weekend?" he asked.

"Yeah." This was a lie. I had no plans. I wanted to have plans with Gage and Sybil, but I didn't yet.

We reached the first floor, and I turned for the second.

"Alright, let me know about today," Wick called after me as he stopped beside Perk. "Nice chatting!"

I wished Amber and Wick would stop being so messed up. I didn't want to be dragged into the middle of their bad romance every time they had a fight. Mostly, the problem was Wick. He couldn't walk away from a challenge. I imagined very few girls had ever turned down the chance to be his hook up, and he probably hated that I did. I just hoped this didn't mean more trouble for Gage. Despite my weakness, I could handle Wick. What I couldn't handle was Gage being hurt again because of my one stupid hook up.

I stood at the stove after school, waiting for the kettle to boil. My mother fussed around with a recipe on her Ipad while I pulled out a mug and some tea.

"I have a skype call scheduled with Thomas," she said out of the blue. She didn't even look up from her screen.

I pinched the cold handle of my spoon between my thumb and finger. "When?"

"Tomorrow afternoon. I made it after school in case you wanted to talk to him, too."

My initial impulse was to scoff and snap *No*. I didn't want to talk to him. I had nothing to say to him, and he had nothing to say to me. What would we talk about? The food in prison? His annoying cell mate? I couldn't bear the insincerity of saying anything to him.

"I'll think about it," I said calmly, despite my anger at her offer. Being decent to my mother was one of the things I learned in therapy. Belinda convinced me to stop making things worse for Mom by taking my feelings out on her.

"Her actions toward Thomas may seem delusional to you," Belinda said. "But it's what she has to do to live with this. Don't judge her for that."

So now, I played the normal game with her. As if talking on Skype to your fifteen-year-old son who's in jail for multiple murder could ever be construed as normal. There was normal family dysfunction and then there was this situation.

Before we left California, I knew these skype calls were a possibility. Skype was one of the reasons Mom agreed to leave. Would it make her feel better or worse? This was the first one so the idea scared me. I knew Thomas's behavior since the shooting had continued to be erratic. Even taking his medication, he was not stable. He lashed out; he berated everyone, his delusions of being under assault persisted. I didn't think I could take being attacked by him verbally, even through a computer screen.

Upstairs with my vanilla chai, I sat at my desk and considered my letters to Thomas. After the shooting, when

121

I refused to see or speak to him, Belinda encouraged me to write him a letter. There were several started on my laptop. They all contained varying degrees of fury and desperation and once I wrote them, I never read them again. For some reason, however, I didn't delete them. What would I tell him if I talked to him tomorrow? I opened my laptop and pulled up a shiny new document in which to write. I wasted five minutes playing with the font and the line spacing and saving it as if it was a diary not a letter. I simply titled it February eleventh. And then, I let it flow. I didn't think a lot about what I wrote in those letters. They were more just a stream of consciousness. Call me James Joyce.

Dear Thomas,

Nantucket is a frozen wasteland. You would hate it here. Not that you probably like it in jail. I'm sure it's awful. I guess I shouldn't be so ungrateful about being here. When compared to you, I've got it good.

Mom is going to talk to you tomorrow but I don't think I can. I hope this doesn't hurt your feelings, but for me, it just doesn't seem right to speak to you and act normal after what you did. When you think about the fact you killed four people, do you cry? Do you wish you could take it all back? They tell me you were mentally ill, but that still doesn't explain it for me. I can't understand why you did it. What did you think shooting people at Beaton would accomplish? I have done some research on school shooters, and I learned that there are three kinds.

You are supposedly the first kind. The psychotic. You did it because you were delusional. The prosecutors think you might be the second kind—the sociopath. These people are thrill killers who have no empathy for anyone. I don't think that is you. The third kind is traumatized. Those are people from messed up families with lots of abuse so that is not you either.

I wish you could have told me about how you were feeling. If you had, none of this would have happened. You could have gotten help. Sometimes, I'm just so angry that you didn't. I'm angry at myself, and I'm angry at you.

Mom told me that you aren't doing very well. You fight with everyone and you won't take your medication and you're mad at her for leaving. She tried to get me to talk to you, but when I hear you are acting like that I don't want to. I don't even know who you are anymore. You're a stranger to me. I miss the way you used to be, but whenever I start to think about that, I also get angry. I'm pissed at you for taking yourself away from me. I've lost you. Maybe forever.

Tears rolled down my cheeks and landed on the keyboard. I slammed the lid down and wiped my eyes. I couldn't finish. I could never finish the letters.

Later that night, as I started to read *Hamlet*, my phone chirped with a new message.

How about that drive?

Even though I deleted Wick, I recognized his number. I added him to contacts again before answering.

Sorry. Homework.

Sounds boring.

Kinda but must be done.

I considered ignoring him. There was definitely a part of me that wanted to be cruel to him because of what he did to Gage. There was another part, however, that saw his possible good side. Clearly, he wasn't all bad, and I found myself wondering about his personality. He seemed to have buried the real him under layer upon layer of bravado and ego and idiocy. Still, it was there. I had seen glimpses of it. He was kind to me in the car after my episode.

Math was easy.

Yeah. Doing English now.

Is your mom home?

Yeah.

Christ, was he going to stop by? I broke out in that tingly feeling like someone was watching me, like he was parked outside waiting for me to invite him in. I wished he didn't know where I lived.

You need more pics on Instagram

Stop stalking me

Send me some

No.

Please?

Not right now.

Friend me on FB. I couldn't find you.

I don't have it.

Why not?

Long story

You going to the dance?

The Valentine's Day dance was Saturday night.

Not sure.

You should. We could hang out before. Have a drink or two.

I rolled my eyes.

I don't think so.

I decided to text Gage and ask about the dance.

You going to the dance?

Me? School dance?

Just thought I'd ask...

Were you asking me as your date?

My face flushed with heat.

No!

Okay. Phew. Because that would be awkward. Since we're friends and all

Right

Sybil's probably going. You could go with her.

Are you trying to set us up?

NO!

LOL!

Just then a new text came in from Wick.

Do you always play so hard to get?

I sighed and stared at the screen, trying to decide how to answer.

Nothing personal. I'm just not into dating right now. Friends?

Sure.

But I knew there was an implied *for now*. For now, we would be just friends. For now he'd stop badgering me. Knowing Wick that probably meant just for that night.

Chapter 16

Lainey

THE THRUMMING BEAT OF THE bass echoed across the street as we walked toward the American Legion Hall. Dances were held there instead of the gym or cafeteria at school just like back in Mrs. Sharpe's time. The building was old and brick, tucked in beside a closed-for-the-season seafood restaurant and an art gallery.

Sybil decorated our exposed skin with neon body paint to fit the rave theme of the dance. Her friend Teal and, surprisingly, Gage joined us as well. Somehow, Sybil convinced him to give us a ride and come in for a few minutes.

"I can't believe I let you drag me here," Gage muttered as we made our way down the uneven sidewalk. I tried to stay upright and keep up which was not easy because Sybil dressed me in a pair of heeled sandals and a mini skirt she found in my closet. They were a few of my favorite clothes from my old life in L.A., but of course I didn't tell her that. That night, I was like her personal Barbie doll that she enjoyed styling.

"Where's your sense of fun, Gage? Consider this your first Rave."

"This is not a rave. This is a bunch of horny teenagers using any excuse to get drunk and grind."

I tripped and stumbled forward. Gage and Sybil grabbed my arms to steady me.

"I don't think those sandals were a good idea," Gage said.

"Of course they were. She looks like a total babe. If anyone should be wearing sandals like that, it's Lainey."

We reached the entrance where Mr. Santoro and a uniformed police officer waited. They gave us a once over, probably checking to see if we are drunk or high, before allowing us to enter and pay five dollars at a table by the door. Save for the special black lights that illuminated everyone's body paint and neon clothing, darkness pervaded the room. A club style song with a fast beat played from the balcony where the DJ was set up overlooking the crowd. Mobs of students stood in clusters, shifting and swaying with the music.

We managed to file off to the side, so we could watch for a few minutes. Sybil already bounced to the beat with Teal while Gage looked tortured. I would have tried to talk to him if it wasn't so freaking loud. Amber and Alex and a bunch of other girls from their lunch table danced nearby with Wick and Perk and others. Unfortunately, Wick spotted me before I could avert my gaze.

I turned to Gage and leaned up close to his ear to speak to him. He bent down to listen. "Please dance with me. Wick just saw me."

He placed his hands lightly on my hips, and his eyes lingered on my cleavage. I instinctively reached up and put my hands on his shoulders. He shouted back, "I hate this music."

I raised an eyebrow at him. "Please? We could pretend it's a slow song and just stand like this."

He smirked and adjusted his hands, pulling me slightly closer, our bodies inches apart. "Okay," he said. "But only because Wick's looking. Touching you like this is the best revenge I can get."

I gaped up at him. Was he only touching me to get back at Wick?

Before I could respond to his rudeness, Sybil appeared beside us. "Come dance with us!" She tugged us both by the arms toward Teal and a bunch more friends that they'd found, including Cassie. She scowled when she saw me, but I still joined the group to dance. After a couple songs, I left to go to the bathroom. On my way, I felt a hand on my arm.

"Hey, hold up," Wick said.

I faced him with more confidence than I felt. "What?" I asked.

"How's it going?"

"Fine."

"Are you high?" He examined my face for clues to my status.

"No. Why would you ask?"

"You came with Pike. And I was hoping to see you happy for once." He chuckled at his own joke.

I rolled my eyes at him. "I'm trying to go to the bathroom." I lowered my gaze to his hand on my arm.

He dropped it, and I walked away.

"You look hot, by the way! In that outfit!" he called after me.

After five minutes in the packed restroom, I steeled myself to walk back out. I hoped I could find Gage and

Sybil and the others before Wick tried to grind on me. I took a deep breath and weaved quickly through the crowd. My efforts were pointless, though, because Wick was waiting. He took my hand.

"Friends, right?" Wick said. "We can dance as friends?"

A comeback was lost on me. I didn't want to piss him off, and I didn't want him going after Gage again. The music pulsed and his hand was warm and his lips, the lips that kissed so well, lifted in a sexy smile. I let him pull me closer. We danced. We shook and bounced and swayed with the crowd—Wick's hands on my hips, mine occasionally touching his chest and arms. I tried to keep from looking him in the eye. My head spun and the music pounded, and I knew we were being watched. Everyone waited to see what would happen. Thankfully, the song didn't last much longer, and when it stopped, the DJ paused to make an announcement. I used it as my chance to slip away.

"Thanks. Bye," I said to him before disappearing into the crowd. Thankfully, he let me go.

When I arrived back at our corner, Gage was gone and Sybil was wide eyed. Behind her, Cassie and Teal and the others all watched me. Their disapproving expressions made me want to flee. Dancing with Wick was a huge mistake. I couldn't seem to get anything right.

"I think I'm going to go!" I shouted over the music.

"With Wick?" Sybil yelled back.

"No!" Tears formed in my eyes. Did she really think I'd leave with Wick?

Sybil must have seen my angst because her face softened. "Gage left, but you could probably text him for a ride. It was just a minute or so ago."

"Forget it. I'll call my mom." I started for the exit.

Sybil called after me, "Why don't you stay?"

But I kept going. The walls were caving in on me. The music assaulted my brain, and my temples throbbed. I shouldn't have come at all.

Chapter 17

Gage

SHE MOVED WITH HIM, HIS hands reaching for her. I couldn't believe what I saw. Wick smiled and ducked his head closer to say something to her. Lainey turned, a faint smile crossing her lips. They danced. Lainey danced with Wick.

I had to get out of there. I should never have come. Two seconds in the door and I insulted Lainey. Then, ten minutes later, she was dancing with Wickersham.

I found Sybil talking to Teal and Cassie. They stopped when I arrived and all peered up at me. I could tell by their faces they were talking about me and Lainey and Wick—a juicy love triangle I never wanted to be a part of.

"I'm leaving!" I shouted over the music.

"Okay!" Sybil answered.

I could see that she knew. She knew the effect Lainey had on me. I hated that anyone could see how I felt, and that I was stupid enough to let a girl as beautiful and unattainable as Lainey get to me. Without another word, I charged toward the door. I dodged bodies and was just about to break free when Andrew appeared in front of me.

"Hey man!" he said. There was a cute freshman in a tight mini dress at his side. "This is Sierra!" Andrew gestured at her.

I shoved my hands in my pockets. "Hi."

"This is my friend, Gage!" Andrew told her. Then to me, he said, "I didn't think you came to these things!"

"I don't usually," I said just as I saw Lainey moving through the crowd. Alone. She was alone. I craned my neck to see where she was headed.

Andrew smirked and clapped me on the shoulder. "Go get her, dude."

I took off, hoping I could catch her before she got outside. Luckily, she moved slowly in her heels, and I managed to slide in front of her right by the entry table.

"Hey!" I shouted over the music. "Where are you going?"

She glowered at me, her lips pursed in a tight line. "Home!" She darted around me and out the door.

Without any internal debate, I went after her. Even though she danced with Wick. Even though I should have steered clear. Even though everything, I could see that she needed a friend, and Sybil and I were all she had in that department.

We walked right past Santoro and the cop. Santoro called after us, "If you leave, you can't come back in!"

Apparently, neither of us cared because we both kept going. After trailing her toward town for a minute or so, Lainey stopped and yanked out her phone.

"You wanna ride?" I asked.

She glanced up at me, anger and hurt clouding her pretty eyes. I knew she was mad at me for what I said earlier.

I didn't mean for it to come out so cold, so thoughtless and rude, but I couldn't figure out how to take it back.

"No. I'm texting my mom."

I crossed my arms. "You can't just run off alone every time something annoys you. It's not safe."

I sounded like a parent, and this irritated her.

"Oh, but you can?" she snapped.

"Yeah. Because I have a car. And I'm not wearing a mini skirt and heels. Sorry if the world was unfair. I didn't make the rules."

She scoffed at me and jammed her phone back in her jacket.

"Does that mean you'll take a ride?" I asked, gesturing at her pocket.

She looked me square in the face and even in the dark, her eyes were dangerously sexy. She didn't answer with words but simply nodded twice. I could tell that she hated giving in to me when she was still mad. I wanted to tell her I knew the feeling. Slowly, gradually, she was wearing me down too. She made me want to give in to her. I only went to the dance because of her, and then to see her dancing with Wick, I almost lost it.

"Great. Let's go," I said.

We walked side by side back to the Cherokee. I kept a slow pace because I knew she had to take it easy in her sandals. Despite my best efforts not to notice, her legs were sexy as hell in them. Leave it to Sybil to deck her out like a model. We got in my car without a word, and I started driving.

Lainey

He seemed to be driving me home. We headed up Main Street toward Madaket Road, but I refused to say anything. Even though I wanted to hang out with him, I had too much pride to ask. He was so rude at the dance. He made touching me sound so mean and petty.

I prepared myself for an awkward goodbye when he surprised me and drove past my house. I snuck a glance at him and tried to read his face, but still, we didn't speak. He continued driving out Madaket Road. I waited for him to take a side street, but we kept going. I knew the end of the road was coming up soon, and just like every main road in Nantucket, this one ended at the beach.

In California, roads leading to the beach were all heavily populated; at least the public roads that allowed traffic. But in Nantucket, pitch dark surrounded us. Few houses near the beach were occupied in the winter.

When we reached the end of the road, Gage turned right and drove over a rickety, wooden bridge. I had been there before with my mother when we went exploring. I knew the road changed to dirt after the bridge and led to the western most part of the island known as Smith's Point. If we drove much further, we'd be on the beach, but instead, we hooked a right and headed the other way. We passed closed-up beach houses along the water's edge as we bounced along the rutted road. We came to a point, the entrance to an inlet. A boat ramp appeared in the headlights. Gage parked on the dock and shut off the car.

I exhaled an involuntary sigh. The night was beautiful but cold. I could smell the salt air even with the windows up. The whole universe of stars lay above us with just a few twinkling house lights on the horizon. The moon illuminated the water. Peaceful. Gage must have liked it there because it was so peaceful.

When Thomas and I were in middle school, we used to sit by our pool at night and talk sometimes. We'd leave just the underwater light on, and he would open up to me. One time, he told me about a girl he liked and another night, about a kid at school that was teasing him. I never looked at him when we'd sit like that. It was a rare and fragile thing for him to feel close to me, and I didn't want to put him off in anyway.

Gage finally broke the silence between us. "I told you those dances suck."

My anger had dissipated with every inch we drove. Now, I just felt sad.

"You didn't really give it much of a chance," I said quietly. "I wanted to dance with you."

Gage sighed. "Apparently you wanted to dance with a lot of people."

"*Want* is a very strong word, Gage."

"Yeah. It is."

We both knew there were layers upon layers of meaning in this conversation. We both wanted things. I wished I knew what he wanted from me, but I felt like I needed to explain myself.

"I told Wick I would be his friend, so he'd stop hating me and chasing me. He sort of accepted that, and he wanted to dance. I got away from him as soon as I could. But I don't want to be a pawn in your battle with him. I don't want to feel like you're only being my friend to get back at him."

"I am definitely not being your friend to get back at Wick. I would never do that. I'm not a fake person, and I don't use people."

"Okay."

"But do you seriously think you can be friends with Wick?"

"No," I answered. "But I'm hoping he'll get tired of being just friends with me and leave me alone. You're starting to act just like him, though. He told me I couldn't go out with him and be friends with you. Are you telling me I can't be your friend and Wick's friend at the same time?"

Gage shot me a dark look. "I don't tell my friends what to do, Lainey."

"Well that's a relief." I squeezed my hands together in my lap.

We sat in silence for a few moments. I watched the way the moonlight played off the water. It formed a long line of illumination stretching across the inlet toward the houses.

"Sorry," Gage said.

This surprised me.

"You do understand that I hate him though, right? He kicked my ass because of you, and I sort of want to get some revenge on him, even if I know I shouldn't use you to do it."

"I get that. And for the record, I know that he's not really my friend. Not in the way you are."

Gage flashed me a wan smile. "I told you being my friend might not be the best choice. Remember?"

"Yeah. But I'll take my chances."

"Alright. So we're all good now?"

"Yeah. We're good," I answered.

"Good. I'll take you home then."

I didn't object even though I didn't want to go home yet. I had too much pride, however, to suggest going back to the basement. I already practically threw myself at Gage while I was high, and I couldn't take anymore rejection from him.

"Sorry the dance was such a bust," he said as he backed us off the dock.

"It was fine. I didn't exactly have high expectations."

"Raves at the Legion not your thing either?"

"No. But I can't wait to tell Mrs. Sharpe we went. She'll think it's great."

"Yeah. Until she forgets it five minutes later."

I sighed. "I know. Poor Mrs. Sharpe."

I wondered if there would ever come a day I forgot things. There were plenty of memories I'd have liked to leave behind.

Chapter 18

Lainey

SYBIL SAT ON THE ZEBRA striped slipper chair in the corner of my room while I perched on my desk chair. "Did you decorate this room?" She surveyed the walls and furniture.

"No. My mom did it," I answered.

"Oh," Sybil said. "It's nice, but it's sort of too perfect."

"I know. Don't get me started. She said I could personalize with posters if I wanted."

"Oh. Cool," she said. "So, let me get this straight in my head. After you left the dance, Gage drove you to Madaket and parked on the boat ramp and still didn't kiss you?"

"Yup. No kissing, no touching, no nothing. Zero romantic contact."

I remembered talking like this with Hannah about boys—boys at the beach, boys at clubs, boys in Santa Monica. We always had some new, pressing tidbit to share about our latest crush. Hannah was in my life—a living breathing person, and now, she was just gone. In the blink of eye. Thinking about Hannah made my playfulness level drop from one hundred to zero. I had no right to be enjoying this moment with Sybil.

"Well, all I can tell you is that he'll have to cave eventually. I know he likes you. I saw the look on his face when you danced with Wick. Which by the way, why did you do that?"

I shrugged and picked up Thomas' horseshoe from its place on my desk; the metal cold against my palm. "I just couldn't say no. He was being nice, and I didn't want to make him mad."

"Have you always been a pushover? Seriously, it's okay to say no. You should learn no. I can give you some assertiveness training if you want."

I found myself wishing I could tell her I hadn't always been like this. I used to be tough, but since the shooting, I feared everything, it seemed. Even being playful with Sybil was scary. I was as prickly as a porcupine when it came to my emotions.

"I guess the truth is I felt bad for him for some reason. I see something in him. Like he's really a very sad person inside."

And saying these words, I realized it was the truth. I saw Wick's damage. I didn't know what it was, but I could sense it, maybe because of my own.

"Really?" Sybil shifted on the seat. "What's your theory on why Wick acts like an asshole, then?"

"I don't know. It's just a feeling really."

I felt kind of embarrassed that I said anything. Since when was I so empathetic? Really, I shouldn't have cared about Wick's issues. He was mostly a jerk around me, and he beat up Gage. That was all that should have mattered.

"Please tell me you're not one of those girls who dates guys to try to fix them or save them?"

"No," I said emphatically. If anyone needed fixing, it was me. I had no business trying to fix anyone else. "I just don't want to be mean to him."

Being cruel to anyone ever again seemed wrong. I regretted all the times I was mean or rude or thoughtless when it came to my brother. Rationally, I knew that I did not cause him to act the way he did. Still, I struggled with a very real sense of guilt as if somehow, I contributed to what happened that day at Beaton—every one of my actions building and adding up until Thomas reached a tipping point.

"So, what about Gage?" Sybil asked. "Are you trying to save him?"

"Definitely not. I just think he's hot and fun and cool." I moved the horseshoe up and down like I'm lifting a hand weight.

Sybil grinned and sat up straighter. "Well, that I can get on board with."

"Thanks. So, any new advice on how to make it happen?"

"None. I say just keep being you. He won't last much longer."

I hoped that what she said was the truth. I had the biggest, fifteen-year-old girl style crush on Gage.

Monday morning, I took my usual seat in Rapisardi's circle of doom. I had Wick on the brain because he kept texting me the night before about doing the Hamlet project together. I pretended my phone was dead and didn't answer. I waited for him to come in, so I could give him the bad news that I didn't want to work with him.

Wick arrived right at the bell and dropped his backpack in the seat beside me. Instead of sitting down or speaking to me, however, he kept walking to Mr. Rapisardi's desk. I watched their conversation. Wick gestured at me at one point, and then they both looked in my direction. Mr. Rap nodded, and Wick returned to his seat.

"I let Mr. Rap know we want to be partners for the Hamlet project," he said.

"I never said that was okay."

"I know, but I definitely need you to help me get an A on it. No lacrosse if I don't get my grade up. What are friends for, right?"

"I'm not doing the project for you." Seriously, he was so manipulative.

"Well, of course not," he said with mock outrage. "I'll do my part."

Despite what he said, I knew I'd end up doing the entire thing. Plus, he'd be spending every meet up scheming how to get me back in his bedroom.

"I'll think about it," I finally said.

It felt easier to be non-committal at that point. During class, I pondered what to do. Partnership was optional, and I could tell Rapisardi I didn't want to be Wick's partner. Plus, Gage would hate it, and I didn't want to torture him. Maybe Wick would give up the idea himself. We had two weeks until the project was due. Hopefully, he'd become bored with me soon. He seemed to have a short attention span when it came to girls.

After class, Wick stayed close by as I packed up. "We should meet today or tomorrow after school to pick a project. My house or yours?"

"Neither. The library."

"We'll never get everything done during library hours."

"We can make it work."

"Don't you trust yourself around me?" He twinkled his dimple at me.

I rolled my eyes in return. "Spare me the narcissism."

"Okay. Whatever that means."

This made me giggle. "You don't know what narcissism is?"

"No. Is it good?"

"No. It means your conceited."

"Oh." He looked confused for a moment and then regained his composure. "I can't help it if I'm adorable." And he batted his eyes at me.

"Go to class," I told him, shaking my head.

Wick was turning out to be sort of amusing even if I should have hated him for what he did to Gage.

Gage

I had English with Cassie first block. She sat beside me, which was normal, but I could tell by her scowl that she wasn't a happy camper.

"Are you hooking up with her now?" she asked.

"What?" I asked reflexively even though she was clearly referring to Lainey.

"You heard me," Cassie said. Her hair was jet black, as if to accentuate her dark mood.

"Am I hooking up with Lainey?"

"Yeah."

"No. We're friends."

"Does being friends with her mean we don't hang out anymore? Because that's what it seems like to me."

"No. It doesn't mean that. You know it doesn't mean that."

"Do I?"

Annoyance flared in my chest. "Well maybe with the way you're acting, it does."

Her cheeks reddened, and her grimace deepened. She started digging around in her bag. "I just don't want you getting caught up in her games. Guys are always blinded by girls like her, with her pouty lips and her I'm-so-lonely eyes. Trust me, that girl doesn't know what lonely is. She's just seeking as much attention as possible."

"You don't really know anything about her."

"I don't need to. I know her type."

Cassie was doing to Lainey what the popular kids did to the rest of us all the time. Judging without knowing. I found my irritation with her growing as class started. Part of me was pissed that Cassie was being so bitchy and the other part wondered if maybe I was being blinded by Lainey. Was she really an attention seeker? Was I, in fact, being manipulated? Perhaps I was too awash in male hormones to see the truth.

More unsure than ever, I ignored Cassie's attempt to speak to me after class. She stormed off, and I finished packing up. When I reached the hall, Lainey walked toward me with Wick at her side. She stopped to talk but unfortunately, Wick did too.

"Did Lainey tell you about our project?" Wick asked.

"No."

"We're doing our Hamlet project together. She's saving

my ass, actually. I need to pull my grade up. So, I might be stealing her in the next few weeks to get our work done."

Lainey gaped at Wick. "I haven't agreed to anything yet," she said.

"I really need this, Lainey. Please don't let me down."

Lainey closed her mouth and glowered at him. "I've got to go," she said.

"Yeah. Me too. See you guys later." Wick sauntered off.

"Hamlet project?" I asked once he was out of earshot.

I needed to get a handle on the hot feeling of jealousy bubbling up in my chest. I had no right to be pissed off or jealous about Wick. Just like at the dance, however, I couldn't seem to swat it down. What the heck was wrong with me? I did projects with Lainey in physics, and it meant nothing. Wick and her talking about Hamlet in a Google doc should be nothing too.

"His latest ploy. Don't worry. I've got it under control."

"I wish you'd just tell him to fuck off."

We walked toward our next classes.

"I know you do, but that's not really my style. I talked to Sybil about this yesterday."

"Oh yeah? What did she say?"

"She told me not to go around trying to fix broken boys."

"You consider Wick broken?"

Seriously, this was a crazy idea. The guy loved himself. He had everything he could want in the world except Lainey. And he was doing his best to remedy that.

Lainey said, "Yeah. Clearly, he is."

"And you want to fix him?" I couldn't hide my skepticism.

"No. I just don't want to further his damage. Sybil was

very good at helping me figure this out. Talking to her, I think I have it clear in my head now."

"I'm glad someone does," I muttered as we stepped aside for pack of giggling freshman girls. "I hope you aren't trying to fix me, too?"

This made her smile sweetly. "What's to fix?" she asked.

My resistance melted by another inch, like an iceberg on a hot day in the Caribbean, I didn't stand a chance when she heaped praise on me. "Um...quite a bit actually, I assure you."

"Well, I don't see it that way." She bumped my arm with her shoulder. "I'll see you at lunch."

Then, she veered off into her history class.

Chapter 19

Lainey

I WAS RIDICULOUSLY GOOD AT SPANISH. In fact, I grew to be Senora Tasch's favorite student more and more each day. She marveled at my proficiency, and I even confided in her that I had a Mexican nanny when she inquired about it.

Leaving Spanish, however, I still got nervous about lunch. I wondered if the cafeteria would ever be a place I felt at ease again. Probably not, but having safe people to sit with made it more tolerable. I claimed the same seat as last week and responded to everyone who greeted me. Gage was still in the line to buy food. As I retrieved my sandwich, I sensed Cassie looking at me.

When Gage arrived, he took the seat beside me. He had other seat options, but he picked this one.

"Hey," he said. "Let me guess. Peanut butter and jelly?"

"Yeah."

"Hey Lainey, did you have fun at the dance?" Cassie asked.

"It was okay," I answered, wondering where this was going.

"You didn't stay long? Did Wick say something mean when you were shimmying on his junk?"

Her words reverberated through me like an echo.

"Cassie!" Sybil said. "What the hell!"

"What?" Cassie asked. "I was just wondering what happened. You know, when she was all up on Wick."

"She was not all up on Wick," Gage said.

My face felt hot and my vision blurred. Cassie's lips moved but the sound faded—unintelligible and getting quieter and quieter. Gage and then Sybil spoke—their lips clearly moving—but I no longer heard anything until a loud bang rang out. A tray on a table? A mop falling over? I closed my eyes.

I put my ear to her mouth. Was she breathing? I should do CPR. I should do something. When I looked up, two police officers entered the cafeteria with their guns drawn. The sight of them struck me with a whole new terror.

Someone touched my arm. "Lainey?"

I opened my eyes. "Are you okay?" Gage asked.

I ran down a check list. Nantucket not L.A. Lainey not Lizzie. Nantucket High School not Beaton Prep.

"Oh my God! Are you serious right now?" Cassie asked. "Nice damsel in distress act."

Blink. Blink again.

"Is everything alright here?"

A teacher.

"Yeah. Fine. But I think Lainey needs a social worker," Cassie said, her voice dripping with sarcasm.

"Shut up, Cassie," Sybil snapped.

"Lainey, are you alright?" the teacher asked.

I didn't know her, but I managed to nod.

"Maybe you girls should split up if you can't stop yelling." The teacher gestured between Sybil and Cassie.

"Sure. No problem." Cassie stood. "I'll give you guys some space to tend to the princess."

Cassie moved to the other end of the table and a few friends followed her.

"Here, have some water," Gage said.

I drank a few sips. Sweat soaked my neck and underarms. I forced a smile.

"I'm fine," I said. But of course, it was a lie. As Gage so aptly pointed out to me last week, clearly I was not fine.

"Do you have plans after school?" Gage asked me as he went back to eating his pizza.

"No."

"Are you supposed to start the project today?"

"I don't know." My sandwich suddenly seemed very unappealing.

"Just tell him you're busy."

"What project?" Sybil asked.

"With Wick. She has to do a project with him in English."

Sybil shuddered. "Has to?"

"Long story," Gage said.

Sybil continued to stare at me. Andrew tried to act like everything was normal. Gage leaned in closer to whisper to me, "Maybe we could smoke later."

"That would be good," I said.

Getting high with Gage sounded perfect. My feelings were too much for me to handle. Was I being a princess? Imposing on these poor people with all my baggage and needs? Guilt started to drag me under its waves. Being friends with me might turn out to be a big job. Gage and Sybil didn't need that in their lives.

Gage said, "Text Wick you'll do the library tomorrow."

"Okay."

"If the snow keeps up, we might have a snow day anyway," Gage said.

"That would be awesome," Andrew replied.

Sybil asked, "Have you ever been sledding, Lainey?"

"Once. In Utah. But it was tubing."

One year, we went to the Sundance Film Festival with my father. I was around ten which means Thomas was around eight. Our babysitter for the trip took us to a tubing hill. Dad was busy at a panel or a screening. We pretty much spent that whole trip with a babysitter. Thomas didn't want to ride in the tube, but the sitter made him. I was the more adventurous one who enjoyed it.

"Tubing is sledding. Was it on a course?" Sybil asked.

"Yeah." Slowly, they talked me off the ledge without even knowing they were doing it.

Gage said, "We'll take you free-styling at Dead Horse Valley. Andrew and I are the kings of stoned sledding."

"That sounds dangerous." My anxiety dissipated in small increments. I focused on sledding with Gage. A visualization. I pictured us sitting on a toboggan, me between his legs, leaning back against his chest. Someone pushed us. Andrew. Andrew could give us the push we needed to start down the slope. Cold air bites my cheeks—

"Hey, we meeting after school?"

I snapped out of my fantasy to see Wick standing beside the table. Tension radiated off Gage. "No. I have plans. Tomorrow we can. In the library."

Wick glanced at Gage and then back to me. "Okay. I could always come over tonight too."

"No. Tomorrow. Library," I repeated.

Despite not getting his way, Wick continued to smile. "Okay. See ya."

Once he was gone, Sybil said, "I'd talk to Mr. Rap if I was you. A project with Wick seems like the last thing you need right now."

I knew she was right. I knew I should try to get out of it. But then Gage said, "Lainey can decide. She's a big girl."

In that moment, I wished it was true. I wished I was as strong as he thought I was—as I should have been. Maybe I could be. Maybe. If I tried.

We didn't go sledding. We went to the basement and smoked a bowl. Gage didn't even care that his step-mom was upstairs.

"She won't come down. Trust me."

After smoking, I laid down. I was like a cat, and Gage's bed was my favorite place to curl up and nap. Gage dispensed with the paraphernalia and joined me just like the last time. Maybe this would be the time he finally kissed me. I hoped it was. He arranged himself beside me, and I wondered if I should be the one to do it. Then I reminded myself that I didn't want to ruin our friendship. It had to be him. He was the one saying no, so he had to be the one who said yes.

"Do you want to talk about lunch?" he asked.

His lips looked soft and pink, his eyes a calming blue. He had one little line between his eyebrows that seemed to form when he was worried.

"Not really."

"I think Cassie feels threatened by you. I'm sorry, though, for how she acted."

"Why are you sorry?" I asked. "You didn't accuse me of being a slutty drama queen did you?"

This conversation was reminiscent of our texts when I apologized for Wick.

Gage smiled shyly, clearly getting the reference. "No. I didn't."

He brushed hair away from my cheek toward my ear. The soft, tracing of his fingers gave me goose bumps.

"I wasn't faking it, by the way. In case you were wondering."

"I know. I didn't think you were."

I wanted to tell him more. As my friend, he deserved to know something, but I had to suppress the urge to confess everything. It must be a natural human instinct, wanting to share secrets with people you care about, because I struggled to stop myself that day.

"I'm kind of messed up," I said. "You probably already figured that out, though."

He ran his hand over my shoulder and down my arm before clasping mine. I thought I'd explode from the sensation of him touching me—warm and gentle and sexy all at the same time.

"I can tell something happened to you," he said.

I squeezed his hand. "I can't talk about it."

"You don't have to. I understand."

"I'm glad someone does."

Gage cared about me. Gage didn't want to use me to make himself feel good like other boys. I shifted toward him, and he met me halfway. We hugged. Our hugs were one of the best things about my new life.

Chapter 20

THE FLAT SCREEN ON THE *wall was paused on a video game—two bloody people lay at the feet of the player while he faced the desolate landscape of a destroyed city. I tore my eyes away from it to find the source of the music. Clothes and books and food wrappers were strewn everywhere. I managed to locate an iPad docked in a set of speakers on the nightstand. I picked my way through the debris on his floor and shut it off. The silence was an instant relief. Thomas's music could only be described as terrible. Acid Metal Punk Rock. Almost immediately after I felt the relief, though, I wondered if I should restart it. I could hit play again and simply turn it down so I wouldn't hear it all the way down the hall in my room. Maybe Thomas was just down in the kitchen getting food and maybe he was going to be really mad when he discovered I had been in his room...*

Lainey

That night, my mother was abnormally chatty. While we ate, she rambled on about salmon with orange sauce and something Graham told her about town politics and new fixtures in the half bath; none of which interested me.

I was rinsing my plate at the sink when she decided to

drop the news she'd been withholding. "I need to talk to you about something before you go up."

She just had the whole meal to talk to me, so I knew it must be something unpleasant—something that would have made me sick and unable to eat. I focused on the warm water as it ran over the congealed remnants of my dinner.

"About what?" I finally asked.

"Some new information I got today," she said.

I shot her a warning look. *Don't do this. Don't.*

"It can't be avoided, Lizzie," she said as if reading my mind.

I finished rinsing my plate and set it precisely in the dishwasher. My heart began to pound in my ears, sweat forming on my neck.

"I need a pill," I told her.

She puckered her face like this was something she really needed to consider.

Before she answered, I stated it again. "I need a pill."

She sighed and said, "I'll meet you in the living room."

I had Ativan pills to take in case of emergency. *PRN. As the situation demands.* That's how they were prescribed and my mother kept control of them so I couldn't abuse them. I was certain, however, this was going to be a PRN moment especially after the day I'd already had.

On the couch, I curled my legs up beside me, covering myself with a fleece throw. Mom arrived with a glass of water and one little white pill. She watched me take it and drink the water, and before I could set the glass down, she blurted out the news.

"A trial date has been set."

I froze and waited for her to say more. When? Why?

They were supposed to make a deal. Plea out. Why couldn't they get it done?

"It's going to start May fifth, and you're on the witness list for the prosecution." Mom took the glass and sat beside me on the couch.

I peered down at my hands atop of the cushy, blue fleece. They were so pale. So thin and so pale. Were they even mine? Were they the same hands that held Hannah's while I watched her die?

"I know this is hard, but we really have no choice. The prosecution won't plea. They want a trial, and Thomas isn't helping his case with all his bad behavior in jail. The defense wants to see you. For preparations. We have to go back—"

"Go back?" My voice cracked as I said it.

"Yes. Just for a day or two. We could do it so no one knows we're there. Your father is working on it now."

Los Angeles. A flight home. A meeting with lawyers. Thomas on trial. My head hurt. In a courtroom, I'd see Hannah's family. I'd see Thomas. My worlds that spun apart would collide. I was torn apart inside, and at a trial, I'd be torn apart on the outside, for all the world to see.

The feelings I had for Thomas jumbled and bounced like lottery balls blown around inside their case. They spanned the spectrum of possibility before shooting out and revealing the winner. Like the numbers, I had no idea what emotion would emerge on any given day.

This ordeal was supposed to be over—at least as well as something like that could ever be over. I wanted to put Thomas and the shooting and Hannah's family and even Hannah in a box, never to be opened again. If I didn't put them there and keep the lid on, all of me might ooze out

154

like blood. Like a hemorrhage. It will be like I was shot that day, too.

Gage. My phone. *Where's my phone?* Without another word, I rose from the sofa to retrieve it. I needed Gage. I needed him more than I ever needed anyone. Gage was now. Gage knew without really knowing anything. Gage saw the bleeding mess I was and didn't care.

"Lizzie? Where are you going?" Mom called after me.

I didn't answer, not because I didn't want to but because I could not. I was struck mute. I snatched my phone off the granite counter in the kitchen and sent Gage a text.

Can you come get me?

My mother followed. "Who are you texting?"

I turned the phone around to show her. As she read, the phone vibrated with an answer.

Sure. Bring warm clothes.

"Where are you going?" she asked again.

I didn't answer. Instead, I strode to the hall and began layering up with clothes from the closest.

"Lizzie, it will be okay," Mom said. "I know it seems terrible now, but we'll get through this. I'll call Belinda. She'll come to the sessions. She'll be there for you if you want. What have you told this boy?" she asked.

I stilled. "Nothing. Of course, nothing." My voice had returned.

"And you can't. Promise me you won't."

I met her gaze—her beautiful blue eyes, her pale skin, the fine lines that revealed her age—and I knew I couldn't make that promise. Someday, I might tell Gage.

"I won't," I told her. "Not yet."

Gage

Lainey must have been waiting at the door because she came right out. She jogged to my car across her slushy driveway, bundled in more layers than I'd ever seen on her. She slid into the passenger seat without a word.

"Hi," I said.

"Hi," she murmured in return.

Her lips were downturned; her forehead creased into lines.

"Everything okay?" I asked.

She shook her head, as a single tear rolled down her cheek. I fought the urge to lean over and brush it away. "Sledding or basement?" I asked.

"Sledding."

It was a relief to hear her voice, to know she wasn't lost inside her own head as sometimes happened.

"And your mom?" I gestured to where she watched us out the side light window.

"She's fine."

I put the car in reverse. "She's not gonna call the cops on me for taking you?"

"No. Maybe Graham but not the cops."

I was glad she still had some semblance of a sense of humor.

Day by day, little by little, the saddest girl in the world was changing me. Lainey was making me different. How exactly she did it, I can't say, but it was happening, and I had no intention of stopping the momentum.

Lainey

A million snowflakes fell. They swirled in the headlights and stuck to the windshield before the wipers could clear them. As far as the eye could see, they continued. Ever steady. Ever determined to land somewhere.

About four inches had piled up, causing the roads to be slushy. Near the Old Mill, Gage took a right onto a dirt road. We didn't drive far before he pulled off to the side in a small parking area surrounded by tall, pine trees.

"Why is it called Dead Horse Valley?" I asked.

Gage shrugged. "Hell if I know. You wanna smoke first?"

"Yes." Getting high would feel good. Getting numb and disconnected was what I wanted to do.

Gage retrieved a joint and lighter from his coat pocket. He lit the joint by taking one puff on it, and then he handed it to me. I only took two hits, knowing that Gage's weed was very powerful, and I'd already taken a pill.

Once we smoked, he stashed the extinguished joint in the cup holder. "You ready?" he asked.

I nodded—my brain already clouding over, becoming anesthetized from the emotional pain of being Lizzie Berringer. Lizzie Berringer had to go home. She had to face her brother and the gun and the bullets and the dead. All the pretending in the world wasn't going to change that.

Outside, Gage retrieved an orange, plastic sled from the back of the Cherokee. It was a far cry from the old-fashioned toboggan I imagined at lunch.

"Flimsy but it works." He flicked on a flashlight, and we walked along the road.

An insulated hush had fallen over everything; the snow

157

forming a white blanket of protection. The only sound came from an occasional car passing in the distance on the main road. The scent of fragrant pine filled my senses as wet snow collected on my cheeks.

When we reached the top of the hill, Gage shone the light down the slope. We saw tracks from other sleds, but no one was left. We were alone in the dark.

"Here, sit down and I'll give you a push."

"No. You have to go with me."

Gage peered at me in the darkness, maybe trying to decide what scared me. The dark? The hill? The snow? Thankfully, he didn't ask. "Okay. You take the flashlight and sit in front."

I situated myself on the front of the sled, gripping a handle on the side with one hand and the flashlight in my lap with the other. Gage knelt behind me because we wouldn't fit otherwise. The sled was made to hold two children; not two full grown people.

He used his hands and one of his legs to inch us toward the tipping point of the hill. This could be a physics lab. At what point will we gain enough momentum to plummet down the incline? Finally, Gage gave us a good shove and retracted his leg. He crouched down and wrapped his arms around me.

The sensation was like careening into blackness. I could only see a small area in front of us where the flashlight illuminated. We sped along, the wind we created buffeting my face. My heart raced with adrenaline—this time in a good way. "Gage!" I hollered.

"Yeah!"

"This is awesome!"

I had no idea how long it would last. The hill could go on forever, and that would have been fine with me—the cold air, the feeling of freedom, and being held in place by Gage all felt amazing. At some point near the bottom, however, we hit a bump. Gage shifted his weight, and we launched off the side of the sled. My face contacted the snow. I shrieked and then laughed as Gage and I laid on our sides, our bodies facing downhill, his arms still wrapped around me. I continued to clutch the flashlight in my hand.

"You okay?" Gage asked as he tried to sit up.

"Yeah. Fine."

We untangled ourselves, and he shined the flashlight near my face. "A smile. That's a good sign," he said. He reached and brushed some snow off my cheek with his gloved finger tips.

I watched his face carefully as he did it. The tenderness of the action was the side of Gage I loved the most. "I guess sledding therapy is the way to go," he said.

"Yeah. I guess so."

"I think we better go a few more times then."

"Okay."

As we climbed back up the hill to take another run, I realized I was still smiling. My brother was going on trial and I was going to testify against him and my best friend was dead, but somehow, I wasn't destroyed. Maybe the only real therapy in this world was friendship. Friendship could fix just about anything.

Chapter 21

Gage

AFTER DEAD HORSE VALLEY, I had to talk to Wick about Lainey. Even though he most likely wouldn't listen because he was a fucking Neanderthal, and he hated my guts, I still had to try, for Lainey's sake.

At school, I found Wick holding court as usual near his locker on the second floor, and I strode right up to him.

"Hey, Gage," he said. He made it sound casual like me approaching him was no big deal, but I could see in his eyes that it was.

"Can I talk to you? Alone?" I asked.

Everyone around him—Perk and Monroe and Amber and Kaitlyn—seemed to hold their breath while they waited for his response. There were many ways it could have gone, too, but luckily, it went my way.

"Sure," he said with a small shrug of nonchalance.

"Okay." I walked away toward the stairs. Wick followed. The stair landing would at least give us a small amount of privacy.

Once the heavy door shut behind us, he said, "What's up?"

I crossed my arms over my chest and made sure I

squared off to him. Even though Wick probably wouldn't fight me in school where cameras were always watching us, I still wanted to be careful.

"It's about Lainey. I don't know if you've noticed, but something's wrong with her."

His forehead wrinkled. "Whaddya mean?"

"I think something happened to her before she came here. Something bad."

Wick crossed his arms, mimicking my stance. "You know this for a fact?"

"No. I don't know anything for a fact. But I'm telling you something isn't right with her, and I was hoping that maybe you'd back off and give her some space because of it."

"She does seem to flake out sometimes. Like disappear into herself and get all sad," he said.

Maybe he wasn't as dense as I thought. "Exactly. And it's worse than she lets on, I think. So, can you stop messing with her? You can mess with me all you want, but don't use her to do it."

Instead of answering me, he asked, "What do you think happened to her?"

"I told you I don't know." I started backing up toward the door. "Just consider what I said."

"I'll go easier but I'm not giving up," Wick called after me. "And I'm not giving up the project either."

"Did you listen to anything I just said?"

"Yeah," he took a few steps toward me. "Thanks for the heads up."

He shoved past me, hitting the push bar on the door hard. Wick always had to find a way to assert his dominance. Plus, it made for a grand entrance back into the hallway.

Whatever happened, it was worth a shot to protect Lainey. He did say he'd go easier. I just didn't know if Wick's version of easier would be enough.

Lainey

"Will all our visits be supervised?" Wick tilted back in his chair and stared across the school library at Gage.

I glanced over, too, where Gage was working diligently on a Chromebook, waiting to give me a ride home.

"I don't know, but could we pick a project and get started, please?"

"Yeah. Sure. Are you artistic? We could do the poster. If not, maybe a PowerPoint."

I examined the assignment page. There were too many choices as far as I was concerned. I wished Mr. Rap just told us what he wanted instead of giving so many options.

"The PowerPoint sounds good, but it needs to be on one of these topics, and they all seem complicated."

"Read 'em to me." Wick dropped his chair down to all four legs and put his elbows on the table.

"Number one, a trial. Put one of the characters on trial for a crime or wrongdoing." I paused and gulped. That one wasn't happening. I kept reading. "Your court documents need to be properly formatted. Number two, a scrapbook. Choose one character and have him/her create a scrapbook of their life and their part in the play. Number three, mental health issues. Research both Hamlet and Ophelia's mental conditions. Provide a diagnosis and then prescribe a course of treatment. Include proper citations."

"That one. That sounds interesting."

I glanced up at Wick. "Seriously?"

"Yeah. They're both messed up, and it'll be fun trying to give them a diagnosis. Plus, we could try to diagnose other people we know. Like Gage. What do you think Gage has?"

I narrowed my eyes at Wick. "We're not talking about Gage. But I'll do this topic if it's what you really want."

"See, I knew all along you were going to give me what I really want." Wick winked at me and waggled his eyebrows.

I sighed. "Seriously, you need to get a grip." But against my will, I also smiled.

"Oh! Oh! I saw that!" he said, pointing at me. He was loud, too. The library monitor frowned over at us, and Gage looked up. "You smiled!" Wick proclaimed.

"Shhhh," I covered my mouth with my hand. I couldn't believe I was even slightly amused by one of Wick's stupid jokes, but I guess it was kind of funny in a totally childish, silly sort of way.

"Sorry. It's just nice to know you don't totally hate me," he said.

"I don't totally hate you. I just dislike you for what you did to Gage."

"That wasn't personal," Wick said.

I scoffed. "Beating the crap out of someone seems kind of personal to me."

Wick laced his fingers together in front of him. "You don't get it. I can't let my authority be challenged. Not by Pike. Not by anyone."

I thought for a moment, wondering what I wanted to ask Wick in this moment of apparent honesty. After a few seconds, it came to me.

"Do you have any friends that are totally real? Not guys like Perk who do whatever you tell them or girls like Amber who you use. I mean people you open up to. People you show vulnerability to?"

"Why would I want to be vulnerable?" he asked.

"Because you're a human being."

He smirked but it wasn't a snarky one. More rueful. "Are you sure about that?"

I was on a roll. "What are you so afraid of that you have to act like this?"

"Do I have to be afraid of something?"

"Everyone's afraid of something."

For once, Wick didn't have a smart answer. He truly appeared to be considering my question.

"I have an idea," I said. "Why don't I tell you something real about me and you tell me something real about you?"

"Like truth without the dare?"

"No, Michael, like being a real person. Not a game. A real friend. I'll go first. My last boyfriend broke up with me through an email."

His eyebrows rose into his forehead. "No way."

"Yup. Truth."

"Wow. Did you cheat on him?"

"Nope. He just thought we needed a break."

I still remember every word of the email.

Lizzie

I'm really sorry about your brother. I know you can't see me right now and that's okay. Maybe in a few months when things calm down, we can hang out. Take care of yourself.

Dylan

There was nothing mean about it. It was sort of a nice email if it had been sent to an acquaintance or a casual friend. The problem was I was not one of those to Dylan. I was his girlfriend. The girl he made love to—the girl who was supposed to be important to him. Not someone he could just throw away.

"He must have been secretly gay." Wick chuckled and sat back in his seat. He then tilted it backward again, balancing precariously.

"Your turn," I said, ignoring his frat boy response. "And it better be good."

He gazed at me, probably trying to decide how real he could be. "Fine. I hate my middle brother, James."

"Why?" I asked.

"Long story."

And I could tell by his expression that he meant it. There was a real story behind his words, something involving deep emotions that might actually explain Wick's power trip at school.

"Well, Michael," I said, leaning across the table. "It appears we have something in common because I hate my brother, too."

He dropped his chair back to the floor. "You have a brother?"

"Yeah. He's back in California."

"Why?"

"Long story. Doesn't it felt good to be real?"

"Kinda. Yeah."

"Your turn. One more and then we get back to work."

"Okay, how about this," he said. "If you make me talk about real shit, I might start really liking you."

"You mean not just as a conquest?"

"Maybe."

"I'll take my chances. Now, about Ophelia."

He pinched his eyes shut and scrunched up his face. "Do we have to talk about Ophelia?"

"Yup. Crazy as she was, we do."

After the library, Gage drove me home. On the way, I decided to tell him about the trip. Mom and I were leaving Thursday after school and flying out of Boston at six. We'd arrive in Los Angeles around nine West Coast time and check into the Embassy Suites at the airport. Friday morning, we'd have an all day meeting with the lawyers in our suite. My therapist, Belinda, had been called in to assist in case I lost my shit. This was a real possibility since they planned to make me discuss every detail of what happened in the cafeteria. Afterward, assuming I was still a functioning human being, my mother and I would take the red-eye back to the East Coast.

"I'm going away Thursday."

"Where?" Gage asked.

"Boston. My dad's going to be there, and he wants to see me."

It's a small lie but a lie nonetheless.

"So you'll miss school Friday."

"Yeah."

"Are you staying the whole weekend?"

"I'm not sure. We might."

"Cool. That should be fun," he said. But I sensed a tension underneath his words.

"Yeah. I guess."

"You don't sound very excited."

I shrugged. "Eh. I'm just getting used to it here, so I don't really want to go."

"Well could I give you some island advice?"

"Yeah. Sure."

"You should call it *going off-island* not *going away*."

"Really? That matters?"

"Just a small thing but yes. You sound like wash-ashore if you don't."

"A wash-ashore?"

"Yeah, a non-local."

"Well, I kind of am."

"But you don't have to advertise it." Gage winked at me as we turned in my driveway.

The silliness of this conversation made my trip seem slightly less horrible. Like it was just a normal everyday thing to *go off island*, and it was just a normal everyday thing that I was going to do.

"And not that I mind driving you everywhere, but the next session of driver's ed starts in March. You should sign up."

"Really? Okay. It would be good to be able to drive." I had to get a whole new license as Lainey Darwin. We could not transfer it in my old name because I was still a junior operator.

"Yes. Freedom. Freedom is always good."

"Thanks for the ride."

"Sure."

"I'll snap you later," I said as I got out, referring to snapchat.

"Saying that still doesn't sound right to me. Someday, distant-future historians will analyze what snapping someone meant."

"No, they won't because they'll all still be doing it."

Gage chuckled "Maybe."

Chapter 22

I WAS SHAKEN AWAKE. I OPENED my eyes to see a man hovering over me. "Were you in my fucking room!" he screamed.

A white-hot feeling of fear flooded my body. Terror. It could only be described as sheer terror. I couldn't move. I couldn't breathe. I tried to focus on his face and that's when I realized it was Thomas.

"If you go in my room again, I'll fucking kill you. Do you understand?" He shook me by my shoulders for emphasis. The music. I shut off the music.

"Okay. Okay…" I managed to answer in a hoarse whisper. He released me and left the room.

Lainey

Travelling to Los Angeles, I descended into faker mode. I pretended nothing was wrong. That was how I got through many days right after the shooting. Faker Lizzie served me well.

I know why people sometimes can't remember traumatic things—their brain simply won't let them. I sometimes wished I didn't remember. What a relief it would have been to just not know. Truly. But since I did recall it, every detail in fact, I had to try a different course of action. I had to try to forget.

I tried a method Belinda taught me where I put the memories of that day in a trunk. I imagined locking the lid on a decrepit, wooden box and throwing the whole thing over the side of a ship. This was a pretty childish fantasy. When Belinda first shared it, I thought she was the crazy one. But then I discovered that it worked, at least temporarily. When everything got to be too much, fantasy was what I turned to. I watched that trunk splash into the ocean and float away, taking my past with it.

I was in the middle of shoving it off the ship when my mother interrupted me Friday morning.

"You need to shower before they come."

I tore the crust off my toast. "I know."

The oatmeal bread at the Embassy Suites tasted terrible. I was an expert when it came to oatmeal bread, and this brand was too grainy and too thin.

"They'll be here in less than an hour, Lizzie."

"I know," I repeated.

I was pissed off about Rosa. I wanted to see her while we were there, but mom said it wasn't possible. *Strict time constraints. Just not going to work.* I hated all the bullshit lines adults used to placate me. Rosa would come to see me if I asked. Anytime. Anywhere. That's how we were. Screw the time constraints.

While I ate, I stared out the floor to ceiling window at the urban sprawl of Los Angeles. It extended all the way to the mountains in the distance, bathed in radiant sunlight. Live trees with green foliage stood in stark contrast to the gray, lifeless landscape back in Nantucket.

After breakfast, I reluctantly prepared for the on-slaught. Mom told me to wear something plain since I'd be videotaped during the interview. The lawyers wanted to be able to watch my testimony later. Technically, no one else would see the recording, but you could never know for sure. It could be leaked. No one wanted me looking trendy and happy after what Thomas did. God forbid I ever be happy again.

I continued to gaze out the window at the palm trees and the planes and the rooftops as the team arrived. I didn't turn around to watch them come in. My mother greeted them, and I didn't even care that one of them was Dad. To me, they were the inquisition—the people there to force me to recall the worst day of my life in elaborate detail.

I thought about a party I went to with Dylan. It was held in a rooftop garden at a house in Hollywood. There were fruity drinks, white Christmas lights, and loads of marijuana. And kissing. Dylan tasted like strawberry daiquiri when he kissed me that night. I sat sideways on his lap, and he nuzzled my neck.

Maybe Dylan thought about me sometimes. Maybe he saw girls who looked like me at the beach and wondered where I was and if I was doing all right. By now, he surely found another girl. A pretty girl. A happy girl. A girl without problems, at least not big ones. That was what I used to be.

I sensed someone approaching, and I knew it was my father.

"Hello Lizzie."

I forced myself to turn around. "Hi."

"You look so different," he said, cocking his head to

the side. "Mom told me about your hair, but it was hard to imagine."

"Yeah." He took a tentative step toward me and opened his arms, so I let him hug me.

I harbored a vague, floating anger at my father. It was a persistent feeling that he was somehow to blame for Thomas. My father was a powerful man. He made stories come to life in his movies. He was given awards for the work he did. He should have been able to prevent what happened. In my mind, I knew that blaming Dad wasn't fair. It was like people blaming me or blaming my mother. But somehow, to me, he was culpable. I wanted to place blame with him.

He pulled back from our hug. He looked skinnier than ever and his tan was not as dark as usual. "We won't start until Belinda's here. She's stuck in traffic," he said. "Come, though, and I'll introduce you to the lawyers."

I followed him over to the dining area. The suite was spacious, the biggest they had. It was decorated in beige and brown and blue with a plush carpet and modern fixtures.

"This is Henry Asiminov. He's the lead attorney for Thomas. This is his associate, Peter Leftwich, who's in charge of witness preparation, and this is their paralegal, Connie Ritow."

They were all dressed for casual Friday, perhaps because they were coming here. Connie had dress pants and a crew neck sweater. She wore rectangular-shaped glasses and had super-coifed red hair. The men wore cotton sweaters with collared shirts underneath. Henry was the older one with almost no hair and Peter was younger with a hipster flair to him despite the fact he was a lawyer.

172

They all acknowledged me kindly as they unpacked their computers and papers on the dining table and desk.

"Why don't we sit on the sofa while we wait for Belinda," Dad said. Always the director. Always staging everyone around the room for maximum effect.

"How was the flight?" he asked.

"Fine."

Gage would scold me for using so many *fines*.

"Mom said school is going okay?"

I marveled at the oddity of him speaking to his ex-wife about these things but not to me, his own flesh and blood daughter. How did that happen? Why was it like this between us? Maybe it was my fault. Maybe I should have called him. Or maybe I should let him know that I wanted him to call me. I wasn't sure talking to my father on the phone from Nantucket would help, though. As I pondered this, a text came in.

Ugh. Physics lab without you

I smiled and started typing back.

"Well, there's a smile," Dad said.

Mom answered for me. "Lizzie has made some friends that she really likes in Nantucket."

I ignored them both and answered Gage.

Sorry ☺ Trust me, I wish I was there instead.

And then I added.

Don't let Smithson catch you texting

A knock sounded at the door. Mom and I both jumped up.

"Check that it's her," Mom told me as I darted to answer it.

When I let her in, Belinda and I immediately embraced.

She was just as I remembered her—young, plus-sized, beautiful smile.

"Your hair!" she gasped when I pulled away.

"I know. It's weird."

"No, it looks pretty. You look great." She rested her hands on my upper arms and leaned back to take me in.

At first, I was unenthusiastic about Belinda. A therapist, I assumed, would want me to talk about all the things I wanted to avoid, but that was not Belinda. She let me talk about whatever I wanted, so I told her all about my life before the shooting. About Dylan and Hannah and more. How I lost my virginity. The first time I got high. How good I was at tennis. Everything. Nothing about Thomas unless he came up in a story and nothing about the shooting. She became my only friend because no one else was speaking to me. I spent all the rest of my time at home with Mom and Rosa, so my weekly trips to Belinda were a highlight for me.

"Do you want to talk alone first?" she asked.

The lawyers were still busy getting all their multitudinous supplies ready for the day.

"Yes. My room's over here."

Inside, I sat on the bed and Belinda took the chair in the corner. She wore the same type of outfit that she always wore when I saw her—knee-length skirt, dressy t-shirt, and flats.

"So, you seem to be doing okay?" she said.

"Well, I'm happy to see you. I've been pretty upset about the rest of this."

"Tell me about your new place? I have no idea where you are so don't reveal that but your dad did say you're going to a public school?"

"Yeah. And it's been okay. A few bumps but I have some friends now. Like real friends so that's good."

"Wonderful. Are you nervous about today?"

"Yeah."

"Did you take your meds?"

I rolled my eyes. "Yeah. Mom let me have an ativan for the plane and one for today."

"What a nice mom." Belinda smiled.

"And you'll stay? The whole day?" I asked.

"Yes. The whole time." Her smile made me feel like I could almost take what was about to happen. Almost.

Chapter 23

Lainey

"Hello Elizabeth. As your father told you, I'm Henry and these are my colleagues, Peter and Connie. We want to hear about what happened that day in the cafeteria in your own words."

I listened closely to him, but I stared into the camera. It sat on a tripod and was aimed directly at me. Belinda couldn't sit too close to me because she wasn't allowed in the shot.

Connie said, "We need you to look at the lawyers, dear, not at the camera. Just pretend it's not here, okay?" She was southern—her twang unmistakable. She stepped behind the camera to make sure the shot was still lined up.

I looked down at my lap and inhaled a huge breath.

"It's okay. Just try to relax," Belinda said.

After a brief pause, Henry continued. "This isn't your actual deposition, Elizabeth. The video tape is just for us to go over if we need to when we have questions about your testimony."

Peter the hipster said, "What we'd like you to do, if you can, is tell us about the whole time in the cafeteria.

Everything you remember. We know that's going to be hard, but it could help immensely in your brother's case. As you know, we aren't disputing that he's the shooter, but we are arguing that he was mentally incompetent at the time of the shooting and, therefore, not responsible."

They overwhelmed me with their legal talk. I wanted to tell them that what I had to say wouldn't help. Everything about that day was normal. Everything was just the same as it always was up until, well, it wasn't.

Henry said, "He'd still go to prison but to a different facility, one for the criminally insane where he'd get therapy and have better living conditions. It's conceivable he could even be released someday, depending on his progress."

The idea of Thomas ever being released felt wrong and frightening. It didn't make sense. It was like a piece of a jigsaw puzzle I kept trying to connect in the wrong place despite how obviously it didn't fit. People who kill other people should not get out of jail. Even if they are fifteen. Even if they are crazy. They still should not be freed.

I hated myself for thinking this, though. I should have wanted him to get out and have a life. I wished I wanted that for him. For my family. But the fact of the matter was, I thought he should pay a penalty. He deserved to suffer. The victims deserved justice.

"We've been going over the police reports, but what we'd like to hear today is your story from start to finish. Then, we'll take a break and figure out the best angle to take with you in your testimony."

I rubbed my hands together because they felt cold. "I thought I was subpoenaed by the prosecution."

Henry said, "You were. But if they end up calling you,

177

we need to be ready to question you to our advantage. Plus, we might want to utilize your testimony too. To help our case."

I gulped back the lump in my throat. "Where do you want to start?"

"The cafeteria. What was going on before Thomas came in?"

I looked past Peter Leftwich's shoulder at a print in a black frame on the wall. It looked like a dandelion.

"I was sitting with my friends at our regular table. We were just eating and talking."

"But you made him wear a condom, right?" Hannah asked Lily.

"I'm on the pill. It's fine."

"It's not fine. You know it's not fine. He's a man whore."

"Stop! He's not that bad."

Hannah rolled her eyes at me. Everyone knew Cullen was a man whore. Cullen's mother probably even knew he was a man whore.

"Was he good?" Hannah asked.

"Hannah!" Our friend, Brynn, said.

"What? I'm just curious. He has enough experience. I would think he would be good."

I giggled and thought about Dylan. Dylan would definitely be categorized as good. Brynn lifted a Vitamin Water to her lips, laughing at Hannah too.

"And when did you first notice that something was wrong?" Peter asked.

If you drew a stick figure of a flower, it was this picture.

"I heard a scream and then a bang. It came from the entrance to the cafeteria."

A momentary hush fell over the room. Everyone looked toward the door. We all looked to see what was going on. I learned later that Thomas had just shot and killed Mrs. Hugo, the guidance counselor, in the hall. But at the time, I didn't know that. I just saw my brother with a toy gun.

"And then I saw him," I met Henry's gaze, and I felt Belinda take my hand. "He was holding the gun. Kids were getting up and running past him. Others were trying to hide under tables. There was more and more screaming."

A whole chorus of screams erupted, high and low pitched, boys and girls. Slow motion took over. Everything started to happen as if we were inching forward frame by frame in a video.

"And what did you do?" Peter asked.

There were just a few downy seeds left on the flower. The artist chose to leave them for some reason. All the rest had blown away. One drifts above the skeleton-like flower.

"I didn't move."

"You didn't hide under the table?" someone asked.

"No. I watched…"

Thomas raised his arm, aiming the toy gun at the wall of windows. Another loud pop sounded and glass shattered—raining down on the room. A unified scream engulfed the cafeteria. Thomas wasn't holding a toy gun. Thomas was shooting a real one.

"And what happened?"

Belinda squeezed my hand. "He shot the wall of windows. And that's when we got down on the floor, sort of under the table."

"Who's we?"

"Me and Hannah."

"And what did Thomas do?"

"He shot Mr. Clinton."

Someone ran toward Thomas. Mr. Clinton. He was a big man, a coach and a math teacher. Thomas pointed the gun at him, pulled back the hammer with his thumb, and shot. Mr. Clinton was hit in the stomach. Blood spurted out of him, a rusty red color. He put his hands over the wound and staggered backwards.

"Do you remember what Thomas looked like in that moment? Did you see his face?"

They called this type of art *minimalist*. The artist wanted to portray a very basic, ugly flower. Not even a flower, really, but a weed. They wanted to express its simplistic beauty.

I glanced at Henry. His lips are very thin. They're thin and pink and I see a few black hairs sticking out of his nose.

"No, but I screamed. I screamed because I saw blood coming out of Mr. Clinton."

A sound came out of me like I'd never heard before, an inhuman, guttural keening like I was an animal in pain. Thomas turned around and fired again—a wild, frenzied shot, as if he thought someone was sneaking up behind him. That was the bullet that hit Olivia Avery in the back as she ran for the door.

"And what did Thomas do next?"

"He shot Olivia but it wasn't on purpose. He just turned and fired randomly behind him."

"Did you see his face then?"

"Yes. He was...determined. Angry maybe?"

My hand was sweating, so I pulled it away from Belinda. I heard my mother murmuring somewhere in the room, but I couldn't tell what she said. There were two more floating dandelion seeds near the top of the print. I didn't see them at first. I was only looking at the flower, not in the space above it. I honed in on them now.

"And what happened then?"

"Thomas walked toward the back-exit door where all the kids were trying to get outside. He was two tables away from me and Hannah. I don't know why it was just me and Hannah left on the floor."

The room fell silent to my ears. Dead silent, like when the action was still happening on the screen but the television is on mute. Thomas cocked back the lever on the gun, and I knew he was about to shoot again. "Thomas! Stop!" I screamed.

"And I yelled at him. I yelled because I could tell he was going to shoot again."

I don't know why I did it. What I thought my order to Thomas would accomplish. It was an involuntary urge—an impulse to try to control my little brother.

"What did you say?"

I focus on those two stray puffs—tiny, black flecks drifting in blank space.

"I said 'Thomas Stop'."

"And what did he do?"

I focus on Henry Asiminov and his hairy nose. "He looked at me."

Hannah jumped to her feet and began to run. And as if by instinct, Thomas aimed and fired at her. He fired two shots in quick succession. He didn't want her to get away. Even though there were plenty of other people to shoot, he shot her. Twice.

"And then what?"

"He shot Hannah."

"Another witness reported that she was running away when he shot her. Is that true?"

I nodded.

"Yes or no, please, Elizabeth," Connie said.

"Yes."

"And they said he shot her twice. Were you aware of that?"

"Yes."

I screamed and jumped to my feet as she was struck in the back. Her body flew through the air before flopping to the floor like a rag doll. I looked back at Thomas, prepared to attack him for what he'd done. Thomas looked at me too. He turned toward the sound of my scream, gun still extended and ready to shoot. When our eyes met, he recognized me. He knew it was me, his sister, and in that moment of recognition, something changed. I saw it in his face because I knew him so well. The firm set of his jaw and the tightness around his eyes all loosened. He saw me and he wasn't angry anymore. His lips quivered and he jerked back the gun so he could press it to his temple. The silver barrel slipped and fell toward his eye before he could straighten it again.

"Thomas! No!" I screamed again.

Still, he cocked the hammer back with his thumb. I closed my eyes and waited for the bullet to pierce his skull. For the searing, awful penetration. He was about to die and there was nothing I could do.

Chapter 24

Lainey

"AND WHAT HAPPENED NEXT?" HENRY asked.

I heard a click and then nothing. Nothing happened. No firecracker sound. No metal ripping through his brain. I opened my eyes and saw Thomas examining the gun, opening the chamber and looking inside. Why didn't it shoot? Why was he unable to kill himself?

I pinched my eyes shut.

Belinda said, "Maybe she should stop." I felt a hand gently touch my back.

Henry Asiminov said, "Elizabeth, if you can, tell us what he looked like while this was happening. His face, how was he acting?"

Belinda moved her hand back and forth on my back, like a mother soothing a baby. I shook my head and dropped my face into my hands.

"What did you do next?" Connie asked.

I ran to Hannah. She lay twisted on the floor, and I knelt beside her. "It's okay. It's going to be okay," I told her. I took her hand as she writhed in pain, blood leaking out of her chest wounds.

"She needs a break. Come with me, Lizzie."

Belinda tried to guide me up by the shoulders but my legs wouldn't work.

I saw motion in my peripheral vision. Someone was running. Thomas turned to look just as Mr. Rivera tackled him. They hit the floor with a thud. The gun skittered across the linoleum in my direction.

"Call 911!" Mr. Rivera screamed.

Thomas wiggled underneath Mr. Rivera's body. Other teachers appeared near them.

"Are there more? Are there others?" someone asked.

"No. I don't think so. Thomas, are there others?" Mr. Rivera yelled.

"Help us," I said. I wanted to scream it, but for some reason, it was weak. Barely a whisper. I gripped Hannah's hand tighter.

"Lizzie," she said faintly.

I met her eyes.

"I don't want to die."

Her lips were blue; her face as white as paper.

"You won't. You can't."

But it was a lie. The last words she heard in the world were a terrible, awful lie.

"I told you this wasn't going to be easy. I told you how fragile she is."

Belinda. Belinda was talking to someone.

"That's why we're doing this now. Why we have to start preparing her."

My mother asked, "Isn't there some sort of exemption she could get? Because of her mental state?"

"Unfortunately, unless she's confined to a hospital and declared incompetent, then no."

"Well that might be what happens by the time you're done with her," my mother snapped.

I rolled to my side and opened my eyes because I wanted them to know that I could hear. I realized I was on the couch. Everyone turned to look at me. Belinda was sitting on the coffee table, closest to me.

"Hi," she said. "How are you feeling?"

"I'm okay." I started to sit up. I didn't want to fall apart. I couldn't fall apart because I had to go back to Nantucket. I wanted to go back to Gage and Sybil. I wouldn't let anyone take them away from me.

"Would you like some water? Something to eat?" my father asked.

He watched me closely with his arms folded over his chest. My father offering to wait on me was strange. I was living someone else's life, it seemed. Someone who had a different father.

"Water would be great."

Connie said, "I'm sorry you have to go through this, Elizabeth. We really hate it, too. We're ready to narrow down our focus now, though, so that's good."

I ignored Connie. Really, I didn't need her fake platitudes. "Where's my phone?" I asked my mother.

Everyone began looking for it as if finding my phone would be the answer to all our problems. Thomas will be free. No one will be dead. We could all go back to normal.

"Here," Mom said. She snatched it off the kitchen counter and brought it to me.

I checked my messages, but I had no new texts from

Gage or Sybil. School must not have been out yet. I sent them each a message anyway.

To Sybil: **Plans tonight?**

To Gage: **How was school?**

Gage and Sybil had become my touchstones to reality. To normalcy. To the person I should have been. When I finished sending the messages, I drank my water and avoided looking at anyone. Connie decided to try again.

"We need to talk about Thomas in the days leading up to the shooting, Elizabeth. You came all this way, and you leave again tonight so we need to find a way to make this productive."

I inhaled a big breath. She was right. I didn't want to come back again.

I asked, "What do you want to know?"

Everyone seemed to drop their shoulders with relief.

"Why don't we bring the camera over here?" Belinda suggested.

And while all the lawyers busied themselves with moving their stuff to the living room area, I observed my parents. My mother rubbed the space between her nose and lips with the side of her hand. Dad ran his hands through his hair, making it stand up on end. I couldn't help but wonder what they thought about one of their children being a killer. Of course, he must be insane. What sane person would ever do a thing like that?

The rest of the day was a blur of questions and instructions.

"Don't ever say he looked normal. Banish that word from your vocabulary," Peter said.

We took breaks and pressed on until it was time for

us to go to the airport. The lawyers packed up and I was saying good bye to Belinda on the couch when Mom and Dad approached.

"Before Belinda goes, we have something to tell you, Lizzie," Dad said.

He held an envelope in his hands, but he faced the side with the address away from me.

Mom said, "We weren't sure about giving this to you, but it seems wrong not to." She wrung her hands. I moved my eyes between each of their faces and tried to decipher the big secret. What was in that envelope and who was it from? Then, I suddenly knew. I knew who wrote it. I knew who it was for.

"I can't. Not right now," I blurted out.

Mom's face softened. "You don't have to right now. But later. Maybe. Only if you want."

Dad turned the letter around. My name was written on it in Thomas's scrawl. "You don't have to read it if you don't want to, Lizzie. We just thought you had a right to know about it."

Belinda said, "Lizzie, look at me." When I did, she continued. "Your mother will keep the letter. If you decide you want to read it, ask her for it. Otherwise, you can just ignore it. It's as simple as that. You are in control of this. No one else. Do you understand?"

Control. Such a strange word. Are we really in control of anything? If my plane crashed on the way back to Nantucket, I'd never read the letter. I'd never see Gage again. We really weren't in control of anything. We were dandelion puffs on the wind, travelling whichever direction it blew us. Control was an illusion. Control was a fiction we told ourselves to make sense of our lives in a world full of randomness.

So, I gave the only answer I could. "Okay." Surrender was what my fiction required. And with that surrender, I rose from the couch and went to my room to finish packing.

Chapter 25

Gage

I SQUATTED BESIDE MY DIRT BIKE, draining the oil. The weather was warm enough Saturday for a ride, but the bike had been sitting all winter. My phone buzzed in my pocket.

Arrive 1:20. Airport. Can you pick me up?

Lainey's texts had been sporadic, and she hadn't even answered my last one. Seeing her words, however, my stomach twisted into a knot of anticipation. She'd only been gone for two days. Missing her was stupid. How did I let that happen? Despite my efforts at deflection, Lainey had managed to flutter her way into my life.

I wiped my hands on a rag before answering.

Sure.

She travelled with her mom so I assumed she didn't actually need the ride. This meant she wanted to see me which caused another swirl of emotion in my otherwise neutral heart.

Your mom?

She has her car.

Checking the time, I decided I needed to change quickly and eat something so I could make it by 1:20.

I partially cleaned up the garage, leaving out the filter and new oil that still needed to be added, before heading back to the house. My dad was at work because Saturday was an important day for real estate brokers even in the dead of winter. Laura, however, was home.

In the kitchen, I scrubbed the black remains of the oil off my fingers and palms before making a sandwich. One good thing about Laura was that she stocked the fridge. She knew what I liked, and she bought it without me asking. I did not take adults with their shit together for granted after the times with my mom when I did everything. It didn't happen all the time, but when she couldn't get out of bed, I fended for myself. At ten, I did my own laundry and shopped for food at the mini-mart.

I slathered mayo and stacked salami and ham and swiss on fresh Portuguese bread from Something Natural, a local bakery. Adding a tall glass of milk and some sour cream and onion ruffles, I balanced the plate and glass and almost made it to the basement door when I heard Laura call, "Gage!" from upstairs.

"Yeah!" I called back. But, I kept going toward the door, hoping I could make it down before she appeared.

"I need to talk to you!"

Shit. She never wanted to talk to me.

"What!" I turned the door knob just as she rounded the corner at the bottom of the main stairs.

"I went down in the basement earlier to put some things in storage and it smelled like marijuana again." Laura planted her hands on her narrow hips.

I smiled. I wasn't even trying to make it my shit eating one either—it just automatically happened.

"So? You jonesing for a toke or something?"

"Gage!"

I pulled open the door and headed down the stairs. Laura stood at the top. "I'm going to talk to your father about this!" she called after me.

"Okay!" I hollered back.

Seriously, it always smelled like pot. I don't know why she got so up in arms about it every few months. Dad would be more upset about my rudeness to Laura than the incriminating odor.

Once in my room, I chowed down my sandwich and changed my clothes. I didn't want to be splattered with oil and grease to meet Lainey.

On the way to the airport, I considered taking Lainey for a ride on my bike. The weather was warm enough, high forties and sunny. Plus, she loved the sledding so much.

I waited on a bench near the arrival gate. The plane was about five minutes late, but I finally spotted it taxiing from the runway. My phone alerted with a text.

Landed.

I see you ☺

It seemed to take forever for her to emerge from the plane. She was wrapped in her usual green fleece, her long legs clad in black leggings and Uggs. She had her arms folded over her chest and her head bowed. Her mother looked sort of stricken as well. Even before they reached the terminal, I knew things hadn't gone well in Boston.

Lainey immediately began searching the gate area for me as she stepped through the sliding glass door. When she found me, her lips turned up in a smile. She strode toward me. "Thanks for coming."

"No problem."

She looked paler than usual with dark circles under her eyes.

"Everything okay?" I asked.

She shook her head, her eyes wet with tears. "Basement?"

"Okay. Do you need to talk to your mom?"

"No. Let's go."

Lainey

I went straight for the bed. Gage's room was almost always the same and that was just how I wanted it to be, especially that day.

Gage asked, "You wanna smoke?"

"No. Come here. Please?" I reached my hand for him, letting him know what I meant. I didn't care if holding me tortured him. He could have me, but he tortured himself, and there was nothing I could do about that.

He sat on the edge of the bed and removed his boots, the muscles in his back straining. He laid himself down carefully and scooted closer to me, exhaling a big sigh as he collected me in his arms. His mouth rested on the top of my head.

I loved being held by him. The feelings I had for Gage were like nothing I'd ever experienced. Before, I was a good time girl, always out for a laugh and a hookup. I never experienced emotions like I did with Gage.

"I missed you," I told him.

Gage's body tensed slightly. I felt it like it happened to me. Then he pulled back and met my eyes; one hand between us was holding mine, the other rested on my hip. "I missed you too."

I lifted my hand and touched his lips with my index finger. "I don't want to just be your friend."

He held our eye contact. "I know."

He licked his lips and moved closer. I closed my eyes and tilted my chin up, willing him to do it. If he kissed me then, there'd be no going back. No more resistance. No more bluebirds and sparrows. Just us. Together.

Finally, his lips met mine. My chest filled with warmth, my whole body vibrating at the soft, pulsing beauty of it. Gage trembled beside me, cupping my cheek with his hand. His lips, soft yet urgent, transported me somewhere else. Some place happy. Some place safe. Some place where only good things happen.

When we pulled apart for air, he pressed his forehead to mine. "Lainey…" he breathed and then began planting a row of soft kisses along my cheek and jaw. I ran my hands up the back of his neck, my fingers lacing in his hair.

"I need you. I need you so much it scares me," I whispered.

"I know," he murmured. "Me too."

Chapter 26

Gage

WE MADE OUT FOR A long time. Holding her and touching her and kissing her was amazing and terrifying all at the same time. I was headed down the rabbit hole, and there was no stopping myself anymore. Her lips, her soft moans, her chest pressed against me—I thought I might lose my mind from all the sensation and emotion.

When we finally stopped because she had to go to the bathroom, I saw that it was almost four o'clock. I moved to sit on the edge of the bed to wait. I needed to get a grip. I needed to figure out what to do. I didn't want to admit it, but I was falling for her, and I thought she was falling for me as well. I was not the kind of guy who usually thought like that, especially after one hook up, but Lainey was different.

Before I had time to fully process all my chaotic thoughts, Lainey emerged from the bathroom, tugging on the sleeves of her sweater. She carefully sat beside me.

"So, what now?" I asked. I took her hand, and clasped it with mine, resting it on my thigh.

She shrugged her shoulders. "I don't know. I understand if you want to just forget it happened."

"No. That's not going to work."

"Okay." She raised our clasped hands and kissed the back of mine.

"Let's just see what happens," I said.

Lainey kept her head bowed, but her lips lifted in a smile.

"Sure," she said. "That's fine."

"Fine?" I asked.

"Yup. Fine," she said again.

"Do you need to text your mom?"

"I should probably go home. The trip was exhausting."

We put our boots back on and headed outside. On our way to the Cherokee, my dad drove in. *Crap*, I muttered under my breath and started walking faster. Dad, however, came to quick stop and hopped out.

"Gage!" he called to me.

"Yeah?" I kept walking.

"Hold up." He jogged to reach us.

"Hello, I'm Gage's father, Marcus Pike." He extended his hand to Lainey, and they shook.

"This is Lainey," I said, unable to mask the irritation in my voice.

"I need to speak to you about Laura and about the smell in the basement."

"Right now?"

Dad glanced at Lainey. "Where are you going?"

"Taking Lainey home."

"Okay. Come upstairs when you get back."

"Fine." I stormed off to the Cherokee.

"Nice to meet you, Lainey," Dad called to her.

"Yes. You too," she answered as she scurried along behind me.

Once in the Cherokee, Lainey fiddled with the radio. I had an old iPod loaded with music and attached with an aux cord. She loved to scroll through the songs. I was grateful that she didn't ask about my dad.

"If it makes you felt better, my dad sucks too," she said when we reached her driveway.

I parked and slumped back against my seat. "Seriously, I think they all do."

"I thought he was cool about the pot?"

"Not exactly. He's more just helpless to stop it, so he pretends it's not happening. But my step-mom, when she gets riled, he feels like he has to do something."

"Sorry."

"Yeah, it's fine."

The mournful guitar solo from the beginning of *Wish You Were Here* came on. Pink Floyd. I forgot that was on there.

"Don't bluebird me," she said with a wan smile.

I laughed. "Is that even a thing?"

"It is now," she said. "You can blame yourself for that one."

"Right. Sorry."

"And don't worry. Nothing really has to change."

The lyrics resonated through the car.

…heaven from hell, blue skies from pain

But it had. Everything had changed. I reached for her hand and she leaned toward me.

"Bye Gage."

She kissed me this time, longingly, her lips supple and searching. The faint flower scent of her hair filling my senses, and I knew I was a lost cause.

Chapter 27

Lainey

G AGE KISSED ME. I KISSED Gage. Finally, kissing happened. I had been wanting it for weeks—craved it and hoped for it, and now, it had happened. This wasn't just an adrenaline rush or sexual excitement like with Wick. This was true and honest and real. I may not have been real but this was.

Maybe it was all a dream. Gage didn't really kiss me. I didn't really go to Los Angeles and talk all about Thomas. Maybe I had just been there, lying in bed with a fever or some rare illness that caused vivid hallucinations.

But as lucidity took hold of my clouded brain, and I oriented myself to time and place and reality, I knew it was all true. Every bit of it. With a moan like I was hung over or very old, I reached and fumbled on my side table for my phone. I should have a message or something, something to confirm what happened yesterday. Once my hand fell on the phone, I hauled it into bed with me. I cracked open my eyes and swiped through the few screens necessary to see there was not one message but two.

Wick: **When will you be home? We need to meet.**

Gage: **Hey**

I wanted to frown and smile at the same time. Relentless Wick and darling Gage.

My clock said it was eleven twenty-four—practically afternoon. The sun shone outside my closed blinds. I needed to get up. I was grateful Mom let me sleep, but I needed to deal with life. First, however, I texted Gage.

Hi. I way overslept.

And then to Wick.

We can meet tomorrow after school.

I threw on some clothes and headed downstairs to eat. My mother wasn't around but left a note that she was running errands. My phone vibrated with a text as I spread peanut butter on a piece of oatmeal bread.

Wick: **Are you home?**

I sighed. I didn't want to tell him the truth because I didn't want to see him. Then, a text from Gage came through.

Plans?

None yet. Wick wants to do project but I said no.

This elicited several angry emoticons from Gage.

My mom's out. Wanna come over?

Sure. Be there soon.

I showered and dressed as fast as I could, but my hair was still wet when Gage arrived. I took him upstairs to my room. Once there, Gage examined everything. He folded his arms over his chest and took in each object and item as if he expected to learn some deep, dark secret about me just from looking at them. I sat on my bed while he did it, feeling nervous that he occupied my space now. I liked it better when I was in his.

"Did you decorate this room?" he finally asked, taking a seat in my desk chair.

"No."

He spun in the chair. "It's very peppy. Were you a cheerleader back in Cali?"

"Shut up," I said and tossed a pillow at him.

He batted it down with a chuckle before turning to explore the items on my desk. This was only fair because I had done the exact same thing in his room—holding every guitar, touching every knickknack, and studying every poster.

Gage picked up Thomas' horseshoe. He turned it over and around in his hands.

"Did you have a horse?" he asked.

"No. It's souvenir from a trip."

"For good luck?"

"I guess." My cheeks felt hot. The bent metal had not brought anything resembling good luck.

Gage said, "You're supposed to place it upwards. Like this." He propped it against the wall behind my desk, the ends facing up. "So the luck doesn't run out."

"Maybe that's why it never worked," I said.

My phone sounded with a new text.

Wick: **Why is Pike here?**

I stared at the message trying to sort out what it meant.

"What's wrong?" Gage asked.

"It's Wick. He must be outside right now."

I wrote back. **Are you outside my house?**

"Seriously?" Gage asked.

"I never answered his text, so he must have just come over."

"What the hell," Gage muttered.

He stood and paced toward the door just as I heard the

front door open. My mother called out, "Lainey! You have a visitor!"

I jumped to my feet. "Coming!"

A scowling Gage followed me down the stairs. In the foyer, we found my mother with Michael Wickersham and four bags of groceries.

Surprise registered on my mother's face when she saw me with Gage. Wick, however, didn't let an ounce of annoyance show. He beamed one of smiles at my mom, smug that he'd wormed his way inside my house by carrying the groceries for her.

"Michael said he's here to do a project with you?"

"Uh-huh." I glared at Wick. "And this is Gage. He came over because I invited him." I emphasized the word invited.

"Nice to meet you, Mrs. Darwin," Gage stepped toward her with an outstretched hand.

I could see the wheels turning in her head. She glanced between the two boys as if trying to decipher the situation at hand. A love triangle? To her, this was probably a sign that I was returning to my old self. I certainly had more than one boy interested in dating me back in LA.

"Why don't I get these bags in the kitchen for you," Wick said.

"Thank you. Right through there." Mom pointed down the hall.

"I'll help." Gage stooped to pick up the two bags closest to him.

As they walked away, my mother caught my eye and mouthed, "What's going on?"

I shook my head at her and followed the boys.

In the kitchen, Mom went to the sink to wash her hands. "Do you boys want some lunch?" she asked.

"No, thank you," they answered, almost simultaneously.

"Why don't we go in the living room," I said.

I headed that way and hoped they'd follow without strangling each other. Michael eased into a chair and Gage joined me on the couch.

"I told you we could work tomorrow," I said to Wick.

"I can't tomorrow. I have conditioning after school."

Gage leaned forward, his elbows on his knees while Wick shrugged off his letterman jacket. He removed his copy of Hamlet from of his pocket.

"If this is going to bore you, Pike, you can go," Wick said.

"No. I think I'll stay."

The boys continued to stare each other down so I asked, "Did you want to ask me some questions about the project, Wick?"

"Yeah. Do you have a computer? I need to show you what I wrote so far." I stood up. "I'll get my laptop. Please be nice while I'm gone."

Gage

"Dude, not cool," I said once Lainey was out of the room.

"We have a project to do. Why are you here?"

I ignored his question. "Can't you just leave her alone?"

"Why? Because you said so?"

"No," I answered. "Because it's what she wants."

"Are you sure about that? She could have gotten out of this project if she wanted."

"Yeah but that doesn't mean she wanted you show up at her house like some creepy stalker."

Lainey's mother walked in and set a tray down on the coffee table with three tall glasses on it. Despite the fact she probably heard all or part of that conversation, she played it completely cool.

"It's lemonade. And water for Lainey," she said.

"Thank you, Mrs. Darwin." Wick said.

I wanted to smack the stupid, ass-kissing grin off his face.

"You're welcome. And you boys can call me Abby."

Mrs. Darwin left as I heard Lainey charging down the stairs. She appeared in the doorway carrying her laptop. "Okay. Did you email it to me or something?" she asked.

"No. I have a flash drive," Wick said, reaching into his pants pocket.

"Ever heard of google drive?" I muttered as I slid down the couch to give them room. I grabbed a glass of lemonade, as Lainey set the computer on the coffee table between her and Wick.

They began talking about the project, and I didn't interrupt. It would be over soon. Hopefully Wick wouldn't create another pretense to be around Lainey. I debated telling him then and there that we'd made out but that seemed too cheap. Plus, I didn't want to share it with him. It might have been overly sentimental, but kissing Lainey was special to me, and I hated the fact that he had kissed her too—first even. I hoped with lacrosse starting, he'd be too busy to continue his pursuit of her.

Wick said, "I don't think he really loved Ophelia. It's

only after she's dead that he thinks he did. He's more just upset that she died."

Lainey pursed her lips. "Maybe. He was really rude to her in that one scene. The *get thee to a nunnery* one. So maybe he just feels guilty about that."

"Exactly. And Mr. Rap would probably love that interpretation so let's go with it."

"Yeah, but what mental illness was that?" Lainey asked.

"I don't know."

"Well that's what you're supposed to figure out. I already figured out depression for Ophelia."

Wick scoffed at her. "Depression is such a cop out. You need to give her something else."

"Cop out? Depression fits her perfectly. She's repressed. All the men in her life are always telling her what to do. She's powerless and that has caused her to become despondent."

"Well I was going to go with depression for Hamlet but it seemed too basic. Too boring."

"Yeah, for him it's something else. He's having delusions."

I couldn't stop myself from jumping in. "Bi-polar. He most likely has bi-polar disorder." They both looked over at me. "When in a manic phase, people can hallucinate and that would explain his visions. That would also explain why he freaks out on Ophelia and then feels so badly about it after."

Wick chuckled. "You seem to knew a lot about this disorder, Gage."

"Actually, Michael, I'm just trying to help you so you can get the fuck out."

Wick started to stand up. "Okay!" Lainey said, jumping to her feet. "Time to go. I'll put this in google drive and share it with you, so we can work on it tonight." She stepped in front of Wick, blocking him from my view. "We can Facetime if you want. Just text me first."

I stood up, too, as Lainey placed her hands on Wick's arms, trying to direct him toward the door. Seeing her touch him, a surge of jealousy coursed through my body. I'd never experienced anything like it before. I wanted to jump across the coffee table, and slug Wick in the face. Instead, I forced myself to remain calm.

Wick eyed me as he grabbed his jacket, and I gave him the stare down right back. "So this is how it's going to be?" he asked Lainey.

"What's going to be?" she asked.

"You can't be around me anymore?"

She set her hands on her hips. "I can do whatever I want."

I wanted to tell her he was baiting her, challenging her to be alone with him, but it would have been pointless in the moment.

"Doesn't seem like it to me," Wick said. "See you at school." He snagged his book off the coffee table. "Later Pike."

I didn't answer. I just stared him out the door. When we heard the front door shut behind him, Lainey sighed and ran her hand through her messy hair.

"Sorry," she said.

"For what?" I sat back down.

"For whatever just happened… "

Lainey dropped herself onto the couch beside me.

"Not your fault," I said.

I leaned toward her, not caring if her mother walked

in. She waited for me, too, the most beautiful expression on her face. She closed her eyes first and I almost wanted to stop so I could just look at her. But I didn't. I kissed her. And it felt so damn good that I deepened it, reaching to wrap her in my arms.

"Why don't we go upstairs," she whispered against my lips.

"Is that okay with your mom?" I asked. I tried not to pant but I was already losing my mind. Kissing her for the second time, the flood gates of feeling opened. I wanted her. I wanted to touch her and kiss her and breathe her in.

Lainey murmured in my ear as I inhaled the scent of her hair. "Yeah. She thinks we're friends."

"We are friends." I nuzzled her ear.

"True," she answered.

On the way to the stairs, I wondered if Wick would be waiting for me in the parking lot in the morning. If he was, I promised myself I wouldn't be blindsided this time. I might lose again, but I'd get a few shots in. If I could remember the feeling of jealousy I just had, it wouldn't be too hard to fight back. I might even stand a chance.

Chapter 28

Lainey

LATER THAT AFTERNOON, WE WENT back to Gage's house. We parked and went to his garage instead of the basement. Gage needed to finish changing the oil in his dirtbike, and then he was taking me for a ride. As we walked to the side door, Gage looked back over his shoulder at the house as if expecting his father to come out again.

"You can have a seat," he said once inside, gesturing at a nearby stool. "It won't take too long."

Instead of sitting, however, I wandered around the large space. The two bays were not cluttered with junk. It was possible to park two cars there by moving just a few items. Along the walls were various storage cabinets and shelves, all relatively organized, and the floor was clean and swept. The mild scent of paint and oil was more pleasant than I expected.

Gage kneeled beside the bike and began to work. "I'm not supposed to go on the main roads, but we have to take a few to get to the back roads. So, if a cop sees us, we might get in trouble."

The blue and black dirt bike stood propped on a

kickstand. I could tell it was full size but it seemed too narrow to hold two people. It barely looked like it could hold Gage.

"Hopefully that doesn't happen," I said. I examined a bunch of small drawers with clear fronts. They contained various nuts and bolts.

The side door to the garage opened, and Gage's father walked in. I stepped back from the drawers quickly.

"Hello again. Lainey right?"

"Yes. Hi." I gave him a lame wave.

Gage scowled. "What's up?" he asked.

"I just came out to see what you were up to."

"Oil change," Gage said, as he continued adding the new oil.

"I see. Have you heard from your mother this weekend?"

"No. Not yet."

"Okay. If you do, tell her I need to speak with her."

"Okay."

"So, Lainey, are you new to the island?"

I nodded but before I could speak, Gage said, "Yeah. She just moved here."

"Oh nice. Where from?"

"California," I said.

"Did your parents get jobs here?"

"No. We—"

Gage interrupted. "We're kinda busy, Dad."

"Lainey's not busy. She doesn't mind chatting, I'm sure."

He smiled kindly at me—his salesman charm unable to be contained. I got the feeling he liked me being there with his son, maybe because I didn't have orange hair and numerous facial piercings.

"My parents are divorced. I'm here with my mom," I explained.

"Ah. I see. Gage, please be sure you don't ride on the main roads, right?"

"I know, Dad. I'll take the path."

I wasn't sure what the path was, but I hoped it was wide and we wouldn't be pummeled by tree branches.

Mr. Pike said, "Lainey, did your mother purchase a home or are you renting?"

"Dad, she has a house, okay?" Gage stood up and tossed the empty oil container in the trash before wiping his hands on a rag.

"I'm just making conversation, Gage," Mr. Pike said. Then to me, he asked, "Where did your mother buy?"

I knew he was just curious because he was a broker, but his questions still made the hairs on my neck rise. The house was bought with a trust so it couldn't be traced to my father, but I didn't really want Mr. Pike to go digging around in the records.

"Near town."

"Oh, nice. What street?"

"Madaket."

"Oh. Well then, have fun on your ride. I'll see you for dinner, Gage?"

"Yeah."

"Nice to see you again, Lainey."

"Bye."

When he left, Gage's posture relaxed. "Sorry about the interrogation."

"No problem. Is it ready to ride?"

"Yup. Let's go."

I plastered myself against Gage's back, my head turned to the side. When I did look around him, it felt like being on a carnival ride or inside a video game. We weren't actually going that fast, maybe thirty miles per hour, but the cold air and the rutted road made it seem so much faster. "You okay!" Gage called to me over his shoulder.

"Yeah! Great!"

Being on the back of the bike with my arms wrapped about him took me completely out of my own head. The rush of adrenaline. The vibration of the bike. I loved the entire experience. The ocean was to our left, the foaming, pale blue surf rolling onto the shore. I watched it and enjoyed the sensation of moving and hugging and being outside all at the same time.

Being Gage's friend was the best thing that happened to me since the shooting, and I planned to hold onto him for as long as I could—as long as the stupid, messed-up world would let me.

Chapter 29

Gage

I SHOVELED LAURA'S VEAL PICCATTA INTO my mouth at dinner.

"Lainey seems like a nice girl," Dad said.

"Yup."

"I looked up the sale of her house. If it's the one I think it is, it was a trust that bought it. Cash deal."

"Don't snope around in her life. It's none of your business." My anger flared like a lit match.

"I was just curious. It was probably part of the divorce settlement or something, but I found it interesting. She must come from money."

I shoved my chair back from the table and stood up. "I don't give a shit if she comes from Mars. Stay of out my business! It doesn't concern you!"

"Sit down, Gage. You're overreacting."

I hated his patronizing tone. How dare he dig around in Lainey's life like that. Instead of sitting back down, I stormed off to the basement. He was such an asshole. He had no right to know anything about her.

"Gage!" Dad called after me but I kept going. And

luckily, he didn't follow. I'd hear about this later, but better later than when I was so amped up, I could have exploded.

Once in the basement, I decided it would be best to leave. I'd drive to Andrew's and smoke or even to Lainey's and pick her up and smoke with her. Either way I wanted to smoke, and I couldn't in the basement because Dad would probably come down. I tugged the key over my head and went to the drawer.

I retrieved my last half bag and some papers and shoved them in my pocket. I needed to restock. I needed to call Zane. That's what I'd do. I'd text Z and drive around until he told me where to meet him, and then, I'd go to Andrew's or just smoke with Zane.

I heard movement upstairs, so I quickly re-locked the drawer and grabbed my coat and keys. Outside, I jogged to the Cherokee. I didn't turn on my headlights, fearing my father might run out to stop me.

Once a safe distance down Surfside Road, I pulled over and sent Zane a text.

Can you meet?

I may have done a lot of things wrong, but texting and driving was not one of them. I also sent a text to Andrew.

You busy?

I hoped he'd answer. Sometimes, he had family stuff on Sunday.

Money. Lainey was loaded with money. I pretty much already knew that based on her house and her clothes. Plus, having money wasn't that unusual in Nantucket. What was sort of unusual was buying a million-dollar house with cash. That was more than just having a good income. That was super rich.

I told myself not to go there. Lainey didn't want anyone to know about her past, and I should respect that. Unfortunately, when you really like someone, it's hard not to think about them.

My phone vibrated.

Zane: Cumbies. Ten minutes.

I headed toward Cumberland Farms. Cumbies, as it was affectionately known, was the busiest convenience store on the island, right by the school and across from the biggest grocery store. Driving there only took three minutes. I parked and waited in the Cherokee.

Zane graduated from Nantucket High School two years before and came back to the island after a semester at a college I couldn't recall. Apparently, he never went to any classes and spent the entire time partying and dealing. As a result, his parents pulled the plug on his college career. Back on the island, he established a lucrative marijuana business. Rumor had it he grew his own plants under black lights.

I debated texting Lainey since Andrew wasn't answering. Before I could decide what to do, Zane's piece of crap truck drove in. You would expect a drug dealer to have a better ride, but maybe, the truck was part of his cover

Once he parked, I got out and walked over. Cumbies parking lot was one of the busiest places on the island; everyone going in to get their dollar hotdogs and cheap pizza slices.

"What up?" Zane said when I slid into the passenger seat.

"Not much. How about you?"

Zane had brown hair down to his chin and always looked like he needed a shower. "Shit, you know me, man.

I heard a rumor about you though. Some hot new girlfriend you stole from Wickersham?"

My face flushed with heat. Seriously, the gossip on this island. I couldn't believe stoner Zane who didn't even go to school with us heard about it. "Yeah. She's cool."

Zane grinned. "So, is she a bad girl or a nice girl?" His face was expectant like he wanted me to tell him a dirty story about Lainey.

"Fuck off," I said. "How much did you bring? I got a hundred bucks."

"I got—"

Someone knocked on the driver's window and a flashlight beam illuminated Zane's lap. On my side, another flashlight beam appeared. I looked back to see a uniformed cop.

"Step out of the car please," the cop on Zane's side said to him through the window.

Holy Crap! My heart began pounding out of my chest.

"Shit!" Zane said.

"Now!" the cop said loudly and tapped on the window again. "You too." He pointed at me and met my eyes.

I opened my door and stepped out with my hands out in front of me. It was just my luck. Just as something in my life was starting to go well, I was picked up by the cops with Zane.

"Put your hands on the car please. I'm just going to pat you down. Anything sharp in your pockets?"

"No."

He quickly frisked me.

"What's your name?"

"Gage Pike."

He removed my phone, my bag of weed, and the rolling papers from my pocket. I pinched my eyes shut and felt my knees getting weak. My father was going to kill me.

"How old are you?" The cop shone his flashlight on the bag of weed and examined it.

"Seventeen."

"Step back, please. Do you live on the island?"

I did as he said and folded my arms over my chest. "Yes."

Zane was being frisked on the other side of the car. "Can I ask what this is about?"

"Yes. Your friend has a warrant for his arrest."

Cuffs were placed on Zane. "You have the right to remain silent…" his cop said to him.

"Why did you get in the car with him?" my cop asked.

"We're friends."

"Is this marijuana?"

I nodded.

The other cop called over. "Found four bags in his coat."

My cop raised an eyebrow at me. "Were you trying to buy some marijuana?"

I didn't answer because I wasn't going to lie. Clearly, they knew Zane was a drug dealer, and most likely, I was a buyer.

"Am I under arrest?" I asked him.

He examined me and looked down at the papers and the pot and my phone. "Have you ever been arrested before?"

"No."

The cop handed me my phone. "Call your parents and tell them to meet us at the police station in fifteen minutes."

I gulped back a golf ball size lump in my throat. "Why?"

"Because I think they should know where we found you. And what you had in your pocket."

"That's really not necessary," I stammered.

"Oh yes, Gage. It really is." The cop's voice dripped with sarcasm, and I wanted to smack him for being such a smug son of a bitch.I stared at him, trying to decide if he'd back down. But from the look in his dark eyes, I knew he wouldn't. He wasn't the backing down kind, and he knew calling home was the worst possible punishment for me.

I exhaled a huge breath and found my Dad's number. It rang twice before he picked up.

"Hi Dad. Um, I'm at Cumbies and I have to go to the police station. They said you have to meet me there in fifteen minutes."

"What! What's going on?"

"I'll tell you there."

"Are you okay?"

"Yeah. Fine," I lied. I wished I could turn back the clock fifteen minutes. I would have made a very different choice if only I'd known.

"Okay. I'll be there," Dad said.

I hit end.

"Let's go," the cop said, gesturing at his car.

The police station in Nantucket was a brand-new facility; a gorgeous building that some cynical town residents called the *Police Palace*. It looked like a building that belonged on a college campus with a brick façade and white trim.

The cop didn't cuff me, but I had to sit in the back. He

told me his name was Sergeant Larson and asked if I had my driver's license on me.

"It's back in my car," I told him.

After going through the security gate, we drove around the back of the building where they parked all the cruisers. He escorted me inside to an interview room that looked very much like the ones on television with the table and the two-way mirror. "I'll go wait for your father in the lobby. You're on camera right there." He pointed to the bubble in the ceiling. "The dispatchers can see you so don't try anything."

Once he left, I rested my head on my arms on the table. Why was this happening? How many times had I bought weed from Zane? Of all the times, that was the night he got picked up for a warrant with me in his car.

I still had my phone, and I debated texting someone. Lainey, of course, was the first person that came to mind, but I quickly dismissed her. It would be better to tell her about this in person. The best person I could think of to talk to in this situation was Andrew. He would calm me down. He was the calmest person I knew. But when I checked my messages, he still hadn't responded to my first text. I sent him another anyways.

I need to talk. It's important.

I was still waiting for his answer when the door to the interview room opened. My father entered with Sergeant Larson. His jaw was rigid, and if he could, I think he would have kicked my ass right there in front of the cop.

"Have a seat Mr. Pike. I had Gage call you because we found him inside the truck of a known drug dealer at Cumberland Farms. The suspected dealer had a warrant for his arrest and was also in possession of several eighths of marijuana that we believe he was about to sell to your son."

"Is this true?" Dad asked me.

"I was in the truck."

"Were you about to buy drugs?" Dad asked. His voice was eerily quiet. I think it was scarier than if he was yelling.

I dropped my head. "I think we should talk about it at home."

Dad turned his attention back to Larson. "I'm sorry Sergeant. I understand if you must charge him with something. I have tried to talk to him about this, but I guess he just isn't listening."

"Is this his first contact with the police?"

"Yes," Dad said. "That I know of. Is it, Gage?"

"Yes."

Sergeant Larson said, "Well, what I would say to both of you, then, is that you have less than one year until Gage is an adult. Right now, I could charge him along with Mr. Bellamy with possession with intent to distribute just because he was in the car. Next year, when he's eighteen, that's what I would do. But since Gage is seventeen and never been in trouble, I'm inclined to give him this one break with the understanding that in the future, we won't be as lenient."

My father's hands were clutched together in front of him on the table. "I appreciate that Sergeant. I really do."

They both looked to me, as if I was supposed to say something. I should have been thankful, I guess, but all I really wanted to do was tell them both to fuck off.

"Thank you, Sergeant," I managed to mutter.

Sergeant Larson said, "I hope that means you plan to stop smoking marijuana?"

My mind resisted that idea. Instead, I thought about being more careful when I did my deals. And then immediately, I was pissed off at myself that I was willing to risk serious criminal charges to keep smoking pot. Was it that important to me, and if it was, did this mean I was addicted?

"Yes."

I had to say something. In that moment, I had to be a liar.

"Well that's good to hear. I'd also like you to possibly help with some community service projects through the Police Charitable Association. It's not required, but I often ask young people like you who are headed down the wrong path to volunteer."

"Sure. Whatever you want."

I never wanted to see Sergeant Larson again but if agreeing was a condition of walking out of there, I was willing to do it.

"Well then, I leave you in the capable hands of your father. Based on this conversation, I don't think you're off the hook yet, Gage. Good luck to you."

Dad didn't speak to me until we reached his car. "Where is the Cherokee?" he asked.

"Cumbies."

We drove there without a word, but my father's white hot anger radiated across the car. I waited for the yelling to start.

"I'll meet you in the basement when we get home. You will hand over all your drugs and all your paraphernalia. If you do not, I will take away your car and your dirt bike and your phone and your laptop. Do you understand?"

I nodded.

"And you will start counseling again this week. You will go, and you will talk about why you feel the need to get high all the time. This stops today, Gage."

"Okay."

The night didn't go at all how I planned, and I wished I had a do-over. I never would have left the house. Staying home and smoking the small amount of weed I had left would have been my best option.

But, maybe it all happened for a reason. Maybe it was my wake-up call so I didn't end up like Zane—twenty, in jail, driving around in a shit box truck and concerning myself with the new girls at NHS. Maybe I needed to see the signs in my life for what they were—signs of things to come.

Chapter 30

Lainey

GAGE TOLD ME HIS STORY on the way to school the next day.

"Wow," I said when he finished recounting his terrible night. "That really sucks."

Deep gray clouds marched in lines across a lighter gray sky. This usually meant rain or snow or both.

"So I can't smoke," Gage proclaimed. "At least for now."

Upon hearing this, my first instinct was to say screw that. Defiant teenager still ran in my veins, and this situation certainly aroused it. I considered offering to be his buyer and for us to smoke in secret at my house. Parents couldn't stop us. We'd get around any and all barriers to doing what we wanted.

But something about the way he told his story made me hold back. A hint of resignation, perhaps. Maybe, he wanted to try. Maybe, he was scared. I knew all about being scared.

"Well that's okay. You can stop for now, right?"

He gripped the steering wheel tightly with both hands. "Yeah. I just like it, you know?"

"Yeah. Me too. But we'll be fine. We'll do other stuff."

He didn't respond to this, and I wondered what I meant by other stuff. We could drink. We could have sex. We could take other drugs. Or we could just hang out. I supposed that's what some kids did.

"My dad's going to make me go to counseling, too."

"Oh," I said and quickly decided to share my experience with him. That was something I could do to help. "I used to go. My parents made me at first but then I ended up liking my therapist."

"I went before and I hated mine," Gage told me.

We drove into the student lot. "No one else knows so please keep it quiet. People have probably heard about Zane, since he supplies the whole school, but hopefully not me."

"Of course. I promise."

He shut off the car but neither of us got out.

"One of us should tell Sybil," I said. "Not about you but about…us."

Gage grinned. "Us?" he asked in a teasing tone.

"What would you like me to call it?" I teased back.

"I'm just messing with you. *Us* works." He reached and took my hand. "I just think it's funny. And you can tell her. I'm sure she'll say something like *Finally*."

I laughed. "Yeah. Probably."

He squeezed and then released my hand. "We better get going or *us* will be late."

"Please, no bad grammar puns," I said.

Gage chuckled about this as he got out, and I was glad I could make him smile after what he went through the day before. Truly, it sucked that he couldn't just enjoy *us* finally being together. At least he didn't get grounded or lose the

Cherokee. And I'd help him. I'd do anything I could to make it work for him and for me.

Gage

I got a new counselor. My father listened to reason and agreed to a fresh start. No more snooze fest with Mr. Ariana. This time, it was a woman—Deirdre Parsons at Island Counseling Service. My dad stayed for the intake. *Intake.* They made it sound like I was there for a serious medical procedure.

"So, what brings you in today?" Deidre asked. She looked sort of like a teacher. She wore dress pants and flat shoes and a tunic style top. Her hair was brown and up in a ponytail.

"My son, Gage, has been smoking marijuana. I don't know how often, but he was picked up by the police in a drug dealer's car on Sunday."

"Okay. Is this court mandated counseling?" Deidre straightened her glasses and re-crossed her legs.

"No. He wasn't arrested. He was given a warning. But the next time, I don't think he'll be that lucky."

"All right. Gage, how do you feel about being here?" she asked.

I met her gaze. She's sort of cool looking for a thirty-something-year old who sits in a comfy chair all day and listens to people's problems. "Fine. I've been before."

"Okay. When was that?"

Dad answered. "Two years ago. I found marijuana in his room."

Deirdre said, "I'd like to hear from Gage, if that's okay with you, Mr. Pike. If I have a question for you, I'll ask."

She looked back to me, but I waited for her to ask another question. You didn't want to be too eager with these people.

"Did you like going to counseling before?"

"No."

"Why not?"

"Because it was stupid." I examined the books on her built-in shelves. You can tell a lot about a person by their books and how they organize them.

Queen Bees and Wannabes
Cognitive Behavior Therapy
DSM V Manual

She managed to keep her expression blank. "You didn't find it helpful having someone to discuss things with?"

"Not really."

"Okay. Fair enough. Do you live with both your parents?"

"No. My dad and his wife Laura."

"I see." She jotted something on the notepad in her lap, probably a big red D for divorce.

"Do you visit your mother?"

"Not lately. She's in Connecticut and she has issues." I finally met her gaze.

I heard dad inhale a breath like he was about to speak, but I turned and glared at him. "She wants to hear from me."

He pinched his lips together.

"Gage, could you tell me what her issues are?"

"She's a bipolar alcoholic."

Deidre finally loses the poker face and frowns. "Are these actual diagnoses she has or is this your opinion?"

"Actual," Dad and I said at the same time.

"She just got out of rehab. Again," Dad added.

"Okay. If you're comfortable with me working with Gage, Mr. Pike, I'm ready to get started," Deidre said.

"Okay. Thanks." Dad patted his thighs twice with his hands and stood.

"See you soon." Deirdre stood and waited for him to shut the door behind him before sitting back down.

Once he was gone, I asked, "Are you going to tell him everything I say in here?"

She examined me with her wide, brown eyes. "No," she said. "I'll only tell him if you are a danger to yourself or others."

"That sounds like a load of crap."

"Why?"

"Because you could make anything you want seem dangerous. Like driving fast or smoking a joint."

She pondered this, glancing off to the side for a few seconds. "I see what you mean, but that is not how I operate. For now, you're just going to have to trust me that I won't."

Instead of continuing our trust talk, I asked, "What time is this over?"

She looked at the clock on the wall behind me. Counselors always have clocks positioned in strategic places around the room, so they know when time's up. Deirdre's had roman numerals and a distressed, wood frame. "Three fifty."

"Okay." I pulled out my phone to text Lainey.

Meet at the Bean? I'll be at there by 4.

She wrote back immediately.

Kay ☺

"Who did you text?" Deidre asked.

225

"A friend."

"Who?"

"Lainey."

"What did you tell her?"

"That I'll meet her at 4."

She set her pad of paper on the table beside her and readjusted herself in her chair. I wondered if she was getting ready to ask me some whopper of a question like how do I feel about my mother. I was surprised when all she said was, "What do you want to talk about?"

I focused out the window. She had several pale blue bottles decorating the sill. Beyond that stood a dormant cherry tree. "I don't know. Don't you have a list of questions you're supposed to ask?"

She laughed. It was almost a giggle which sounded sort of weird coming from her. "No. No list. How about school? Do you get good grades?"

"Yes."

"Like honor roll kind of grades?"

"Yes."

"So you're smart then?"

"I guess."

"But you enjoy getting high?"

"I did, yeah. But I can't anymore."

"Did you get high with your girlfriend?"

"I didn't say she was my girlfriend."

"Are you just friends?"

"I don't want to talk about Lainey."

"Why don't you tell me who you usually get high with."

"Lainey, my friend Andrew, my friend Sybil. I used to get high with a few others but that's mostly it now."

"And how have they been about you getting picked up by the cops."

"Fine. Andrew is the most chill person in the world and Lainey has been… supportive I guess."

"Does she still want to get high."

"I don't know. She hasn't asked. I was always the one who had the pot and she just went along with it."

"Have you smoked since Sunday?"

"Nope."

"And how's that going?"

"Fine so far."

"Why do you think you smoked so much?"

I shrugged. "It felt good."

"What felt good about it?"

I had to think about this question. What did I like so much about getting high? "I think it's the release. The stress and bad feelings just dissolve away when you get high."

I kept my focus out the window while Deirdre kept hers on me. I hated being stared at, but it was inevitable in that situation.

"So, I guess we just need to figure out what those bad feelings and stress are caused by and get rid of them?" she asked.

I snorted a breath at her. "Yeah, because that's so easy to do."

"Well, it might be easier than you think. But we could talk about that later. Why don't you first tell me what upsets you?"

So, I did. I don't know why Deidre made it okay to talk about, but I just unloaded everything about my mother and my father and my life that pissed me the hell off, and she listened. She was way better than Mr. Ariana, or maybe it was just me. He probably asked this same crap back then, but I just wasn't ready to hear it.

As I left, she shook my hand at the door. "Have fun with Lainey."

"Thanks."

And amazingly, I felt sort of better.

Chapter 31

Lainey

THE BEAN IS ONE OF too many coffee shops in Nantucket. In the downtown area alone—which is barely two by two city blocks—there are four of them. As far as the most authentic coffee shop vibe, the Bean wins followed closely by the Handlebar Café.

Wick caught up with me and Sybil on the way to her car and invited himself along.

"The PowerPoint is due tomorrow," he said.

"I know. It's done," I answered.

"But we need to practice presenting."

"Sybil and I are going for coffee."

"Great. I'll come along."

Wick and Sybil were probably the most unlikely pair ever to sit together at a table in the Bean. Sybil sipped her white chocolate mocha, and Wick had a regular with cream and sugar. Coffee beige walls along with white, marble-top tables and dark wood chairs fill the space. The hiss and swirl of the cappuccino machine combined with the heavy scent of coffee roasting filled the air.

"Are you gonna tell Gage if I flirt with Lainey?" Wick asked Sybil.

"Maybe," Sybil said.

"Well, if I can't flirt with her, maybe I'll flirt with you." Wick flashed his best grin at her. Most girls would have swooned, but not Sybil.

"Sorry. You're not my type."

"So, the rumors are true?" Wick cocked his head to the side.

I shifted in my seat, worried this was going to take a turn for the worse. Neither Wick nor Sybil was the backing down type.

"Are you asking about my sexual orientation?"

"Maybe. Maybe I just want to get to know you better. I'm trying to expand my friend group."

This made Sybil laugh.

"Why is that funny?" Wick asked, genuinely confused.

"If you don't know, I can't explain it," she said.

Wick turned his attention to me. "So, are you and Pike like official now?"

"Official what?" I asked, purposely playing dumb.

"You know what. A couple. I saw his arm around you the other day in the hall."

I sipped my chai latte. "Gage and I prefer not to label our relationship."

"But yeah, they are," Sybil said.

"Sybil!"

"What? It's not a big deal. I don't get why you can't just acknowledge it. Am I right?" She tipped her head toward Wick in a bizarre moment of solidarity between them.

"Are you ganging up on me with Wick?" I asked, incredulous with her.

"Maybe," Sybil replied.

Wick extended his hand, and they fist bumped.

"So now that we're friends, Sybil, I have a favor to ask you."

"What?"

"Someday, purely for research and not for sexual pleasure, I was wondering if you'd let me touch your boobs."

Sybil tossed her head back and laughed. "Seriously? You did not just ask me that."

Wick grinned. "Come on, I've never touched boobs like those." He gestured at her formidable chest.

Sybil was still laughing, thank God. Their exchange could have gone either way. "They're E cups, just for the record."

Wick hung his head. "Sweet Jesus," he muttered under his breath. "Well I might never have the opportunity in all my life to touch anything remotely like them so you'd be doing me a solid. Someday. Maybe. When you realize I'm really not such a bad guy."

When she stopped laughing, Sybil said, "I don't know how you managed to do it but you just made me actually sort of like you. Normally, a comment like that would have resulted in a slap across the face."

"Well, thank you," Wick said. "Under Lainey's influence, I have decided to try to be myself more often."

"I'm not sure you should try that line with every girl you meet though. Probably won't go as well," Sybil said.

"Are you two done?" I asked. "Or do you want to get a room and give your little research project a whirl?"

Who knew the Bean with those two would turn out to be sort of fun.

"We should probably talk about the presentation," Wick finally said when our laughter had subsided.

"It's easy. You do the Hamlet slides. I do the Ophelia ones. You are not coming over to work on it," I told him.

"But I bet your mom would like that."

"Ew. Stop." I said. "But that reminds me. I saw Amber sitting with another guy today, and they looked awfully flirty."

Wick frowned. "Yeah. Aiken."

"Well, what are you going to do about it?" I took another sip of tea.

"I don't care who she sits and flirts with." The expression on his face, however, defied his words. "Where's Pike, anyway?" he asked.

"Aw, you miss your buddy Gage?" Sybil pouted out her lip.

"He's coming in a bit. But back to Amber. I bet she'd be excited to hang out with the new and improved Wick."

"What are you doing?" he asked me.

"What?" I tried to make my voice sound innocent.

"Why are you trying to push me back to Amber?"

"I'm not," I lied. In truth, I thought we had a better chance of being actual friends if he was dating someone else.

Wick continued to stare me down. "Did she put you up to this?"

I laughed and covered my mouth with my hand. "Really? You think Amber talks to me?"

Wick sipped his coffee, his eyebrows drawn together in a unibrow.

"I just thought maybe you still wanted her," I said. "And if you do, you should move fast before what's-his-name scoops her up."

"Aiken couldn't scoop shit with a shovel. Amber's just messing with him, probably to make me jealous."

"Either way," Sybil said, "you better decide. Prom's coming up, and you don't want to be stuck with me and my E cups. Your reputation would really be shot."

Wick grinned broadly. "I like you, Sybil. How come we've never hung out before?"

"Dear God," Sybil said, shaking her head.

The door to the Bean swung open, and Gage walked in. Seeing him, my chest inflated with air as if I might float up to the ceiling. It happened every time, even if we'd only been apart an hour.

He wore his blue fleece, but unfortunately, a thunder cloud seemed to darken his expression when he saw we were with Wick.

"Hey," Gage said as he took a seat.

"Are you getting anything?" I asked.

"No. I'm good."

Gage nodded at Wick as he pulled his arms out of his jacket.

Sybil said, "We were just discussing if Wick should try to get Amber back."

"No. We weren't. You two were. Not me," Wick said.

Gage frowned. "You've bonded with Michael, Sybil?"

"Yup," Sybil said.

"She even offered to go to prom with me," Wick added.

"I definitely did not offer that," Sybil said. "I was just saying you might be stuck without a date like me. And then we'd have to take awkward pictures together."

Gage looked at me. "Am in some parallel universe where these two are now friends?"

"Apparently, yes."

And I wondered what other strange bedfellows would be created before I left Nantucket. Maybe, if I was lucky, I'd make it until prom to see how it all played out.

Chapter 32

Lainey

GAGE SAT ON THE EDGE of the bed and strummed his guitar. He repeated the opening cords of *Wish You Were Here* while I laid on my side—gazing at his back and biceps. This after-school-together-in-the-basement-time was the hardest for us. We both wanted to get high; Gage seemingly less than me. Perhaps it was because I hadn't gone through what he did with the police. He was resolved. I was just along for the ride.

"You should start a band," I said.

"We tried. No one will sing."

"Who's we?" I propped up on my elbow.

"Me and Andrew and Cassie."

Cassie? I wished I hadn't brought it up. "I bet you can sing."

He chuckled. "Ah, no."

"Sing something. I'll tell you if it's good."

"Seriously. No."

He switched to playing a tune I didn't recognize. I scooted closer and hooked my fingers in the back of his waistband. Gage, however, didn't miss a note. He continued to pick away at the strings even when I gave a little tug.

"What song is that?" I asked.

"It's called Little Surprises."

I sat up and kissed the back of his neck. "As opposed to big surprises?"

Gage stopped playing. "Are you teasing me, Lainey Darwin?"

"Maybe." I kissed him again, exhaling a breath near his ear.

Gage pulled the guitar strap over his head and spun into me at the same time, making me squeal like a middle schooler at a boy band concert. He wrapped his long arms around me and eased me back toward the pillows, planting kisses on my lips and face as we went.

Our making out had gradually escalated. We may not have called ourselves a couple, but when it came to our time on Gage's bed, that's what we were. Still, neither of us cared to give our relationship a name. Friends with benefits. Hook ups. Fuck buddies. None of those fit. We were close. We were friends. We were more than that too.

My shirt and bra came off first. Then, I yanked his t-shirt over his head. Soon after, his hands ran down my sides and met at the front of my jeans. He fumbled there with the snap and zipper until I slid my hand down to help.

Once we removed mine, I went for his. We were practically naked, only underwear between us.

He breathed in my ear. "I want you so bad."

"Me too."

"Are you sure?" He stilled and made eye contact.

"Yeah. I'm not a virgin," I said, in case he was worried that he had to make it all special and sappy.

"Okay." Gage's smile was not usually that broad or that excited. It made me happy to see him that way.

We kissed again, and I could feel how ready he already was. I reached to slide off his boxers.

"Wait" he said.

He hovered over me—his lips red and puffy, his hair a tousled mess.

"What?" I asked.

"I am," he said. His blue eyes were dark with lust as he gazed down at me.

I squinted back up at him—trying to register what he meant.

"I thought you should know," he said. "Not that I don't know what to do. I do. I just—"

I put two fingers to his lips. He stopped talking. "I think you should just kiss me, now," I whispered.

And he did. He tasted sweet, too, a hint of orange juice. His musky cologne filled my head. Together, we got rid of our remaining clothing, and with his strong arms braced on either side of me and my legs wrapped around his hips, he finally did it. A long, low moan escaped him as it happened, and then we found a rhythm together.

When it was over, we lay breathless and sweaty and satisfied. I couldn't believe that I was Gage's first. How had I not figured that out? A part of me felt guilty about it afterward. He didn't know the truth about me, and he'd surely be some degree of hurt when he found out. I only hoped I could make him understand when the time came. My feelings for him were real. Despite my lies, I was in love with him. The real me loved the real him.

Gage

I tried to catch my breath. My head was spinning like a frigging weather vane in a category five storm, but I tried to keep my shit together. I didn't want to turn into a puddle of feelings in front of Lainey.

"I totally forgot the condom," I said.

I was on my back at that point, and she was pressed against my side, her face tucked into my neck the way she liked. I felt her smile against my skin. "It's okay. I'm on the pill."

Thank god.

"Was it what you expected?" she asked.

"Better," I said. "Because it was you."

She lifted her head and flashed me a wry smile. Her hair was mussed, her eyes bright green, and I wanted to have sex with her again. And again.

"You don't have to flatter me," she said. "We already did it."

I chuckled and stroked the soft skin of her shoulder. "This might actually be the best day of my life so far."

Lainey traced circles on my bare chest with her finger. "That's the endorphins talking."

After I took her home, I went online to look for something to give her. I was probably still high from the sex, but even if we didn't use the terms that accompanied a normal relationship like boyfriend and girlfriend, I wanted her to know she was special to me. I didn't imagine ever saying I love you to her. That would probably scare the crap out of her. I knew I had to tread lightly with Lainey.

Hell, a gift might cause her to panic too, but I still wanted to get one.

The first thing that came to mind was a bluebird. That was our special symbol. Even though us being together didn't really make sense, we still were. I google searched bluebird necklace and was brought to a website called Etsy where people sell jewelry and other stuff they make. I only had to go through one page of items before finding one I loved. As soon as I saw it, I knew—a small turquoise bird on a silver chain with a leaf clasp. It was $30, so without overthinking, I bought it. Maybe I would never give it to her, but I wanted to have it just in case.

After that, I laid on my bed, replaying every second with her. I hoped I'd satisfied her. I heard girls faked it sometimes so how were you ever to know really? Regardless of all that, it had gone well. I was certain of it, and it would only get better from there. To quote Wick, I no longer played for the JV squad. I was full on varsity, my friend. I smiled to myself at how lucky I was. Truly, that day, I thought I was the luckiest guy in the world.

Chapter 33

Lainey

MRS. SHARPE HAD A COLD. She sniffled and wiped her nose on a tissue.

"I told you, Tammy, if you just waited, the right young man would come alone. Hank is just that man."

"You were right, Grandma," I agreed. "Hank's a great guy."

I sat beside her at a table in the community room. Gage and his grandfather sat across from us. I glued pink and green elbow macaroni onto a paper plate in the shape of a flower. In addition to the residents working on their manual dexterity, Carol planned to put the finished products up on the wall to signify that spring was coming. Realistically, however, it didn't feel at all like spring outside. Winter was a stubborn beast in Nantucket.

"Looking good there, Tammy," Gage said. "You have a real talent for macaroni art." Gage handed Big Hank a piece of a cookie.

I was tempted to throw a piece of macaroni at him, but I didn't want to set a bad example. Instead, I smirked.

"Mrs. Sharpe, where does Tammy live?" I asked.

"Off-island. New York, I think. Is it New York?" She

pondered this—mentally reaching into the recesses of her brain to find the information. At least she tried but it was doubtful she'd retrieve the correct location.

"Oh, city girl." Gage raised his eyebrows at me a couple times, his lips looking more kissable than ever. We'd already kissed twice that day. In my old life, I would not have kept track of how many times I kissed a boy during a day at school, but then again, I didn't usually date boys at school. Lainey Darwin did though. Lainey was so smitten with her high school boyfriend, she accompanied him to a nursing home and made bad macaroni art.

Carol joined us and looked over my work. "I think Tammy lives in Texas, Mrs. Sharpe. Houston maybe?"

"Oh, that's right," Mrs. Sharpe said. "I told her to find a nice cowboy. I've never been to Texas. I'd like to go there someday."

Mr. Pike shook his head and nibbled on his cookie. Even though he couldn't talk, he seemed to understand everything going on around him. I imagined the delusions of his fellow residents were annoying to his lucid mind.

"When's opening day?" Mr. Kemp boomed at us. "I always watch the Red Sox on opening day!"

"A few weeks away, Mr. Kemp. Don't worry. You won't miss it," Gage said.

"Maybe you could find a nice ball player, Tammy. I could come to the wedding. Maybe your mother would come and get me out of this place if you got married."

"I already have Hank, Grandma. He's the only guy for me." Gage tried to hide his smile with the side of his hand while Mr. Pike grunted and muttered something.

"I know, Grandpa. She's always flirting with me."

Mr. Pike banged his hand up and down on the arm of his wheelchair and grinned at me. I smiled back at him and placed the last piece of green macaroni on the stem of my masterpiece.

On the way home, Gage streamed one of his new playlists on his phone. I didn't know the song, but the lead singer called in plaintive tones for his lover.

Come to me
Come home to me
Come for me.

The sadness of it made me think of Thomas. Thomas in a cell. Thomas all alone. Thomas writing letters. Thomas taking medications that made him drugged and sick.

"Why do you like it there?" Gage asked.

I was momentarily confused. "What do you mean," I asked in return.

We arrived at my house, Gage parking beside my mother's Volvo. "Why do you like going there and pretending to be Tammy and putting up with all their craziness?"

I gazed out the windshield at the dead hydrangeas around my house and tried to formulate an answer. Not a bluebird answer, either. The truth.

"I just do," I finally said. "Tammy is useful. Mrs. Sharpe loves Tammy and it makes her happy when I'm there."

"Even if you aren't really Tammy?"

"To Mrs. Sharpe, I am. And it feels good to make her happy. Not many things make me happy like being there."

Gage stared over at me. I glanced at him but then back out the window. What did he want? More?

"Why?" he finally asked.

The fifty-million-dollar question. I supposed I should

have seen it coming. Someone as honest as Gage was not going to be satisfied with my pretending forever. It felt like a piece of dry macaroni had lodged in my throat.

Before I could answer, he said, "My mom is bipolar. That's the real reason I can't live with her."

What was he doing? I wasn't ready for this. There was no lead up, no warning his confession was coming.

"No one at school knows about her," he continued. "And I'm not trying to force you to tell me about yourself, but I wanted you to know about me. I have problems too. Everyone has problems, Lainey."

He kept his hands on top of the steering wheel and hung his head.

"I know that," I said, my tone defensive. It felt like he was invading my space; his revelation wielded like a weapon. I wanted to tell him the truth but not because he was insisting. It had to feel right. It had to come from me.

"You can trust me," he said.

"I know that," I repeated, crossing my arms.

If I told Gage my secret, he'd never reveal it. He'd hold it tight inside of himself as if it was his own. Even if we broke up or I cheated on him or made him hate me, Gage Pike would still carry my secret. That was the kind of person he was.

"Is she okay? Your mom?" I finally asked.

"For now, yeah. But she goes in the hospital sometimes, and she drinks too much as a way of dealing with stuff. That's why my dad got so upset about the pot."

Finding out Gage's secret was like finding out the names of the colors. Red was red. Blue was blue. Gage had a messed up mother. His story made perfect sense. Unfortunately, mine did not.

"Do you miss her?" I asked.

"Yeah, but I'm used to it now. I know it's better that I'm here even if my dad's a pain in the ass."

"I'm glad you're here," I said.

He needed to know that he mattered to me. I needed him. He was the most important part of my life now, and if I didn't have him, I'd be lost.

But Gage didn't respond. Despite saying that I didn't have to tell him anything, he was waiting. He revealed his secret, and now, it was my turn. I should have spilled it, too. All of it. This was my chance. This was as close as Gage would come to asking for it.

But the other truth that became clear to me that day was that I didn't want him to know. Not yet, anyway. I wanted to be Lainey to him, to stay just Lainey a little bit longer. I didn't want him to know about Lizzie Berringer and her psychotic, homicidal brother because it might change things. It might make him stop loving me.

My refusal could be construed as a betrayal, but to me, it wasn't. In my mind, it was a gift. I was sparing him the pain of knowing what happened to me. What I was a part of. What I was unable to stop.

"I should go in," I said.

He nodded, denying me his eye contact. I was letting him down. In return for his revelation, I gave him silence. As a consolation prize, I leaned across the seats and planted a kiss on his cheek. He closed his eyes as I did it, his face pinched in a grimace as if I was hurting him. I did it twice, two soft, lingering kisses, before he finally turned and kissed me back. Hard. His frustration came through with every pulse and push of his lips and tongue on my mouth. It wasn't the way we usually kissed, but I didn't pull away. The chorus of that song ran through my mind, even though a new one was playing.

Come to me
Come home to me
Come for me.

When he stopped kissing me, he pulled away quickly, leaving me teetering and unbalanced. I fell backward toward the door and caught myself awkwardly with my hand on the dashboard.

"Bye Tammy," he said.

"Bye Hank," I replied.

And as I walked to my house, I knew I had to find a way to tell him, and I had to do it soon.

Gage

I went on a Call of Duty rampage when I got home. Everything in my path was shot and destroyed. What was I thinking? Just spilling my guts like that? For some stupid reason, I thought she'd reciprocate.

After losing two games due to killing the hostages I was supposed to save, I threw my controller against the wall as hard as I could. It smashed into several pieces and landed on the carpet below. Then, I grabbed my head in my hands and roared like a caged animal.

I hadn't been that mad in a while, and it made the craving to smoke stronger. I considered stealing something from the liquor cabinet upstairs. Drinking wasn't usually my thing because of my mother, but I wasn't totally opposed to it either, especially in this situation. Andrew still had pot. I could always call him, but then Deidre popped into my head. Great. Deidre would have something to say about how I was dealing with this particular life stressor.

Leaving the pieces of the controller on the floor, I snatched up my phone and flopped on the bed. I had no new messages. Not from Andrew or Lainey or Sybil or anyone. When I really started thinking about it, my anger was mostly at myself. Lainey was doing better. She was stronger. But something about seeing her playing the part of Tammy didn't sit well with me. I didn't understand it, I guess, and then I pushed her too far. I acted on impulse with something that was clearly very big for her and that was stupid. I decided to send her a text.

I'm sorry.

She responded right away.

Please do not say that.

Why not? I was a dick.

No. You were just trying to be a normal person with someone who is not a normal person.

That's not true.

Yes. Sadly, it is.

Please accept my apology.

No. You accept mine.

Are we going to fight about being sorry now?

Maybe...I'm glad you told me about your mom.

Yeah. Is there any booze you can easily steal at your house?

Yes.

Okay. Can I come over then?

YES.

Without hesitation, I grabbed my coat and headed back to Lainey's house.

Lainey

My mother was conveniently out to dinner with Graham, so I snagged a bottle of wine from the rack. There were six there, so it was possible she wouldn't notice. If she asked, I would confess. A bottle of red wine was the least of our problems.

After uncorking it, I went to the back hall to look for my tennis racket. I hadn't touched the thing in a long time. I didn't want to remember the last time because I knew it was before the shooting. Perhaps team practice. Perhaps with Hannah, but none of that mattered. I wanted it now, and that had to be some kind of breakthrough.

I located the racket on a shelf along with my mother's and some tubes of balls. I took mine out of the case and gripped it by the smooth, leather wrapped handle. The expensive lacing and carbon fiber shell were still in great condition. Of course, it was top of the line. I had the best of everything.

I grabbed my mother's racket, a tube of balls, and a tote bag to carry everything in. Then, I bundled up and waited at the door for Gage. As soon as I saw his headlights, I ran out.

"What are we doing?" he asked when I got in.

"Can you take us to a tennis court?" I took a slug of wine from the bottle before handing it to him.

He took a sip. "Sure."

As we drove, I told him about tennis.

"I was on the school team back home. I was good too. Not to brag, but I was."

"I can imagine you being good at tennis," Gage said.

"I was also super competitive but not with my own teammates like some of the girls were. My friend Hannah and I were a very even match. Sometimes, I'd win and sometimes, she'd beat me."

I sipped the wine again and thought about some of my matches with Hannah. She had a weaker serve but a better backhand. I was faster and more agile and therefore able to be more strategic with my shots.

"I really feel bad about before," Gage said.

"Stop. I don't want to talk about it. Where are you taking me?"

We maneuvered through narrow streets near town.

"Jetties Beach to the public courts. But you do realize it's winter and they're closed, right?" He eyed the bag stuffed at my feet.

The wine tasted sweet and burned on the way down. My head had already begun to lighten from it, so I took another sip.

"We can still hit to each other for a few minutes. Will you?"

"Yeah. But I don't really know how to play."

"That doesn't matter," I said.

We took Cobblestone Hill and arrived at Jetties Beach. On one of our other drives, Gage told me it was big tourist beach, popular with families with little kids. It was on the harbor side of the island with gentle waves plus a playground, restaurant, and the public tennis courts.

As expected, the courts were empty and missing

their nets. The gate in the huge chain link enclosure was padlocked.

"Do you think we can get in?" I tipped the bottle back and took another drink.

"Maybe. But there's still the problem of no net."

"We can just hit it back and forth."

"If you really want, we can climb over or walk around and look for a hole."

"Climbing seems dangerous." I peered up at the top of the fence which was as tall as a one-story building.

"Let's walk then."

The walk around felt like an adventure. Beach grass from the nearby dunes butted right up to the fence. Thankfully, Gage carried the bag because I kept having to grab the fence to steady myself. About halfway around, we found a place where the metal mesh at the base was bent up. Gage pulled on it some more and then held it up for me while I slid through. Gage followed.

"How do we play without a net?"

I handed him my mother's racket and dumped a ball from the tube. "Just one bounce and try to hit it to each other. Stay here."

I walked a short distance away toward where the net should have been. "Ready?" I called.

Gage crouched awkwardly—holding up his racket like he expected me to spike it at him. I laughed and bounced him a soft one.

He hit it back too hard. I managed to get my racket on it, but it flew off to the side.

"Softer!" I called.

"Got it."

Gage retrieved the ball, and this time, we got into a rhythm. I swung. The ball popped off my laces. It bounced. Gage hit it back. The crisp air no longer chilled me. My body felt heated. My blood flowed. We sustained several volleys.

"You had enough?" Gage asked after missing a ball.

"No. But we can stop."

Back in the car, Gage said, "You should try to join one of the clubs. Or play here."

"Maybe."

I sipped the wine, and Gage made no attempt to drive away. Instead, he scrolled through his iPod until he landed on a song I'd never heard—its soft melodic tones meant to be relaxing, I think.

"I had no idea you played tennis," he finally said.

He kept his eyes focused out the windshield, as if pondering what else he had no idea about. This time, however, it wasn't tense. It was just stating the facts.

I reached across and gently turned his face to me with both hands. "I know," I said. "That's why I told you."

He held my gaze, our eyes having a conversation more filled with meaning than any words could ever be. And when we kissed this time, it was soft and sweet, his arms pulling me closer to him.

After, while he kissed my neck, I murmured in his ear. "I'm trying. I'll keep trying."

Chapter 34

Lainey

GAGE WAS TAKING ME TO see the lighthouses. Well, not the lighthouses exactly but the lighthouse beacons. His dad had a listing that boasted a view of all three island lighthouse beacons at night, so he wanted us to see it for ourselves.

"I think it's a load of crap. There's no place you can see all of them except for a plane or maybe Altar Rock."

From our drives, I knew that Altar Rock was the highest point on the island. The house where he took me wasn't far from there, and it was more than just a house—it was a sprawling estate with a pool, a tennis court, and a guest house.

"This place looks really nice."

"Five point eight million of nice. And I got the alarm codes." Gage waggled his eyebrows at me.

"What!"

"Yeah."

"I thought we were looking from outside."

"No. We need to be on the second floor at least."

Rebellious excitement filled my chest. "You're crazy."

Gage gave me a simple wink in return as he parked the

Cherokee next to the garage, as hidden from view of the rest of the driveway as possible.

"What if the codes don't work?" We walked toward a side door holding hands. I tugged a bit on his arm, trying to contain my nervous energy. I was very familiar with alarm codes. Both of my houses in California had them, and I knew the police or a security firm would come if you entered the wrong code.

"We run like hell and get out of here before the cops come."

Gage felt around for a key behind a huge garden urn. Once he had it, we went to the door. The alarm sounded and even though I knew it would, I still felt unsettled by it. In the back hall, Gage punched in the codes on a keypad and the noise stopped. I exhaled the breath I was holding.

"Told you," Gage grinned and flicked on a light.

We tromped upstairs, going from room to room to find the right vantage point. The décor, of course, was nautical; everything soothing shades of green and navy blue with wicker and pillows and huge paintings of ships and beaches. After checking several rooms on the north side of the house, Gage settled on a picture window in the master bedroom. He pulled me to stand in front of him and wrapped his arms around me like we were taking a cheesy prom picture.

"Right over there should be Brant Point. That's the easiest one to find. It's red or green, I can't remember, but it flashes for a while."

I peered out the window. The lights of town illuminated the shoreline and distinguished it from the water of the harbor. "Oh! I see a red light," I said.

"Yup. That's it. It stays lit longer than it goes out."

We watched it come again, and I counted the seconds in my head. When it blinked off, I said, "It was lit for four seconds."

"Yeah. Great Point should be out there." Gage pointed out into the blackness. "Watch for a flash. It flashes faster than Brant Point and it's just white."

"There! I think I saw it," I said.

"Yeah, that was it." He gave me a squeeze with his arms.

We waited, and it came again, a quick flash in the darkness. "I don't think I've ever seen a lighthouse at night before," I told him. "And now I've see two."

"Cool, huh?" Gage said. "Sankaty should be way over there." He pointed off to the right. "It's brighter than Great Point—there! I just saw it. Watch right there."

The beacon flashed and disappeared. "I saw it," I said.

He dipped his head down to kiss my cheek. "I have a present for you," he whispered in my ear.

"You do?" I turned into him, and he kept his arms around me.

He removed a white cardboard jewelry box from his coat pocket, and I realized that bringing me there wasn't just about the lighthouses. He planned it so he could give me a present.

Inside was a sterling silver necklace. I lifted it out of the box, revealing a small, flat bird pendant made from a piece of blue turquoise. The necklace was a lariat style with no clasp. The bluebird looped through a silver tree branch and then hung further down. Tears formed in my eyes. This was possibly the most thoughtful gift I'd ever received.

"I love it," I managed to say. I separated the bluebird from the branch to put it around my neck. My hands felt shaky, but I slipped the bluebird back through. It fell just above my cleavage. "It's perfect," I said.

"It looks beautiful on you."

I stepped to him, and we kissed. And as usual, we could not just kiss a little. It quickly became more, and I walked him backward toward the bed.

"What are you doing?" Gage murmured against my lips.

"Walking," I said. "Toward that bed."

"It's kinda cold in here. Are you sure?"

"I think that right there is called a comforter, used to keep people warm."

That night, nothing else in the world existed except us. Our hearts beat in rhythm under the blanket as we made love. The lighthouse beacons flashed in sequence outside that picture window, and Gage and I were the only two people left in the whole, wide universe. If only that could have been the truth. If only it could have lasted.

I had a plan and it went like this.

1. Tell Gage the truth.
2. Tell him I'm sorry for lying to him.
3. Tell him he must forgive me because I love him.
4. Gage will say it's okay.
5. Gage will say he understands.
6. Gage will say he loves me too.

I envisioned myself handling the revelation and the trial and life afterward. I believed it was possible for me to face what happened, but I knew that feeling was mostly because of Nantucket—because of Gage and Sybil and Mrs. Sharpe and even Wick and Cassie and Amber. All of it was real. I was not damaged beyond repair. I could be a person again. A different person but still a person worthy of friendship and love.

The timing would be everything. Part of me thought the sooner the better with Gage. My confession was long overdue. But every time I tried to start, I couldn't do it. I couldn't hurt him. I couldn't face the potential that I might ruin everything for both of us because he might not follow the plan. Step four through six rested solely with Gage, and Gage did not like lying.

Thus, April progressed without implementation. Bright daffodils sprung up across the island landscape. Yellow forsythia bushes joined the daffodils. Sunshine and temperatures in the fifties caused students to linger outside in the courtyard at school—chatting and laughing and discussing prom dresses. Spring in Southern California was not nearly as special as it was in Nantucket.

One day, I noticed that I hadn't felt panicked or scared in a while. I sat beside Wick in English, unable to remember the last time the twisting vine had choked me. After a few moments of trying to recall when it had, I told myself to stop. Searching for that feeling was like searching for a skunk. Why go looking for trouble? The realization that I was better, however, only made what I had to do more difficult. Nobody in their right mind would want to risk going back.

Even my mother was blossoming with the flowers. She'd fallen in love with Graham, and she'd gotten a part time job. She was doing bookkeeping work for a friend of Graham's.

Still, May approached. Like an albatross, it loomed before me. I had to leave. Thomas had to go on trial. Websites and news outlets were talking about us again. Every day I got up and vowed it would be the day I told Gage, but every day, I failed in my mission. Every day brought me a little closer to the end.

Chapter 35

Gage

I T WAS ALMOST MAY, BUT a spring storm lashed the island with high winds and rain. There were cancelled boat alerts and coastal flood warnings. Spring was on hold a while longer.

Prom and AP exams were the topics on everyone's lips. Girls in English discussed spray tans and hair styles while others planned study sessions for AP bio. I was lucky because Lainey didn't seem to care one bit about how she was going to do her hair or what color my cummerbund should be.

At lunch, she chatted with Andrew and Sybil about summer jobs, and I marveled at her ease in being there. Her expression was soft, her posture relaxed. Lainey was better. Being here with us, she was okay.

She wore her necklace. She'd worn it every day since I gave it to her—the blue bird lying perfectly against her smooth, pale neck.

Her zone outs continued but had grown less frequent. Plus, she was not in a constant state of avoidant sadness like before. At lunch that day, she was just a normal girl talking to her quirky friends. I remember it clearly because of what happened next—the events so jarring, so upending to everything I thought I knew about her. About us.

Cassie and Teal and Dakota were looking at something on a phone. Their eyes darted up and down from Lainey to the phone. Then, Cassie spoke.

"Hey, Lainey. Is this you?" She turned the phone around to show us a picture.

"What?" Lainey asked.

"The girl in this picture." Cassie rose from her chair and walked around the table. "It looks like you with blond hair."

Cassie held the phone in front of Lainey. I craned my neck to see it as well. There was a picture of a girl with blond hair wearing a school uniform. I studied her. Her lips, her eyes, her cheeks. Lainey. It was Lainey.

Cassie said, "It's the sister of that school shooter in California. The director, Roland Berringer's kid."

A strange coldness spread outward from my core. The realization was like rain—a few drops at first, quickly growing stronger, a downpour washing over me in a matter of seconds.

Cassie pulled the phone away, and Lainey gazed up at her. "Yes," she said. "That's me."

Lainey

Gage looked as though the wind was knocked out of him. His mouth had fallen open, and he didn't seem to be breathing. I scraped back my chair and stood up.

"I need to talk to you," I said. When he didn't answer, I gestured at the door. "Let's go to the hall."

Without a word, he went, and ignoring the eyes of the

entire table, I followed. The rest of the room had yet to be informed, but something like this would spread quickly—a stomach bug of gossip infecting everyone soon.

Gage stopped at one of the built-in benches under the whale, but he didn't sit down.

"I've been trying to tell you," I said.

He crossed his arms over his chest. "Really? I don't remember that."

I gulped. "My name is Elizabeth Berringer. My father is the famous director, Roland Berringer. My brother, Thomas, is about to go on trial for murdering four people."

I recited this like a prisoner of war who could only give out certain information to her captors.

"So who's Lainey Darwin?"

"Me." My voice cracked and tears filled my eyes. "Everything else is real. I am her. I just changed my name."

"Kind of like Tammy? Like a silly little game you play with Mrs. Sharpe? Except you play this one with me?"

"No." I wiped a streak of moisture from my cheek with the back of my hand. "Not like that at all."

"Yes," he spat. "Exactly like that."

His eyes burned with rage. I reached to touch his arm, but he jerked it away.

"Gage, nothing between us was a lie. Being with you, being here, it's the best thing that's ever happened to me."

He scoffed and paced away, running his hands through his hair. "But you couldn't tell me. You continued to lie even after I told you about my mother."

"I know. I was scared—"

"Scared! Don't you think I was scared too?"

"I know. I was going to tell you, I swear. I have to go

259

back for the trial. That's why my picture is showing up again. I was waiting for the right time."

"I always knew you'd do this," Gage said. "I knew you'd end up crushing me."

Mr. Santoro appeared beside us. "Where are you two supposed to be?"

"Lunch," Gage said. "But I'm going to the bathroom."

He stalked off, leaving me with Santoro.

"And you?"

"I need to see Mrs. Duncombe."

I was waiting for my mother in Mrs. Duncombe's office when I heard Sybil outside. "Is Lainey here?"

I quickly went to the door and pulled it open. "I'm here. Yes."

Sybil glared at me. "You could have told me."

"I know."

"Then why didn't you?"

"I was afraid. I didn't want to ruin everything."

"But now you have."

"I know." I stepped to her—close enough to hug, but instead, I took her hand. "I'm sorry. Truly I am. You have been so good to me. You helped me at my lowest point."

"Are you saying goodbye?" Sybil looked indignant—shocked I could just walk away after what I had caused.

"For now. I have to go back for the trial." Everything started to spill out of me. "I was going to tell Gage. I kept trying but there was no way to do it. I let it go too long. I would have found a way, though. I would have had to."

Sybil's expression remained one of confused anger. "Will you be back?" she asked.

"I hope so. And I hope you're still my friend."

My mother walked in behind Sybil.

"You should go back to class, Sybil," Mrs. Duncombe said gently.

But I didn't let go of her hand. She had to pull away from me. Once apart, she headed for the door. I had never seen Sybil speechless before, and her silence wounded me more than if she'd screamed at me to go to hell.

Wick started texting me when I was on the way home with my mother.

Where r u?

I can't believe it.

You could have told me.

I didn't want to answer him because my words might be too cruel. Of all the people in my life in Nantucket, Wick was not the one I would have trusted with my secret. But, I had no right to hurt him more. He could vent at me through texts all he wanted, but my mind was too cluttered with thoughts of Gage to care. Gage was the most wounded by all of this—the one person who meant the most to me was the one I hurt the worst.

"What do you want to do now?" my mother asked.

After thinking for a moment, I said, "I guess go back for the trial."

"It's not for two weeks," she said.

"It doesn't matter."

What had we been thinking? We were so foolish to

imagine this would work out well for anyone. I started to feel angry at my mother for not knowing better. She was the adult. She should have told me how stupid this idea was. But then I remembered how much better I felt. I was stronger. I was happy. I had a life again. What I said to Gage was true—being in Nantucket was the best thing that ever happened to me.

As we pulled into the driveway, I typed a series of texts to Gage.

None of it was a lie.

I love you.

Please forgive me.

Chapter 36

Gage

I WENT HOME. AFTER THE BATHROOM, I went to the nurse and got myself dismissed for the day. In the basement, I laid on my bed—the place where it all began. It felt like someone had taken a chisel in woodshop and hollowed out my insides. I was a shell—empty and sick. I hadn't cried since I was thirteen when I found out I wasn't going to live with my mother anymore. I didn't think anything could feel worse than that. Unfortunately, discovering that Lainey didn't exist was something that did.

The tears came after I read her texts. I hated the pathetic noises that came out of me. After a while, when the sobbing finally subsided, I texted Andrew. I had to make it stop. I had to make the feelings go away.

I need to smoke. Bad.

Are you sure?

Positive.

Come pick me up.

Before I left, I went into contacts and blocked Lainey's number.

I went to school the next day. Of course, it had to be a gorgeous spring day with birds singing and the sun beaming. I was ripped apart inside, but the whole world was coming alive again after the storm. Still, staying home seemed a worse option. I needed to be distracted. I needed to stay out of my room where all the memories of her clung like static electricity.

At school, I ignored everyone on my way to first block English. Wick, however, must have spotted me in the Hall of the Whale.

"Gage!"

I pretended not to hear him. I reached the first-floor corridor when I heard him again, this time closer. "Gage! Stop for a second."

Anger started to boil inside of me. Did he think we were going to have a vent session about Lainey in the hall? There was no way that was going to happen. He needed to leave me alone. This was not the day for him to mess with me.

I was almost to my class when he grabbed my arm. "Dude, stop for a sec."

His contact infuriated me. I swung around and shoved him away. He stumbled backward. Pushing him felt good, too. Using my strength and anger against him as if he was to blame for my pain was like a remedy.

Wick must have read this in my expression because he came back at me with a small shove. "Feel better?" he asked.

I shoved him again. Harder. My hands contacted his chest, and he grinned as he faltered backward from it. People started to gather around us to watch.

Wick came back at me again, so I swung a punch at

him. He ducked and said, "This would be better after school, Pike."

I charged him and drove him backwards as hard as I could, crashing us both into the lockers.

The assembled crowd gasped a loud, "Ohhhh!" just as a voice somewhere hollered, "Hey! Hey! Break it up!"

I jerked away from Wick, afraid he was going to grab onto me and fling me to the ground. He certainly could have because I was way off balance. But he didn't. Instead he asked, "Better?"

I stood panting from my exertion as Mr. Rap arrived. "What's going on?"

"Nothing," Wick said. "It's cool. We're just messin' around. Right Gage?"

I hesitated before nodding my agreement. I hoped Mr. Rap would let it go, too. The last thing I needed was to be suspended for fighting.

"Go to class. Both of you," Mr. Rap said. "Everyone else! Go to class!" he hollered.

As the crowd dispersed, Wick said, "Meet me in the weight room after school. We can have a go at it if you want."

Then, he was gone.

Cassie watched me at lunch. Her pity and confusion, which were etched like words on her face, only served to piss me off. In fact, everyone and everything was pissing me off. Plus, I had to decide if I should meet Wick. I was grateful that Sybil and Andrew ignored me and discussed one of their mutual classes.

I was looking at my email on my phone when a text came in from Wick.

Are we meeting at 2:20?

No

Come on.

No.

Don't be a pussy.

Fuck you.

Just fucking show up.

"Gage?" Cassie plopped into the seat beside me.

"Not now," I said.

I stared at my phone and tried to come up with another answer for Wick.

"I just wanted to say I'm sorry. I don't know what I thought would happen, but I never meant for you to get hurt."

I refused to look at her. "What part of *not now* didn't you understand?" My tone was horribly cruel but I couldn't help it. Maybe, if it wasn't for Cassie, Lainey would have told me herself. But I'd never know and that was because of Cassie.

"Fine." She sighed and stood up. "I just wanted you to know."

As Cassie left, my rage felt as if it might blow my head off my shoulders, so I texted Wick back.

See you at 2:20

The weight room smelled worse than the locker room if that was possible. All around me, various jocks did workouts, clanking machines and grunting with their exertion.

Wick was already there, talking with a cluster of his friends. They fell silent as I walked in. Wick walked over and wordlessly handed me a wrestler's head protector. He put one on too before removing his shoes and laying out the blue mats. The attendant, Mr. Kingsley, sat at a nearby desk correcting papers.

I took my shoes off and tried to calm my jitters. Wick had the advantage here. I knew nothing when it came to wrestling.

When he finished his preparations, Wick moved to the middle of the mats, shaking out his limbs. "Come on," he said, waving me in.

I walked toward him, unsure what would happen when I got there. Wick crouched with his arms extended in front. Mr. Kingsley looked up. "Go easy, Michael!" he called.

"I will!" Wick called back.

Wick shoved me in the arm and jumped back. I tried to do the same to him, but he grabbed a hold of me and started pulling me toward him. Instead of fighting it, I pushed into him. Wick fell to his knees and pulled me down as he went.

After a few minutes of full on struggle, arms and legs grabbing and pulling and pushing, I was flat on my stomach.

"Tap out," Wick said through clenched teeth. He was using all his weight and strength to hold me down.

"Fuck you," I spat back.

He laughed. "Just tap out. We can go again."

So, I did. I lost count of the rounds but Wick gave me pointers and lessons along the way, and I even got him down once. After about an hour, my body was exhausted. I had no idea struggling with another person like that could be so tiring, but I did feel better. I'm not sure why or how, but fighting with Wick was helpful.

"Where is she now?" Wick asked as he folded up a mat. Apparently, he'd earned the right to ask me questions.

"I don't know," I said.

I went to work on the other mat and Wick helped me place it back in the rack. All the other kids had drifted away during our matches when they realized Wick wasn't going to kick my ass, and I wasn't going to flip out on him.

"She won't answer my texts," he told me.

I scoffed in return. "I blocked her."

"What?" Wick gaped at me.

"I blocked her. I'm done."

"Dude, you knew she was messed up," Wick said. He sat down and grabbed his shoes. "What did you think? She just had Daddy issues or something? She watched her brother murder people in cold blood. Didn't you look it up?"

"Yeah. I know. And I knew she had stuff going on, but she could have told me. She had a million chances to tell me, and she never did."

"I'm sure she had her reasons. That doesn't mean she didn't love you."

I washed my hands in the nearby sink. Was I really getting dating advice from Michael Wickersham?

"Love? You claim to know about love?" I chuckled as I dried my hands, oddly amused despite my terrible pain at Lainey's betrayal.

"No, but I knew her." Wick finished tying his sneakers and grabbed his letterman off a chair. "And I know how she felt about you."

"Fuck off," I said.

"Sure, but you know it too." Wick body bumped me one last time on his way to the door. "Let me know if you want another go."

Chapter 37

Lainey

MY DAD'S HOUSE IN MALIBU was situated on a bluff overlooking the Pacific Ocean. A wall of windows led to a wrap-around deck which led to the dunes. When I visited him, even before the shooting, I often found myself gazing out at the ocean. The foaming, blue surf rolling into shore endlessly fascinated me. The view of it was why this property was so coveted. People spent thousands on beach vacations for a view like that for just one week. The sea was a source of great power—ever changing, ever moving, infinitely mysterious.

Sometimes, there were a few surfers in sight. They were the brave ones who had tread over private property to get to the nearby break. Dylan told me it was called Loopy's Ledge, and the waves there had taken on mythical greatness because they were so hard to reach.

When we returned to California, my mother and I stayed at my father's house. It was big enough that my parents could avoid each other and isolated enough that we wouldn't be bothered by paparazzi, newly inspired to snap photos of us because of the upcoming trial.

After breakfast the first day, I took the crinkled envelope

containing Thomas' letter to the deck with me. I was back, and it was time to face things—Thomas and Hannah and everything. Nantucket showed me that you can't run away. No matter where you go and who you try to be, your past will follow. Unless you make peace with it, you will never be able to move on. I might never make peace with what happened, but I at least had to try.

I sat for a while on a cushioned chaise, the letter resting in my lap. I watched three seal-like figures bobbing around on Loopy's, waiting for just the right swell to crest and break. Surfers were the most patient people. Lack of patience was the reason I never liked surfing myself. The momentary thrill of the ride was offset by so much downtime—all dependent on the vagaries of the sea. Lizzie wanted fast. Lizzie wanted everything right now.

Lainey, however, waited. Now, I was waiting for the right wave of feeling to roll in and push me in the direction of the letter. It was supposed to feel right to open the letter, but perhaps that emotion would never come. Few things had felt *right* since that terrible day. Gage had been one of the things that had. Waves like him didn't wash in from the ocean very often, and yet, I let him down. I held back. I refused the ride, unsure I truly wanted it, and now I was paying for that decision. If only I hadn't been so selfish with my secrets.

Tears stung my eyes. The stupid letter didn't really matter anyway. Just open it, Lizzie. Just get it over with.

I did it quickly, then. I tore away the cheap envelope and pulled out a single sheet of lined paper and immediately began to read the words of my brother.

Dear Lizzie,

I know you might never get this letter. I know that even if you do, you might not read it because you hate me so much. I hate everything about my life. No matter how many drugs they give me, I still wish I was dead.

I won't insult you and tell you that I'm sorry because there's really no point in that. Obviously, now that I'm stuck here in jail, I feel sorry. I'm not really sorry for them, though. For Hannah and Olivia and Mr. Clinton and Mrs. Hugo because they are the lucky ones. They are free of all the bullshit. So mostly, I'm sorry for myself.

I should have just run away. I could have stolen some money and gone to the beach or something, but nothing made sense at the time. I had reasons, but they make no sense to me now. I was fucked up.

When you come back for the trial, you should come with Mom to see me. I would like that even if you are mad at me. You should think of me and how terrible it is here and just come. You made Mom move away so you owe me something. That means you should come.

I guess that is all.
Not sure how to sign off.

Thomas

Lainey

Because of the nature of his case, Thomas was held in special, isolated lock up at the L.A. County Jail. Walking into a jail to visit a prisoner was not something I ever imagined myself doing. No one ever does, I supposed. Crime and accidents and terrible things just happen. Prisons are one of the ways we deal with the aftermath.

In truth, I almost didn't go. Who could really blame me after that letter? Thomas was as messed up as ever, and who knew what would happen when we were face to face.

I wasn't, however, putting myself through the ordeal for him. The visit was all about me—part punishment, part effort to move on. I knew that facing him was necessary if I had any chance of a normal life again.

I hadn't been in a room with him since that day at Beaton, and I didn't ever have to see him again if I didn't want to after the trial. But that day, I would face him. I would try to put him and all his anger and craziness into clear focus for myself. That was what Belinda thought. She thought I should try, and I finally agreed.

Dad's car service drove us as close to the stark, cement entrance as possible. The California sun beamed down on us like a heat lamp when we exited the car. I had grown unaccustomed to its constant presence, and even wearing sunglasses, I squinted under its power.

Once inside, the process was lengthy. It involved showing identifications, signing in, metal detectors, and drug dogs. Because of Thomas's youth and special circumstances, we wouldn't have to talk to him on a phone through plexi-glass like other people accused of crimes as serious as murder. Instead, we were put in an interview room very much like the one we were in on the day of the shooting at the police station. As we walked along the hall, a din of voices from a nearby cell block reached us. The air was stale with many conflicting odors—overcooked food, a bathroom nearby, lingering disinfectant. In our little room, we sat in silence—a scared little trio. Dad had tried to prepare us before we left the house. Once we were in that room, there was nothing left to do but wait.

When the door finally opened, my chest tightened. All the breathable air seemed to leave the room, and sweat sprouted on my neck. This was a mistake—a terrible error in judgement.

I almost didn't recognize the person being led in as my brother. His hands and feet were shackled, forcing him to shuffle along. A deputy held him by the arm. His hair was shorn off in a buzz cut, and he had gained weight— his face chubby and very pale but still acned. He wore a tan jumpsuit.

Mom gasped, putting her hand over her mouth. She pushed back in her chair like she was going to get up and run to him.

"Audrey," Dad said to her in a warning tone.

She halted, remembering that touching was not allowed. The deputy helped Thomas sit down across the table from us before walking away and sitting in a chair by the door.

From the moment he walked in, Thomas and I stared at each other. It was as if no one else was present. Just us. His lips twisted in a strange smile—not a sweet or happy one but more of a sneer.

Before I could think of what to say or do, Thomas said, "Hi Lizzie."

I sat frozen, unable to respond, still trying to process that I was in his presence again.

"I guess I made you feel bad enough in that letter to actually show," he said with a chuckle.

I narrowed my eyes at him. He hadn't changed at all. Perhaps jail had made him worse.

"I didn't come for you," I said.

I surprised myself, and speaking the truth, finally not hiding or lying, felt good. This was my chance to do it with him unless I wanted to come back again.

Thomas scoffed. "No?" he asked, his tone mocking. "Did your therapist tell you to say that?"

"Thomas," Mom scolded him.

He glanced at her and then back to me. He wanted to see my reaction. Would I dissolve into a puddle of mush at the slightest provocation?

"Why are you so fucked up?" I asked him.

"Lizzie!" Mom said.

Dad placed his hand on her arm, and Thomas laughed again.

"I know, right?" He licked his lips and twitched his eyebrows. "They say mood disorders are hereditary, so you better watch out."

It occurred to me that he was enjoying this. Our tense exchange was fueling him. He needed the conflict. He needed it like air.

"I'm sorry I didn't see how fucked up you were," I told him.

"It's surprising that no one did," he agreed.

"But you are still to blame. For all of this."

"Ouch. Thanks for the vote of confidence. Does that mean you aren't going to help me at trial?" He shifted in his seat, adjusting his leg shackles.

"No," I answered. "I'm just going to tell the truth."

"And you know the truth?"

I thought for a moment. Did I? What was the truth really? Everyone spun their own story—their own version of the things that happened to suit their own needs.

"Yes," I said finally, "I know mine."

I stood up. "I'll be in the waiting area," I told my parents.

The bailiff got to his feet as well.

"Lizzie, don't!" Thomas shouted.

I halted, focusing on the door. It had a window in it with metal grating covering it. My exit. My way out of this nightmare, at least for now. "Don't what?" I asked.

"Don't go," he pleaded.

"Goodbye Thomas," I said.

He called after me—my name echoing down the corridor over and over, growing more distant as I went. I reached the waiting area and found the bathroom. There, I stood at the sink, surrounded by other women and their children, all there to visit the lost people in their lives. It felt like I should cry. Tears would not be unexpected in this situation. But as I gazed at myself in the mirror, my eyes were dry. That was not a day for tears. That day, my heart, for once, was sure. That was the day I was done being his victim.

Rosa was late. I waited in the foyer of my father's house

and peered out the window. Rosa was one of the people I missed the most from my old life. Her kind smile and warm presence; I could always count on Rosa. Even now, when I knew I could count on my mother more than ever before, I still missed Rosa.

I knew she'd come even if she was late. She'd never stand me up, but a pang of jealousy pinched my heart when I wondered about her new family. Mom said the kids were young, like Thomas and I when she started with us. Rosa was in her early fifties. She must have been tired at the end of the day after chasing them around. Perhaps she'd watch them more closely—be on guard for any "not normal" signs of growing up after Thomas.

When her Honda CRV finally eased up the driveway, I opened the door and stepped outside. After what seemed like a very long moment of her fiddling with her purse and her keys inside the car, she pushed open the door and started to get out. I sprinted towards her. When she saw me, her face broke into a huge smile. "Lizzie! Hello!"

We embraced beside the car like a long-lost mother and child in one of Dad's movies. In some ways, I guess we kind of were.

"You look so pretty, mi'ha! And so tall!"

I giggled. "I haven't grown, Rosa."

"No? Well it seems to me, yes."

"Come inside. I'm so glad you came."

I clutched her hand in mine and shut her car door, in case she was thinking of getting back in and driving away.

"I have trouble finding you. I never been to your Poppy's before."

This was true. If we needed a ride there, Dad sent a car for us. Rosa was strictly a Beverly Hills employee. "I was getting a little worried," I confessed.

I led Rosa inside, refusing to let go of her hand. I took her to the living room.

"I'm so glad to see you. So glad," Rosa said once we were seated on the sleek, white sofa.

"Yes. Me too."

"You like your new place? You happy there, Si?"

"Yeah. I was."

"I miss you but I'm happy if you happy. You going back?"

"I'm not sure. We're deciding after the trial. We have to wait and see how it goes," I explained. "Your new family, are they nice? Do you like them?"

"Si, si. They very good. The kids, they are little but so sweet. Three girls. Oh, so busy. And their Mama, she very strict. I do their hair, and it has to be so good and matching."

"Really? I remember when you used to braid my hair. Mom didn't care at all as long as I was happy." I reached up and smoothed down my hair.

"Si si!" Rosa grinned. "You such a pretty girl." There was a tinge of sadness around her lips and eyes even though she was smiling. She took my chin between her thumb and forefinger.

"You sure you okay? It must be so hard," she said to me.

"Yeah. I'm doing the best I can."

Rosa sighed, allowing her hand to stroke to cheek. "You know," she said softly. "No matter how many little girls I take care, you, my little Lizzie, you will always be my girl. And I will always be your Rosa, right?"

"Always."

She pulled me into another embrace. "Siempre… Siempre…" She murmured in my ear.

And I knew in my heart that it was true.

Chapter 38

Los Angeles Daily News
May 5th, 2016

L OS ANGELES, CA: THE MURDER *trial of Thomas Berringer began today at the Stanley Mosk Courthouse with jury selection. The selection process is expected to take three days and then the prosecution will be ready to present its case for why Thomas Berringer is responsible for his actions at Beaton Prep on September twentieth. The defense is not planning to dispute the facts, but instead argue that he is not responsible for what happened due to mental disease or defect.*

May 8th

The prosecution got underway today with it case against Thomas Berringer. Their first witness was the teacher who subdued Thomas in the cafeteria that day after his gun ran out of bullets. To say that the prosecution wanted to start this trial off with a bang would be an understatement. By choosing this witness, Mr. Rivera, they are sending a strong message that they intend to play hard ball in this case. We are seeing why they didn't plea out like the defense requested.

Mr. Rivera testified that he was hiding behind a column in the cafeteria, waiting for a chance to bum rush the defendant. He heard everything but only saw bits and pieces of the murderous rampage. He said when he heard the shooting stop, he peeked out and saw the accused opening the chamber of the gun. The gun was the pearl-handled colt 45 that was used in the movie, Deadwood Falls, directed by the father of the accused, Roland Berringer. Mr. Rivera has been hailed a hero for stopping the shooting which could have gone on if Thomas Berringer had a chance to reload.

Lainey

Because I was a witness, I could not attend the trial or watch the coverage on television. I spent my time at the beginning of the trial at my father's house lounging by the pool, playing tennis with his boyfriend Curtis, and doing my school work for Nantucket. My teachers agreed to let me try to keep up and pass for the year. If I was not back for finals in June, however, I would receive incompletes until I could return to take them.

Finally, after jury selection and opening arguments, the witnesses began. And when the lawyers believed my turn on the stand was imminent, I made the trek to the Los Angeles County Superior Court with my parents. The Stanley Mosk Courthouse was a high-rise building with a cement façade. There were large numbers of law enforcement and press vehicles stationed on the streets all around it. As we drove into the underground parking, photographers swarmed our car, trying to snap pictures of us. Thankfully, they were not allowed inside. We descended into the bowels of the building and were met by a court liaison at the elevator upstairs.

"I love you," Mom said, hugging me before we were separated.

"I love you too."

I waited in a small room off a back corridor near the judge's chambers. My testimony could not be tainted by seeing or speaking to anyone else. They had a bunch of these rooms to stash people like me.

Even though I should have been expecting her, the bailiff still startled me when she opened the door and called my name. "Elizabeth Berringer."

She said it as if there was someone else in the room she might be coming for. I sucked in a breath and got to my feet slowly, smoothing down my skirt and then my hair, now dyed back to its natural blonde.

I can do this. I can do this.

Entering the courtroom was surreal. I felt exposed as if I was naked. Autopilot was the only way I made it to the stand. I caught of momentary glimpse of the jury before tunnel vision collapsed in on me. It wasn't until I laid my hand on the bible and swore to tell the truth, the whole truth, and nothing but the truth so help me God, that it subsided. I had been practicing keeping my expression blank and unreadable but all of that was forgotten. In the courtroom, I simply tried to stay upright moment to moment.

"Take your seat," the court officer told me.

I arranged myself and prepared to look up. The weight of everyone's eyes on me was almost too much to bear. I touched my bluebird. I could do this. I had to get through it to make it out the other side. I decided to look for my mother. She'd give me the reassuring look I needed. When I tried to find her, however, my eyes instead fell on Thomas.

His expression was a cross between a grimace of pain and a smirk of sarcasm. He was told to stay emotionless—to try to look remorseful—but after seeing him last week, I knew he wouldn't be able to pull those off.

The cameras, two of them, dominated on either side of the room along with rows and rows of inquisitive people all staring at me.

Peter Leftwich oversaw my direct examination.

"Good morning, Ms. Berringer, could you state your name, date of birth and address for the record," he said.

Peter prepared me for this at dinner last night. I recited the information into the microphone.

"And for the record, could you tell us your relationship to the defendant?"

"He's my brother."

That was a simple enough fact to state, but one that also bore such pain.

"And have you always resided with Thomas?"

"Yes. Until last September."

"And how would you characterize your relationship with your brother before September of last year?"

"We were not close. Not anymore. Not since we were little."

"And why was that?"

"Thomas was a loner. He liked to be alone, playing his video games."

"So did you ever spend any time with him?"

"Yes. When we were little, a lot of time. In the last few years, I drove him to school and we ate some meals together."

"What did you talk about during these drives and meals?"

"Not a lot. We mostly only talked about stuff like getting rides and school schedules. Sometimes he'd be mad at mom for checking his homework or telling him to do something, and he'd complain about it to me."

"And how would you describe his mood overall during the last two years?"

"Objection! This witness is not an expert in moods."

"Sustained, rephrase please," the judge said. Her name was Iris Fernandez and she was around forty. She had tan skin and light brown hair.

Peter Leftwich cleared his throat. "Elizabeth, how many times do you recall hearing Thomas laugh in the last two years?"

"Umm, I need to think about that." I tried to recall ever hearing Thomas laugh in recent memory. "Umm, one time he laughed because mom spilled her wine."

"A wine spill?"

My cheeks flushed with heat.

"Yes. That's the only one I can think of right now."

"Was it good natured laughing or mean spirited?"

"Um…mean. Thomas wasn't very good natured."

"What about when he was a young child?"

"No. He had his moments, but he could also be difficult."

"In what way was he difficult?"

"He complained if he didn't get his way and threw tantrums."

"Do you have any good memories of Thomas in the last two years?"

I prepared for this. I resisted at first because I didn't

know if I wanted to help him, but I finally agreed to do it for Mom, not for him.

"Yes. One time we were at a premier together for dad." I found my father behind Thomas, his face frozen in a grimace. The sight of him made me lose my train of thought. I dropped my eyes to my lap.

"And you and Thomas had fun together?"

"Yes. A little."

"Any others you can think of?"

"No. Not that I can recall right now."

"So two years and only one good memory of your brother?"

"Yes." I sucked in a breath and looked up at Peter Leftwich.

"Now could you tell me what happened between you and Thomas the night before the shooting?"

"Yes. I was going to bed and Thomas's music was really loud. I went down the hall to ask him to turn it down, but he wasn't there so I turned off the music."

"And then what happened?"

"I went looking for Thomas, but he was gone. He'd taken my car and left even though he didn't have his license."

We later learned that he was at Dad's getting the gun.

"And did you see him later that night?"

"Yes. He woke me up around three in the morning because he was mad I went in his room."

"What did he say to you?"

"He grabbed me by the arms and shook me and said '"If you go in my room again, I'll fucking kill you."'"

There were murmurs in the courtroom about this. Peter Leftwich shuffled papers, letting it sink in.

"Did you believe him, Elizabeth, that he'd kill you?"

"No. I just thought he was angry. I thought it was a figure of speech. But it was weird that he got so mad about such a small thing."

"Had Thomas ever told you'd he'd kill you before?"

"Yes. As kids, we both said it to each other when we were fighting, but we didn't really mean it. It's just a saying. Like 'if you touch my popcorn I'll kill you' that kind of thing. But he'd never been so physical with me before that night. That was the part that scared me."

"So you were scared of your brother?"

"Yes. I guess I was."

"Why do you say guess?"

I paused and looked at the jury. "Well, at the time, I just felt like I needed to walk on eggshells with him because he was so moody. But now, looking back, I see that I was afraid."

"Okay, I'm going to move on to the day of the shooting. Did you drive Thomas to school that day?"

"Yes."

"Did you know he had the gun with him?"

"No."

"If you had known, what would you have done?"

"I would have tried to take it away from him. Or told a teacher."

"And did you talk to Thomas in the car that morning."

"Only about a ride home. I told him he needed to call Mom."

"And what did he say."

"Nothing. He just kind of scoffed at me like I was stupid."

"Was this type of response typical?"

"Objection!"

"Overuled. Answer the question."

"Yes."

"And at lunch, when did you first know that something was wrong?"

I paused and blinked at Peter Leftwich. "I heard a scream and a noise like a firecracker. I thought someone had set off firecrackers."

"Permission to approach the witness, your honor?"

"Granted."

"And looking at this overhead drawing of the cafeteria, could you show me where you were seated?"

They already had my table labeled on the drawing, so it was easy to find. "Right here."

"And what was the next thing you remember after the scream and the noise?"

"People near to the door started getting up and running."

"And when did you see Thomas."

"That's when. He started walking across the cafeteria. He had the gun in his hand."

"And did you witness him shoot Mr. Clinton?"

"Yes."

"And did you witness him shoot the windows?"

"Yes."

"And then he shot Olivia Avery?"

This would be the worst part. I had to keep myself together even though it felt like the pit in my stomach was about to explode.

"Yes."

"And where were you during that time?"

"I was with Hannah. We were standing and then at some point, we got under the table."

"And what happened next?"

"Thomas was walking toward the back exit. He was pointing the gun at the crowd of people trying to get out, and I thought he was going to shoot again."

"Objection! Witness can't speculate about what the defendant was going to do."

"Sustained. Please rephrase."

Peter Leftwich said, "Elizabeth, did you see Thomas cock back the hammer on the gun?"

"Yes."

"And what did you do when you saw him do that?"

"I yelled 'Thomas stop!'." My voice was small now—tiny but still magnified by the microphone in front of me. I didn't want to say this part. The part where he shot Hannah was the worst for me.

"And what happened next?"

"Thomas looked at me. He stopped walking and looked at me."

"And what did Hannah do."

"Hannah got up and tried to run away." I clutched my hands in my lap, hearing the tremble in my own voice. I looked at the jury. Their eyes were glued to me, their bodies poised on the edges of their seats.

"And what happened next."

I turned to the judge, wishing she'd interrupt and keep me from having to answer the question.

"Please answer Ms. Berringer," she said.

I looked down at my hands in my lap. The hands that

held Hannah's as she died. The hands that Gage used to hold. "He shot Hannah." My voice cracked.

"How many times did he shoot her, Elizabeth?"

"Twice."

"And what did you do."

"I screamed. I think I screamed 'No'."

"Then what happened?"

I brushed a tear from my cheek and decided to focus on the jury. "He looked at me and his face…it changed."

"What do you mean it changed?"

"He looked like he was just waking up. Like he was—"

"Objection!"

"Overruled. Continue Ms. Berringer."

"He looked like he recognized me and he was scared or sad all of sudden."

"And then what did he do?"

I wiped my forehead with the back of my hand. Sweat beaded up along my hairline. Water. I took a drink of water. "He put the gun to his temple."

"And did he pull the trigger?"

"I didn't see because I closed my eyes, but I heard the gun click."

"And what did you see when you opened your eyes."

"Thomas was looking the gun. He had the part where the bullets go open."

"Do you believe your brother tried to kill himself when your eyes were shut?"

"Objection!"

"Overruled!"

"Yes."

"But he didn't."

"No."

"Why not?"

"Because he was out of bullets."

"And that's when Mr. Rivera tackled him?"

"Yes."

"Thank you, Ms. Berringer. I have no further questions."

"Would the witness like a recess before cross examination?" the judge asked me.

"Yes." I touched my fingertips under my eyes to clear the moisture and any runny mascara.

"The court will recess for fifteen minutes," the judge said.

"All rise!" called a male Bailiff. Everyone lurched to their feet, and my bailiff came over to escort me back to my witness room. My mother and father watched me go with worry etched on their faces. Having to witness one of your children speak about the other one trying to kill themselves in court must have been the worst moment of their lives. It could be a scene from one of Dad's movies except now he was on the other side of the camera, not in control of any of it. They both leaned on the railing in front of them for support, and I wished I could help them. I wished I could erase what Thomas did for so many reasons. More reasons than it's possible to count.

Chapter 39

Lainey

I KNEW THE RECESS WOULD PROBABLY take longer than fifteen minutes. A break with this many players to assemble would drag on. I sipped my water and thought about Gage. I had been blocking him out, only focusing on the trial, but now that my part had begun and could end soon, my mind jumped ahead. Could I call him? Text him? It had been four weeks since I left. Did he even want me to come back?

Finally, the bailiff escorted me back to the stand. Some of my nervousness had filtered away because I knew what to expect, but now it was prosecutor's turn. They considered me a hostile witness. This meant I would be under attack. The way they'd treat me and the questions they'd ask would be aimed at discrediting and harming me.

After the judge reminded me I was still under oath, we resumed.

A prosecutor named Claire Cox stood at the lectern with the microphone. "Good afternoon, Ms. Berringer."

Our lawyers told me that most likely they'd chose her from the team to do my cross examination. Claire was well put together in a gray, tailored pant suit with a lavender blouse.

"Hello," I answered.

"Why do you think your brother tried to kill himself that day in the cafeteria?"

"Objection!" Peter Leftwich stood up. "Asking for another person's state of mind!"

"Your honor," Claire said, "the defense has used this witness as an expert on the defendant's state of mind. The state should be able to do the same."

"Approach," the judge barked at them.

They seemed to talk forever. I found my mother while they did and we exchanged a smile. Thomas had his head down on the table in front of him and one of the cameras was pointed at him.

When they finally concluded, Claire Cox asked her next question. "Ms. Berringer, if you feared your brother, why didn't you tell anyone?"

"I didn't think I was scared at the time. At the time, I just thought he was being moody."

"So when he said 'I'm going kill you' in the middle of the night, you weren't scared?"

"No, I was. But I didn't think he would—"

"Just answer the question, yes or no, please. Were you scared that night when your brother was shaking you and telling you he was going to kill you?"

"Yes."

"But you didn't tell anyone?"

"No. I was going to tell my—"

"Just yes or no, please, Ms. Berringer, did you tell anyone what happened?"

"No." Anger boiled in my throat. This woman was very smart and very mean.

"Did you eat breakfast with Thomas that next morning?"

"Yes."

"Were you alone or with your mother?"

"My mother wasn't home. Our housekeeper, Rosa, made us breakfast."

"And you didn't tell Rosa about what happened the night before."

"No."

"And you just sat there with your brother even though he threatened to kill you in the middle of the night?"

"Yes."

"Did Thomas seem different to you that morning?"

"No. Not really."

"What do you mean not really?"

"Objection!"

"Overruled. Answer please."

"No. He didn't seem different."

"And what did he eat for breakfast?"

"He had cereal and bacon."

"Was this a normal breakfast for him?"

"Yes."

"And what did you have?"

"A smoothie."

"And did you speak with Thomas?"

"No."

"Where were you eating?"

"At the breakfast bar in our kitchen."

"Was Thomas wearing his Beaton Prep uniform?"

"Yes."

"Did he look disheveled?"

"No."

"Was his shirt tucked in?"

"Yes."

"And in the car, you testified that you told him he needed to call your mother for a ride because you had plans?"

"Yes."

"What were those plans?"

I glanced at Peter Leftwich, hoping he'd object. When he didn't, I answered.

"I was going to Pepperdine."

"Why were you going to Pepperdine?"

"To see my boyfriend."

"How old was your boyfriend?"

"Twenty."

"And how old were you?"

"Objection your honor, this witnesses plans that day are irrelevant." Finally, Peter had something to say.

"Sustained."

"Did your brother know about your twenty-year-old boyfriend?"

"Yes."

"So you confided in him? I thought you weren't close?"

"Objection! Two questions and badgering."

"Sustained."

"Did you confide in your brother about your twenty-year-old boyfriend?"

"No."

"How did he know then?"

"He heard at school."

"And what did he say when you talked about it with him?"

"He asked if it was true and I said yes."

"And he didn't care?"

"Objection," Peter Leftwich said. "She couldn't know his state of mind."

"Sustained. Rephrase."

"Did you have a conversation with him about your twenty-year-old boyfriend?"

I cringed every time she repeated *twenty-year-old boyfriend*. She was trying to shame me. "Yes."

"And what did Thomas say?"

"He said people at school were gossiping about me and calling me names."

"What names?"

"A slut."

"And that was it?"

"No."

"Tell us everything you remember him saying about your boyfriend, please."

This was when I could lie. I could have said I didn't remember. I couldn't be expect to remember every detail of my life, right? But I didn't want to lie anymore. The truth would, as the cliché went, set me free. Maybe, anyway.

"He said he was going to tell our mother and I said if he did, I'd tell her about him smoking marijuana at the skatepark."

"So you blackmailed him to be quiet?"

"I guess. More like bribed."

"Did your brother smoke a lot of marijuana?"

"I don't know."

"How did you knew he smoked at all?"

"School. Kids at school talked about it."

"Was he high the morning of the shooting?"

"I don't think so."

"But you don't know?"

"Not for sure."

"Have you ever been high on marijuana, Ms. Berringer?"

"Objection! Relevance?" Peter Leftwich calls.

"Goes to her ability to determine if someone was high or not."

"Sustained. Move on Ms. Cox."

"Did Thomas talk to himself in the car that morning?"

"No."

"Did he seem any different than any other morning?"

"No."

"And during the morning at school, did you see Thomas at all? Before the cafeteria?"

"No."

"So there was nothing unusual about that day and your interactions with your brother before you saw him with the gun in the cafeteria?"

"No."

"And you testified that if you had known he had a gun, you would have tried to take it or tell a teacher about it?"

"Yes."

"And when you saw Thomas in the cafeteria, did he look different?"

"I'm not sure what you mean by different."

"Was his shirt untucked?"

"I don't remember."

"What kind of expression did he have on his face?"

"None. He looked blank."

"The whole time?"

"I can't say for sure if it was the whole time. I wasn't looking at his face the whole time."

"Well you saw him right?"

"Yes."

"You testified that you saw him shoot three people. What did he look like while he did it?"

"He looked—" I almost said normal but I knew that was the wrong thing to say. It would help the prosecution. I needed to say something that wasn't a lie but wasn't normal either. "Stone faced I guess."

"Did he smile at all?"

"No. Not that I saw."

"Did he look angry?"

"I don't think so."

"Did he look normal, like he always looked?"

"Objection!"

"Overruled. This witness knew her brother and can answer."

"He just looked blank. No emotion. Like a robot."

"So pretty much the same as he always looked?"

"I don't know what that means."

She paused and shuffled her papers on the lectern. I wondered what her notes about me said. Go for the jugular? Make her look like a lying, spoiled bitch?

"Can you tell the jury what went through your mind when your brother was shooting people in the cafeteria that day?"

"I was thinking it must be a nightmare and that I was going to wake up. But then I knew it wasn't."

"And when he shot Hannah, what did you think?"

"I thought he was insane."

Someone in the gallery gasped. The judge banged her gavel in response. "One more outburst from anyone, and I will empty this courtroom for the remainder of this trial."

Claire Cox said, "Judge, I want her last statement stricken. She is not qualified to make that statement."

Peter Leftwich countered. "Ms. Cox has been using this witness as an expert on her brother all afternoon."

"Side bar."

After another lengthy talk, they returned to the tables. The judge said, "You may continue, Ms. Cox."

Claire Cox moved on and there was no further mention of my statement so I assumed it stayed in evidence.

"Ms. Berringer, how old are you?"

"Seventeen."

"Do you have a degree in psychology?"

"No."

"Have you graduated from high school?"

"No."

"So you aren't qualified to make that statement are you?"

"I'm his sister. I knew him. I knew by the look in his eye that something was terribly wrong with him."

Claire Cox paused and met my eyes—sizing me up, knowing I scored another point against her.

"Does insanity run in your family, Ms. Berringer?"

"I don't know."

"Have you yourself ever been treated for mental illness?"

"Objection! Relevance?"

"Goes to credibility, your honor."

And this would be her revenge.

"Approach," the judge said.

They huddled together again in a short meeting. The defense team warned me about this and I knew we'd most likely lose.

Two men and one woman on the jury were watching me intently, even during these lulls. The others fiddled with their notebooks or zoned out. I smiled at the ones that were looking. Not a brilliant happy smile but a weak, sorry kind of smile that was meant to tell them I was sorry they had to be there. Like me, they were here because of Thomas.

The lawyers returned to their places, Mr. Leftwich shook his head at my father.

"Ms. Berringer, have you ever been treated for mental illness."

"Yes."

"What was your diagnosis?"

"After the shooting—"

"I didn't ask when," she interrupted. "I just asked what your diagnosis was."

"Yes, I'm telling you. After Thomas—"

The judge interrupted me. "Ms. Berringer, just answer the question you were asked." I sighed and looked at the jury. Some of them appeared upset, their foreheads wrinkled, and lips pursed.

"Depression and Post Traumatic Stress Disorder," I said.

"And how were you treated for this?"

"I took medication, and I went to therapy after the shooting."

There. I got it in again.

"Why were you depressed, Ms. Berringer?"

"Because of what Thomas did. I saw no way that I would ever have a normal life again."

"So you felt victimized by your brother as well?"

"I felt depressed about my life."

"Did your treatment work?"

"Yes."

"And are you better?"

"Yes."

"Unlike the other victims who were killed that day? You get to have a life?"

"Objection!"

"Withdrawn. No further questions, your honor."

Chapter 40

Legal Talk with Leslie-CTV-9 pm

"WELL THE BIG BOMBSHELL FROM *today was Lizzie Berringer. We finally got to hear from her. Lizzie had previously refused to give her account to police because she didn't want to further incriminate her brother. But today, the defense let it all fly, and they tried to use her as means to show that Thomas had to be insane."*

"That must have been a tense scene, Charlie."

"Yes, it was, Leslie. After her brother's murderous rampage in which her best friend Hannah Pearson was killed, Lizzie Berringer admitted to becoming depressed and needing treatment—therapy and medication. And I have to say that I think the prosecution made a misstep here the way they went about revealing this."

"How so?" Leslie asked.

"Well, they helped make Lizzie a sympathetic player who was truly devastated by what her brother did."

"Interesting. From what you saw in court today," Leslie asked. "How do you think the jury responded to her?"

"They looked very concerned when the prosecution went

after her. She's a young, pretty girl who looked vulnerable up there, so I don't think it sat well with them."

"So you believe her, Charlie?"

"Yes, she seemed very genuine. She didn't contradict any of the other testimony. I think she came off as a believable, sympathetic witness. Despite some early speculation that she knew more than she was letting on, I think it's been revealed that she truly didn't."

Lainey

The trial continued for another two weeks, culminating in two and half days of deliberations. The jury returned early on the third day with a finding. We were summoned to the court and hustled in to sit behind Thomas for the reading of the verdicts.

"All rise!" called the bailiff. My heart raced and my mouth went dry. My brother could go to jail for the rest of his life. This fact seemed both impossible and totally appropriate all at the same time. There were consequences. Our choices had consequences, and he was the one who had to answer for what he did. Either way, he was lost to me. I'd forever have to decide how to share the tragic secret of my one sibling with the world, and the people I cared about in it. I gripped the wooden railing that separated us from him, my knuckles turning white.

"Has the jury reached verdicts on all counts?" the judge asked them.

The forewoman stood. "We have, your honor."

She handed the verdicts to the bailiff. He walked them over to the judge. The judge scanned through all the pages, one for each case. Four first degree murder charges. Time inched forward. Slow motion. My mother put her arm around me. I could see the tension in Thomas's body in front of us.

The judge handed the pages back to the bailiff who returned them to the forewoman.

"Will the clerk please read each charge?" the judge asked.

A woman I barely noticed before began reading one of the charges against Thomas. "In the above entitled action… murder in the first degree… how do you find?"

"We find the defendant—guilty."

My mother gasped. Tears stung my eyes. The second count was read. "In case number…how do you find?"

"We find the defendant—guilty."

It continued on like that. We heard it four times. Each time, I watched Thomas' back, trying to gauge his reaction, but I could see no change. His body remained rigid, his posture the same. I was sure if I could see his face, it would look the same too. Behind the prosecutor—Hannah's parents and all the other families were crying. Their distraught faces erased any sense of injustice I felt. There were no winners. No good endings. Thomas would probably spend the remainder of his life in jail. Hannah and Olivia and Mr. Clinton and Mrs. Hugo were still dead, and the rest of us would never be the same. Did I count myself among the injured? I did at one time. I saw myself as another one of Thomas's victims. But now, I felt like a survivor. I was no longer a person scarred by this horrible event, but a person who had come out the other side. Regardless of where Thomas went for what he did, I could begin to move on.

I sat in the grass cross-legged beside her stone. She shouldn't have been there. Hannah should not have a white marble headstone with her name carved into it. She and I should have been at school. We should have been laughing at lunch or studying for a test or even crying about a boy, but one of us should not have been dead.

"I'm sorry," I said out loud.

Hearing my voice in the quiet, plush surroundings of Holy Cross Cemetery was strangely comforting. If ever there was a place where the dead could hear you, it was there. I could pour my guts out to the grass and the leafy trees and the white marble and somehow, I'd be heard. What I said would matter.

"It should have been me."

I never said those words out loud before. They always seemed too awful to speak even though I often thought them.

"But it wasn't. It was you."

I closed my eyes and pictured Hannah. I drew up the memory of her, not from when she died but from before. Laughing on her towel at the beach. Her long, brown hair and pretty, pixie face.

"I have to live, whether I deserve to or not."

I touched the velvety petals of one of the twelve roses I brought. They lay at the base of her stone. "I'll try to live for us both."

Chapter 41

Gage

L IFE WENT ON. I ATTENDED school and went to see Deidre and visited my grandfather. I still got high sometimes. I went to Andrew's house and paid him for it. I never bought my own. I never had it in the basement again.

I read all about Lainey online. I devoured every article, video clip, and tabloid image. Her mansions, her school, her classmates. Everything. She was like a girl from a television show—90210 or Pretty Little Liars. Not a real girl. Just a figment of my imagination. Except she was real. She'd been there with me in my life, and now she was gone.

It was like a form of torture I put myself through looking at it all. After a particularly bad run, I'd tell Wick I wanted to wrestle. He always obliged.

The day of her testimony, I stayed home sick. Although the trial was not carried live on television, it was being streamed online on a site called Court Chatter. I held my breath when an attorney called her name as the next witness.

And there she was, live on the screen of my laptop. She walked into that courtroom with her head bowed, led by a bailiff to the witness stand. Not a figment. Very very real.

Blond now but otherwise just the same. I blinked back tears when she touched the bluebird around her neck and swore to tell the truth the whole truth and nothing but the truth.

I remained riveted by her testimony on the screen, waves of varying emotions washing over me—anger and sadness and regret. I was so cruel to her that last day. Why? Why was I so angry? I grabbed my phone and unblocked her number. I wrote her multiple messages.

I'm sorry.

I love you.

I hope you're okay.

I deleted every one of them.

She got teary on the stand.

"He shot Hannah," she told the jury.

Hannah was her best friend. Her brother shot and killed her best friend.

"And what did you do then?" the attorney asked.

What do you think she did, you idiot! I hated all those people for putting her through this. I hated the people on TV and online who implied she could have stopped him, that she should have known. Of course, she didn't know, and of course, she would have stopped him. She wasn't to blame for any of it. No one who knew Lainey could ever think otherwise.

By mid-afternoon, I re-blocked her number. I wasn't ready. I couldn't re-connect with her while she was three thousand miles away testifying at her brother's murder trial. That would never work.

At dinner, my father said, "I saw on the news that Lainey testified today."

"Yeah. I watched it online."

Laura and Dad exchanged a look.

"Is that why you stayed home?" Dad asked.

"Yup."

"Do I need to be worried about you?"

"Nope. I'm fine."

Fine was a lie, but he also didn't need to worry about me. I'd bide my time until the end of the trial, wait and see what happened. Where would my little bluebird land when this was all over? Anyone's guess was as good as mine.

Lainey

When I returned, Nantucket was different. Summer had made her grand entrance. Lush grass covered the lawns; trees overflowed with green. The air was warm and scented with flowers. Everywhere I looked, there were roses and lilies and hydrangeas. The streets were crowded with cars and people and bikes.

School had just ended. Summer break had begun, but I had to take four finals in two days. English was my only exclusion because Mr. Rap allowed me to write two essays instead of taking the final.

I sat for the physics exam with Mr. Smithson first. He greeted me with his usual formality, referring to me as *Ms. Darwin* as if he had no idea what had caused me to leave.

"This is a timed exam. You will have…"

He explained each part to me. Out of habit or perhaps something more, I sat at Gage's black-top lab table. Maybe there were some new marks or graffiti on it that might give me a hint about how he was doing.

After slogging through Physics, I went back to guidance to check in with Mrs. Duncombe. I was taking the rest of my exams in her office because the teachers were already gone for the summer.

"Why don't you go out and grab some lunch," she said. "And I'll see you around one."

I had packed my usual sandwich, so I made my way to a picnic table in the courtyard. Since being gone, I had left everyone in Nantucket alone, but now, I knew I needed to try to reconnect. Even if they wanted nothing to do with me, we needed to make peace. I would surely run into them. I had arranged to do an internship with Carol at the Island Home two days a week, and I was going to look for a real job, too. Plus, school. Next year, we'd all be seniors together. I hoped we could at least be civil in the future and hoped for more too.

I had convinced my mother to stay another year in Nantucket, so I could finish high school there. She had resisted at first. She felt obligated to be in California near Thomas because of his conviction. She wanted to be able to visit him and work on his appeal. It was Dad who finally convinced her to come back for me. She could return after my senior year, and have a lifetime of working on Thomas' behalf.

I nibbled my sandwich and constructed a text to Wick. He would be the easiest to deal with. He'd been contacting me on and off for the entire two months. He'd even told me that he and Gage were 'sort of friends' since I left, and that Gage was doing 'as well as could be expected'.

Hey, I'm back.

Wick answered almost immediately.

No way!

Yeah. Taking my exams. How are you?

I'm good. Sorry about your brother. I saw it on the news.

I sighed. Leave it to Wick to just blurt it out there.

Yeah. I'm okay. Glad the trial is over.

Have you talked to Gage?

No. I think he has me blocked.

He does. Can you have coffee?

Maybe. Gonna try to talk to Sybil first.

Okay. Good luck. I'm glad you're back.

Thanks.

Wick went so well, I was less afraid to try to contact Sybil.

Hey. I'm back on island and I'd like to see you.

But I understand if you don't want to.

Sybil didn't answer until later that day. I was already home, laying on my bed in my peppy orange and blue room reviewing for pre-calculus.

What did you have in mind.

Coffee?

When?

Tomorrow?

Okay.

Bean at 8? I have to be at school at 9.

Sure.

I sighed with relief that Sybil had answered and she was going to meet me. I'd only been back a day and a half, but things were going sort of well. I guess I wouldn't count any of it a success until I got to see and speak with Gage. Why would he still have me blocked? I was discouraged by the fact he never tried to reach me while I was gone. He never even responded to my texts that last day—my declaration of love still hanging out there in the land of cellular data somewhere—possibly lost forever. Because of his total black out, I feared the worst. He might never take me back. Perhaps, it was truly over.

Gage

Sunburned and sore, I shoveled my last load of mulch under Mrs. Dodson's hydrangeas. Dropping to my knees, I spread the pile around with my gloved hands. It was my first day back, and after two lawns and too many loads of mulch to count, I was exhausted.

As we cleaned up, my phone vibrated in my pocket, but I waited until I was in the truck to look at the message. It was from Wick.

She's back. I thought you should know.

I blinked and read his words again. *She's back.* Lainey. Lizzie. Elizabeth. Whatever she was called, the girl I loved had returned to the island.

I wrote back quickly. **For how long?**

For good I guess. She's taking her finals.

Thanks.

I put my phone away because I didn't want a lecture from Wick. I could see how that would go.

What are you going to do? Are you fucking kidding me? Call her!

A Neanderthal like him didn't understand the nuances of what happened between me and Lainey. It was intense. It was complicated. Lainey understood my anger better than anyone, and she'd left me alone to deal with it. But, the time to face it had come. If she was back for good, we had to deal with everything.

My co-worker Carlos steered the truck back to the

offices of Halloway Landscaping. "Good to be back?" he asked.

"Yeah. Exhausting but good."

I tried to decide what to do the entire way home. Should I call her or text her or just unblock her? Should I drive over to her house? Should I just leave her alone? I knew what I wanted to do, what I felt compelled to do all of a sudden, but I had no idea if it was the right thing.

It took fifteen minutes and almost an entire bar of soap to scrub the caked-on dirt and sweat from my skin in the shower. Afterward, I got dressed quickly in shorts and a t-shirt. I combed my hair and put on deodorant and once I looked presentable, I jogged to the Cherokee.

As I was driving, I realized I had been waiting for this. I had been waiting and hoping I'd get a chance to see her again. To talk to her. To figure out what really happened between us—what was real and what was lies.

Texting first seemed wrong. Calling wasn't right either. I needed to see her. I knew it was presumptive to just drive over there, but it made sense at the time. She was back. I had to see her.

Once I parked in her driveway, however, I found myself unable to get out of the car. Her mother's Volvo was there, but that didn't mean anyone was actually home.

I took out my phone and unblocked her number. Then, I tried to compose a text, each one more stupid than the last.

Hi

Hi Lainey

Hi Lizzie

I'm in your driveway.

The last one was downright creepy.

I considered texting Wick for advice. Michael Wickersham—relationship guru. What kind of idiot was I! Even though it was a stupid idea, I immediately knew what he'd say and that he was right.

Man up and knock on her door.

Wick, however, would have inserted an f-bomb at the beginning for good measure.

Taking a deep breath, I got out and did just that. Maybe she'd slap me. Maybe she'd tell me to fuck off. Maybe she'd slam the door in my face for abandoning her. But whatever was about to happen, I knew I was exactly where I needed to be.

Lainey

I had no idea how long he'd been there. I happened to come down the stairs on my way to the kitchen for a snack when I spotted the Cherokee parked in my driveway. Gage. Gage was in my driveway. My heart took off like an Olympic sprinter.

Seeing the Cherokee filled me with nostalgia. I recalled the very first time we drove out of the parking lot at school in it with all the jackets watching. Then there were the trips to the Island Home, and the time at Old South Market in the freezing cold when I was supposed to be at the sleepover. Then there was sledding and tennis and all the other little times of no consequence. All of it, both the good and the bad, had transformed me. Healed me. I was not my old self anymore but someone new and different and possibly better. I truly became Lainey.

I waited in the front hall to see what he would do. How did he know I was back? Maybe he didn't. Maybe he came here and sat in my driveway sometimes when I was away. That was something Gage would do. He wouldn't unblock my number, but he'd do that.

He got out of the car. Long and lanky and tan already—he wore shorts and vans. I waited off to the side of the foyer to see what he'd do. Of course, it was logical for him to knock, but nothing could be assumed in this situation.

The reality of his visit caused a storm of emotions to swirl inside my chest. I hadn't prepared for him. I thought I had more time to think of what to say and how to act, but instead he was suddenly just there. Gage must have known what he wanted to say, and the idea of what it might be terrified me.

Gage

I knocked, and she opened the door. It happened fast, too, as if she'd been expecting me.

Seeing her again, in the flesh, I couldn't move. I couldn't look away. First of all, she was blond. I saw her during the trial this way but in person, it was different. She wore black leggings and flip flops, and a t-shirt, and she was fucking beautiful—more gorgeous than I even remembered if that was possible considering how I'd built her up in my mind. On top of that, she was Lainey. Seeing her ignited all the feelings I had for her. For talking to her. For holding her. For laughing with her. It wasn't just because she was beautiful that I loved her. It was so much more.

After standing there gazing at each other for far too long, she stepped outside with me.

"Should we drive?" she asked, gesturing at the Cherokee.

Driving made sense. We had our best talks in the car,

but I shook my head. I didn't want to drive. I didn't want to drive, and I didn't want to talk; I just wanted to pull her into my arms and hold her. I wanted to take her to her bedroom and lay on her bed and kiss her until she understood how sorry I was for being such a jack-ass.

"I'm sorry," I said. "I'm sorry for everything."

Lainey

It took a few minutes to register because I wasn't expecting it. An apology? I was the one who lied to him. I hurt him. What was he apologizing to me for?

"Gage," I said, shaking my head. "Please don't—"

"No," he interrupted. "Let me say this. I need to say it." He stepped closer to me and looked me up and down as if checking to see if I was real. "I was angry. I didn't understand how you could keep something like that from me. I still don't fully understand it, but that doesn't mean I don't love you. I do. I'm in love with you. Even though I've been trying not to be, I still am."

Tears brimmed in my eyes. "I love you too." I swiped at my lashes. "And I missed you so so much."

I stepped toward him and within seconds, he swept me up in his arms and we kissed. It was pressured and warm and filled with every emotion all at the same time—relief and joy and loss. It was a kiss from the movies—something my father would have directed except this was better. This was real. This was unscripted.

"I've missed you so much," he murmured in my ear as he kissed my cheek.

"I missed you too," I answered, unable to stop kissing his face. "And I want to explain. Please, let me try."

Gage shook his head again. "I don't care about why. All I care about is if you're back to stay? For senior year?"

I cupped his cheeks with my hands, smiling so big I thought it might break my face. "Yes. I'm here. I promise. I'm staying."

"Then that's all that matters," he said before kissing me again.

I had returned home to Gage. He was mine and I was his and for the time being, at least, we had each other. Temporary as it may be, as anything in life may be. Whatever direction we flew, I was ready, and I was better for having known and loved him. My sparrow. His bluebird.

Epilogue

I DISCOVERED THAT PERFECT BEACH DAYS did exist on Nantucket. In fact, once summer arrived, there was a seemingly endless string of warm and sunny and beautiful. Finally, I understood what everyone was talking about. Finally, I saw paradise.

My birthday, July twenty-fourth, was no exception. After a day of interning with Carol at the Island Home, my friends were taking me to Madaket Beach for a sunset cookout. Wick brought the grill, Sybil brought the smores, and Gage and I brought everything else—chairs and drinks and burgers and more.

Once we set up, Wick hovered over the small, rectangular grill with an automatic lighter.

"Don't tell me you don't know how to light it," Sybil said to him.

"I do. I'm just trying to be careful. I don't want to blow myself up."

Gage sat in a beach chair, and I sat on a blanket beside him, leaning on his leg, one arm draped over his knee. Just being there at the beach with my friends, I had a perma-smile on my face. The greenish-gray surf crashed and rolled onto the shore. The sun sat low on the horizon like a giant pink ball, and I felt like the luckiest girl in the world.

"You two bicker like an old married couple," Gage said to them.

"Shut up, Pike," Wick muttered just as he hit the igniter. There was a puff of flames, and the grill was lit.

"Finally," Sybil said.

Wick checked that it was working properly before dropping to his knees on the blanket and pulling open his cooler to reveal a six pack of Corona.

"Party time," he said before popping the tops and handing them out one by one.

Sybil said, "We should have a birthday toast."

Everyone extended their arms, placing the bottles together.

"To Lainey," Sybil said. "And to second chances. May we all get as many as we need."

"Here, here," Wick said.

We clinked the bottle necks together before drinking, and as I swallowed the bitter liquid, I met Gage's eyes. He was staring at me. Watching me. After taking my sip, I leaned into him for a kiss. A peck and another peck and then a longer kiss. He tasted like beer and salt and smelled like a sandy beach. When we deepened the kiss, and he wrapped an arm around me, I heard Sybil say, "Okay, Okay, save it for later." And Wick, "Get a room."

Gage and I separated, but I pecked one more kiss on his cheek as the breeze ruffled his hair. The setting sun illuminated him in a warm glow, and I knew I was finally home.

Acknowledgements

First and foremost, I must thank my family—Angus, Eileen, and Joel—for always trying to accommodate my writing in our busy, everyday lives. Between work and school and sports and housework, I sometimes wonder how we get it all done. I appreciate all your support and encouragement.

To my agent, Meg Ruley, for believing in this book. You read countless drafts, provided such great writing insights, and helped me navigate the big wide world of publishing.

To my editor, Stacy Juba, for her brutal honesty and thoughtful advice.

To my writing friends: Elin Hilderbrand, Mary Fan, Elizabeth Corrigan, Kimberly Giarratano, and Stephen Kozeniewski, for always being willing to talk or take a quick look at some little tidbit or other.

To Linda Muhler for always being my friend without rules or strings attached.

To my parents, Richard and Susan Brooks, and my siblings, Seth and Emily for too many things to name.

And lastly, to my lunch crew at CPS—you know who you are—for the laughter and the help and the encouragement in the crazy world of middle school.

About the Author

Melissa was born and mostly raised on Nantucket Island, and she currently lives there with her husband and two teenage children. When not being a wife and mother and teaching writing to seventh graders, she enjoys binge watching shows like Big Little Lies, House of Cards, and Outlander. Despite the rumors to the contrary, she does not actually wish she was a teenager again, nor does she see ghosts like the main character in her first novel, Ever Near. She does, however, love to hear from readers so send her a message on social media or at her email: melissa.macvicar@gmail.com

Twitter: @MelissaMacVicar
Facebook: Melissa MacVicar
Instagram: melissa.macvicar

Other titles

EVER NEAR: Secret Affinity Book 1
EVER LOST: Secret Affinity Book 2